RIGHT ON TIME

SANDEEP PATEL

COLOURS OF ENLIGHTENMENT

Colours of Enlightenment

Right On Time

Sandeep Patel

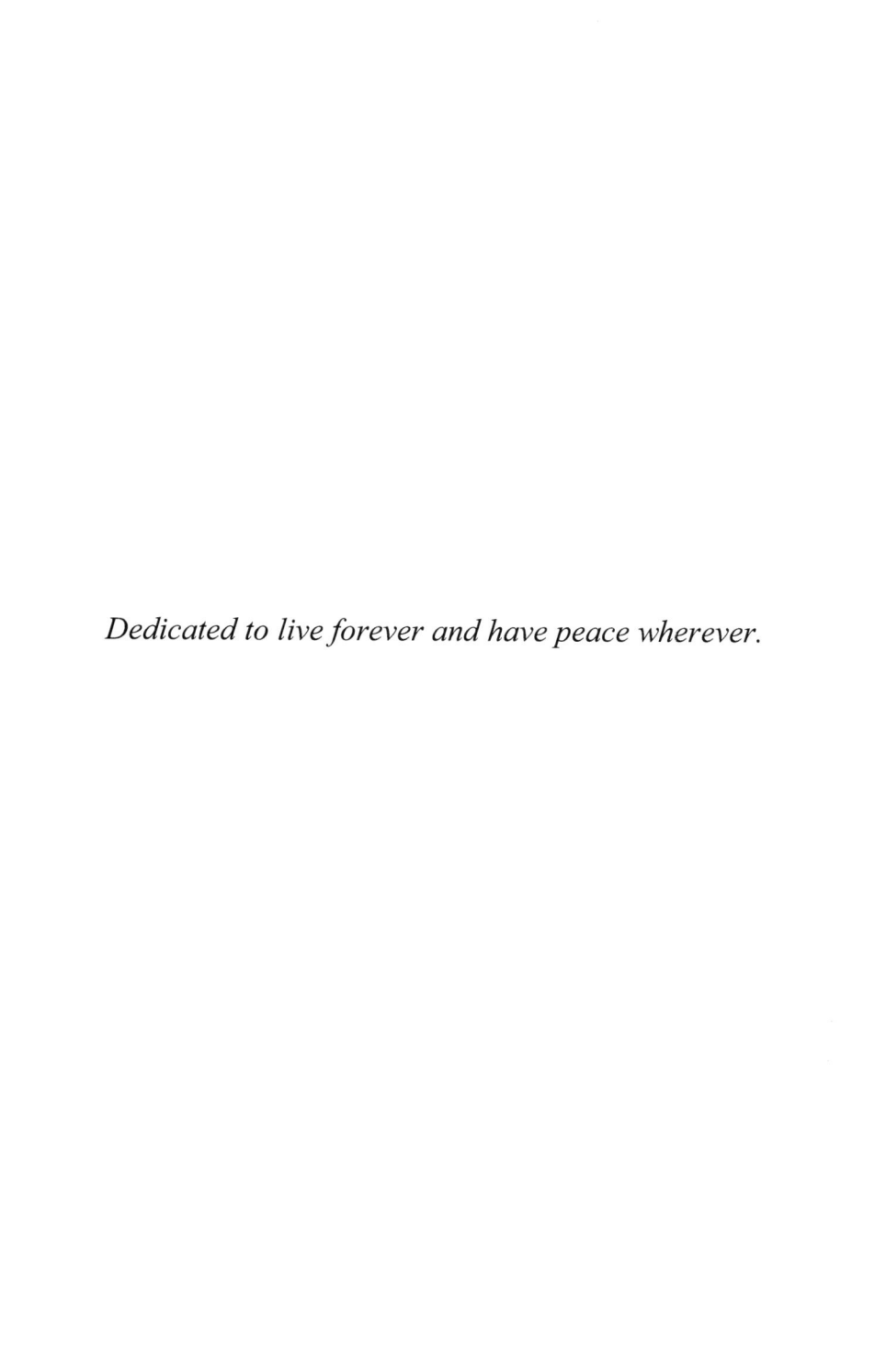

Dedicated to live forever and have peace wherever.

Contents

Prologue			ix
I – III	Family	Black	11
IV – V	Life	Violet	22
VI	Intimacy	Black	28
VII – VIII	Leisure	Indigo	31
IX – XII	Friends	Black	36
XIII – XVII	Math	Blue	51
XVIII – XX	Library	Black	68
XXI – XXVI	Relations	Green	78
XXVII – XXIX	Sport	Black	93
XXX – XXXV	Nutrition	Yellow	109
XXXVI – XXXVIII	Future	Black	125
XXXIX – XLI	Evolution	Orange	138
XLII – LIV	Religion	Black	146
XLV – XLVIII	Love & War	Red	163
XLIX - L	Finale	Black	175
Epilogue			186

Prologue

When a light ray is beamed into a right angled
triangular prism
the light is fractioned between 40° - 42° to reveal seven
distinct colours.
Newton (1672) first degreed this rainbow for five
colours;
red, yellow, green, blue and violet.
Only later he derived
orange and indigo
to match the colours to a musical scale:

I: Family
BLACK

The night was still young. The snow had already fallen. The ground had cooled. To be asked to walk from the shades of streets darkened by dust or lack of light was imagined impossible as snow fell mostly all days of the year. The columns of buildings lined the streets of Moscow with blind out road markings that could not be seen even if they had happened to be painted in. Regardless with what had been studied; a large empire over the Himalayan Alps, covering much of Siberia, became Russia.

Nothing was occupied before the twenty-first century for most of Russia. Nothing could grow as the ground remained cold. Mostly cedars and pine trees covered in snow and patches of black mixed with the earth moving brought gray to several days. The land was bright but there was no light to shine through their environment into the naked pupil of a wondering eye. Indoors was the only place where the atmosphere could be greatly appreciated, not because these caverns were lit with log fires or that vodka was distilled to keep bellies warm, but because the animals prowling Russia warming in these caverns were men.

Practically everything that lived over the Himalayan Alps fell into coniferous trees in mixed forests giving a tundra terrain over the mountain one.

Sandeep Patel

Life members from the south vowed themselves to walk further north to find a new terrain and eastward they found a small stretch of water separating what we now know as North America from Asia. The terrain west was changed by the climate becoming colder. Finland was separated from Norway by Sweden, and each country established themselves from one another in the strong hold of the Russian Orthodoxy.

Regarding that the Russians existed to classify themselves for something that they believed in, they used their beliefs to breathe better. With practice and theory they calculated calm degrees of wind currents into measuring air flow to allow their blood to become saturated with oxygen easier. They learnt how to reside in the northern hemisphere together. Close to Finland, cities like Moscow and St. Petersburg, flourished as poppies with white petals. A delta flowed from the altitudes above Moscow and into the Black, and Caspian Sea. The stream of the water system dividing in two to reach a larger body of water was brought to life by Reko Moskva, which flowed through Moscow. Either side of the river lived the city.

Imagine close to a rhythm nothing but words in another language helping them get along and across oblivion. Music that rides along with bike tracks pressed into the snow intentionally hitting the awe. The feeling of music riding through his body from fogged shadows casting movement off walls of buildings over the metro as he rushed home. Beating over bumps that carry fog lights into eyes would hit him and us harder. The bright light would not reflect the road or a wall any better but carry on driving faster. Let go from the hand of grace, swift and the sudden left to save, not to tell where he had been, close your eyes and you shall see.

There he goes, and again, and again, gunshots fired for more than flesh, not crossed through a flake of quadriceps, but instead through the spleen with weight. Slowly now, and slowing down was not printed on his cards just as the ground he could not see. His road was static from the snow and shadow it's a mystery how he stayed free.

Practicing the will to become closer to Derrick Tarasov, worked to become worthy to speak of his will. The matter of fact was that he compelled to educate himself further; this was to understand how to get to know him better, to hear his conscious play music with the snow would make us fall in love with him forever.

Derrick was from some bay across the Isles, and across some pond, and into seeing Montreal from every glance around any corner he kept his mind on. There he shadowed himself from lights and ravens' caws as they shattered their shadows in synchronized form when casted metal bullets were fired from Moscow's haven.

New bullets can only be placed into new shells just as gunpowder can only be lit. Shine in between the horizon and between the air and edges of buildings. Crosses of cables along, along, along, and through each other as they fall back to where they came from. Refugees with music not sound, and with darkened creaking wood with insects that collect dust to hibernate in. Nicely lit with wax-and-wick, the candle kept alight as midnight oil burning to where the young man had to be going.

Flying over Tagansko-Krasnopresnenskaya Metro, from Sbarro, Derrick dropped his bike to his liking, and reacted with pupils dilating, along with a smile stretching to the sound of music beating from within his theatre. The clock had struck pass ten post meridiem in the first month of 2010. As he opened the door to his building the mix of cold and warm air sparked a shiver through his chest as he stepped inside.

II: Family
BLACK

Derrick's best friend, a megastar in his own right, and in his own name, a true talent to bring a cascade of fire down the forests of Russia. To be reckoned with volcanoes that spit ash to humidify areas close to trees without leaves like evergreens. Along with the earthquakes, the forest-fires allowed resolution, and from Kamchatka Peninsula, came evergreen lad Tyler Hussain. No matter how wide Tyler could see he always tried to look into gray, and what Tyler found was that in Russia hot springs brought cold floods.

Tyler prayed towards the walls of Moscow everyday. Standing beside Moscow Grand Mosque, he prayed by the wall and up close to master that the true horizon was only from above. He would attend prays to share what he had learnt from his beliefs to the younglings that only knew old language. A construction of a new mosque with light walls was to be established in celebration for a hundred year survival, Jumah Mosque. From where Tyler had seen the likelihood of expanding knowledge for the meaning of nothing could only be for the well.

Jumah Mosque would be more of a liking to Tyler once remodeling was done. Nevertheless standing for long hours in gray mists of cold was tolerated by most worshippers who prayed together and amongst each other. Waiting to exit Propekt Mira Metro, the time was to get the blood flowing back to his head. He rubbed his hands together even though they were in mittens and exhaled over his path. Propekt Mira was by the Moscow Grand Mosque, and prays were everyday from one till six. A pleasant probability of a fifty point average was hoped for Jumah Mosque to become refurbished with side seats and tables.

Hundreds of Muslims attended prays on times they felt comfortable attending. Most if not all days people would stand in the cold of Moscow avenues around the mosque to have pray. Mats stretched out onto the cold concrete stone foundation around Moscow Grand Mosque, and swift pray rituals throughout the day. If space was available indoors then people moved in without disturbing those who were already praying. A reconstruction to pull new generations to understand the needs to pray was the focus for a new mosque as Jumah.

Fasting Tyler could do without, nor alone did he only eat halal, not because of any religious verdict, or any verdict of religious letter, but as he didn't understand why that he should eat. Closing in from his diet Tyler gave thanks and ate well. He aided in assistance with Derrick on relaying on his judgment as close to any friend can have on one. What Tyler harnessed was the darkness in a flame and that flame was ignited through Derrick. As with any being the existence can only be by the existence of another, and as for one being the only other was communism. Meaning diplomatist around Moscow would be in better understanding to thank another communist. It would just be easier if everyone could trust one another. Just like these friends', their souls would never spend time without one another.

Tyler's fuel was poured from his knowledge and harnessed by his love to read. Also he joined rampaging crowds of supporters watching the Soviet Union change from athletes for war to patient grazers of ice for the Russian Hockey Federation. From the wooden box and screen within Derrick's basement theatre, Tyler would watch the National Hockey League of the United States, and admire how the best there, were not at all as close to the best of all Russian twig and biscuit leagues.

So from escalating cheers and chants of victories to calming whispers and echoes in the wind, Tyler Hussain, maintained in spirit as Muhammad Ali, maintained righteous worship in transition to be delighted in being called Cassius Marcellus Clay, once again. Forever passing through eternity and through the metro rails of Moscow, Tyler studied within dimly lit libraries, strobe movie cuts and illuminated walls of religion. Praise was only to one, and to that one Tyler shared time with when he wished to relax and pay thanks to where he knew passion rested.

III: Family
BLACK

Turgenevskaya Metro was attached to Chistye Prudy Metro, where the orange line met the red one. That stop was the one used to unwind Tamana from thoughts of work, and was used to born the reasons for one to live life, i.e. to reapply dried lip gloss. That one stop was also used to remove the day's mutiny, reflect immediate rescue to be taken by wisdom, and to neglect the day's events to affecting her relationships to who she was to have coffee with. From Medvedkovo, Tamana would travel to meet Derrick arriving from Cherkizovskaya, to meet her at Chistye Prudy, before meeting Tyler at Okhotny Ryad Metro.

Dark hair mostly jet-black with a few blonde streaks waved with a lift that most models would crave to have had Tamana. Smooth northern skin with a hint of Portuguese tan left by inheritance from her grandfather covered her all over. Full bodied lips, long eyelashes and a perfectly occluding white sparkling dentition, an athletic body accompanied with dark hazel eyes in a sea of corneas, and to match all a thirst for knowledge alongside a fast right hook.

Looking like a million dollars scratch free and unmarked was never to be affected even with a poor diet for Tamana. Overall most days of the year Tamana was covered by different fabric scarves, wooly hats,

Colours of Enlightenment & A Potion

mittens or leather gloves, large black coats and boots to match. The only personality seen on the surface from a stranger would be a stern appearance on thoughts she would have had been having throughout her day. These thoughts would be a mixture of her work or her past.

So the three of them would meet in amongst hundred others to exit the station. Okhotny Ryad Metro led out to Lomonsov Moscow State University, where the three of them studied. Around Red Square, and the Kremlin, sat millions of years of knowledge, never minding that the university held the second largest number of books in Russia. An amazing amount of life kept the university holding sixty-six thousand bodies of power alive.

Tamana was born Russian Orthodox, being aware of the history their city had struggled from forest-fires to warlords. Blessed was she to be born into a strong household in Moscow. Tamana Rostova, loved to visit the old monuments celebrating St. Basil the Blessed prophecy. She admired things that she could not understand; this she felt gave meaning into her life.

From reading the start of the magnificent Cathedral Square, to accommodate beauty and afterlife, that the Ninth Chapel was built to grave St. Basil, beside St. Basil's Cathedral. Before the Ninth Chapel was built St. Basil rested on the site of Pokrovsky Cathedral, a.k.a. St. Basil's Cathedral; nine chapels were founded on Trinity Cathedral over Okhotny Ryad.

Moscow Kremlin was beside the Red Square, and homed two cathedrals and a chapel to tighten trinity hope in Moscow from forest-fires, wars and earthquakes. Alongside Reko Moskva important and incredible drops of heaven stand watching the water flow through the city. The mentality of fifteen century humans built more. One that Tamana joined with her family was through the Metropolitan Peter, which was built initially during 1475-1479, but was torn down once built and when refurbished an earthquake tore it down once more. The building was built once more and now is known as Dormition Cathedral at Moscow Kremlin.

At times Tamana would travel with Derrick to Aleksandrovsky Sad Metro, have lunch and walk over Red Square back to Okhotny Ryad, or to work at the European Medical Center at Tverskaya Metro. She would begin to ask Derrick weird questions to find reasons on what kept the buildings intact. He would not know much about the reason for why they were built, but relied on love that kept them standing. Head over heels Tamana was over Derrick. Her thoughts ran for her to return to sleep close to the hospital and luckily close to him by Tverskaya Metro.

Tamana had two frequent occurrences in her life, both that she enjoyed. One was sweet kisses shared between the hospital and her beeper, and the other was sweet kisses shared with her boyfriend. She had found her foundation relationship with a healthy social life and a hectic working life, which was made easier by Derrick allowing her to have a key to his place. He was the only person that she was close to as a friend and as a person. Everyone else surrounding her life like her hospital family was loved, but anytime she had away from rotations she spent catching up on sleep.

When her thoughts became her own she wondered about her brother. Her only sibling left the family when she was close to fifteen and spent time working abroad with the Russian Army. There had been no contact after the fall out between her father and him that there were no letters sent in either direction, frankly Tamana had no idea if her brother was alive or not. So she studied into a full working career to keep her mind occupied, and hugged Derrick tighter when she thought the worst for the one she loved the most.

Krasnaya Ploschad, (Red Square). 'Krasnaya' meaning, 'beautiful', was paved in the seventeenth century on the high altitudes of Moscow. A beautiful red hue throughout the sky reflected light of the sunrays to hit the clouds that reflected a strong red light over the ground of Moscow, giving the ground its name.

They knew all there was to know about each other. Their love was strong without concern on outside interferences. In laymen's term they looked out for each other. If the three were not together then they would be at prays, working, exercising or spending time on their interests. Tyler attended prays and at all other times with Derrick. Tamana would be with Derrick, or with the faculty members of the university and sick people. Derrick would mostly be at the university's archives or humming to himself behind the screens of the New Opera Theatre, jotting new ideas of interests with his surplus supply of black ballpoint pens on blank paper, or white chalk on several non-rotating sixty-inch blackboards. The dust settles as the dawn rises till the day falls back to dusk where the friends work for no more dust as the dawn rises.

IV: Life
VIOLET

Venezia Restaurant, served the best Italian food for any person especially those close to veterans. The restaurant sat close to the theatre and if Derrick Tarasov was not ordering pizza in then he would order creamy bacon and mushroom fettuccine pasta from Strosney Boulevard's Venezia's. One phone call with half an hour waits for warm food or a ten minute dash, voluntary conversations, tasters in mind and food sealed to stay hot for his ten minute dash back to his villa in the basement of the theatre.

Working with values of each other and violet lily storks resting on Derrick's table, through watching the monitor of his television glow violet light to lighten his living quarters, he was not to be seen as he was closely camouflaged into his surroundings. Derrick's thinking gowns were of one shirt. The only shirt the he wore when he sat alone at home, a light shade between purple and pink collars he wore with buttons of the same shade to match with thread dyed of the same shade. He felt well spending time by amusing himself with comedy as his brain waves worked. So he wore his shirt hiding himself from the light of the television and the flowers on his table, and thought of the values he had for Tyler Hussain and Tamana Rostova.

Colours of Enlightenment & A Potion

In early years the friends of three grew around graffiti painted on mostly every surface of their surroundings. The suburban housing estates would often receive a handful of paint. Some were valued respectably whereas others were tags by local gangs that feared vengeance from the local law enforcement; however both groups of artists forced themselves not to rush their work. Any implementation of reapplying great or better art was offered condolences by the communities to have their art kept for longer. The artist would learn, adapt, practice, and strengthen their works of art just as flowers, like numerous violas species breeding to survive.

From a very long time ago, from a time when young lads were lost to value love, from a time when men thought reading was not cool, from exchanging approval of varied values of trust Derrick and Tyler had got to know the other. From the age of twelve they had shook hands and shook aerosol cans. They repainted surfaces white to improve their skill when all was blackened out. Luminous violet was their shade as this was ambiguous to the nightlight. Their tags were totally represented for recognition as they tagged three hundred foot train carriages. No matter what time Derrick would call on Tyler to keep guard he did as the other painted onto the carriages. When two limbs tired or when two lungs filled with enough toxins to make one of the brothers faint they would shift rotations to ensure their mark was finished. The last project of painting dark galloping horses with light manes in black and violet proved to be their most memorable.

As for the third musketeer; Tamana knew very well of the boys since she was young and found encouragement to listen in with Derrick's mother in the kitchen. Her life had been as beautiful as Christina Aguilera, her valentine Derrick Torosov to always be forever. Medvedkovo was where she was from; Krasnosel'skaya was where he was from; however vibrations from Derrick's and Tamana's views with Tyler had gained reputation amongst their peers from Shchelkovskaya to Yugo-Zapadnaya.

    A delivery was received one night as Derrick caught up to his artwork to sign his signature before the carriages began moving. Unfinished work, but the carriages were back the next night unexpectedly as the adolescents painted surfaces as vents, meter boxes and the valet sections of virgin trains. The previous night's work had been left outside the train garage inviting a perfect opportunity for Derrick and Tyler to pursue the thought of reason. Was the train outside as to be soon in service? Was the train left out the garage as it needed to be cleaned? Was the reason that due to humid summers the controller felt shy not to park it inside? Or was the train delivered from God to help them express their work to a wider Moscow? As the previous night's work had departed into the tunnels as unfinished, the violet paint from the aerosols had to be packed in haste regardless of the paint drying; the lads had jumped the fence just in time to see the rear lights of the train disappear into the darkness. The paint on the returned carriages was retouched just as they had started; the art was finished with ideal calligraphy. The horses were stern to the finish leaving room for their signatures.

V: Life
VIOLET

Through where Derrick kept his vase of flowers there laid paper work across most of the floor in his new home from Krasnosel'skaya to Tverskaya. Along with his own plants of exotic colours Tamana had brought him her own. The violet lilies brought life to Derrick's inspiration, along with a fold out couch-bed, and enough space to allow room for more paper work to fall in. Living for his idea he was not shy of cash but shy to embarrass his Father. Through his own experience he placed his Father's words to practice and marvelous things began to happen.

The other plant in the room was a clematis flower. The flower had its own vase and the flower was replaced unknowingly. As the three of them circled away and into the New Opera Theatre, rotationally reaching to adulthood the flowers always seemed to bloom. There was plenty of space for Tyler to live with Derrick, as for no apparent reason besides the escape of reality for Tyler's past and Derrick's love for him. Tamana loved Tyler as Brendan Fraser would love to keep valuing that flowers remained vertical.

Usually Tyler would sit on a beanbag and entertain himself with videogames and books. Now the men were old enough to appreciate that silent company was golden, and with this respect Tamana was considered mostly like them. Within Derrick's living quarters some areas were decorated venerably, Tyler had added a few photos of women torn out of magazines to decorate Derrick's coffee table with. Tamana also placed photos of herself amongst the growing wall of glossy pages. Derrick had no pictures of people, just pages of black ink sometimes as words, sometimes as diagrams or sometimes as equations.

The kisses between Tamana and Derrick began once Tamana had received an official position at the medical centre. She was just as the men realized, she was as cool as she would be versatile. And by far there is no doubt about a little bit of hugging, a little bit of kissing and a little bit of loving. If this needs to be speculated then the hugging came from Tyler, the kissing came from Derrick and the loving came from above, as most likely Tamana would have been a vigilante.

Living close to sun beds was not desirable for most people in Russia, however there were few who would rather bathe directly in sunlight. Going far enough to feel relaxation that one person could sleep without being disturbed in broad daylight came as a surprise. This fault would lead to possibly laying around for longer and through a ray of light as ultraviolet burn a hole close to the infraorbital nerves of the trigeminal maxillary branch, cranial nerve V. The burn from a ray of light not the heat, the fixed position of laziness, unlike distinguishing shorter wavelengths than that of the hue of Derrick's shirt, can lead to malignancies. A necrotic development of automatically degrading cells later following the nerve to indefinitely erode the outer ear, but most soon likely the loss of vision, personally whined the violin. The metro station to the emergency room in Moscow is pronounced as Tagansko-Krasnopresnenskaya. The gift shop takes VISA for flowers as clematis, tulips and orchids.

"Would they be able to see me if they were around? And what if I sat absolutely still?" he thought to himself. "Where would we go from here?" Derrick mindfully asked whilst mapping himself an answer.

Mapping was performed by first having the hands together at fingertips, or staring at an open palm protected by other palm, and then pushing the vision into the horizons of perplexes. Derrick moved his fingers through each other and out from one another with this view, sometimes with hands close to touch, and sometimes away from his body like he was describing why his victim should stand on guard.

Over and over again Derrick read words through the digits and palms of his hands. Multitude of times variables changing, expanding, stretching, climbing, falling like charting vectors on maps. All concluding to non-variable factors, like when and how the final line of mapping would be drawn, as a conclude thumbs up, as a strike through his words, as a stop from dance of his fingertips to attract his indexes, or a value to closing on a word scribed by his thumb on his pinky. He flicked his right pinky on his left and drifted away to another view.

VI: Intimacy
BLACK

Good things don't usually fall out of thin air nor do they fall from somewhere far. These matters of principle become evident when they were to be matched. The sounds of popping firecrackers, beating drums, chattering people, and the unzipping of Tamana's dress was heard as they amused love far from Moscow in the year 2011.

She held herself tight to allow no resistance for Derrick to unveil her beauty easily. The beat of their hearts pounded in one rhythm as they undressed each other. Kissing and holding themselves close to one another in case the other at that very moment would try to escape. They brushed fingertips along the other's body. Pulling back the top four buttons Tamana forced back Derrick's shirt and slowly unbuttoned the rest just to touch a damp vest. He helped her with the sleeves and slipped off her dress to the floor.

Both concealed in the bodies of Adam and Eve they began to experiment with each other. A warm wind blew the curtain drapes a float and caused the impulse of their action to fall into more comfortable pressures.

Derrick laid over Tamana and kissed her curves from breast through to pelvis. She placed her toes on his chest and kicked him back to stand; unbuckling his buckle she climbed her weight onto his shoulders kicking his pants to the floor with her tongue in his mouth. Derrick grabbed hold of her below the waist line with one arm and climbed out of his foot holes.

He found it amusing letting her bra fall free. She touched herself to warm Derrick further. He pushed her onto the wall beside the air vent and stood erect as the sweat from their bodies raised goose-bumps on excitement.

The evaporated air chilled their skin further making them hold each other tighter. She tried to turn herself away from him but he marked her move to plant her above him. They covered the night in pleasuring each other all through to the morning where the firecrackers were still crackling.

Their souls had intertwined both mentally and physically. They lived with each other knowing very well of their lives. The believed in living for the a God, for a Light, this light was their life that they were presented to live. Both of them required peace, Tamana through her work and Derrick through the thought of his future. This peace was felt to be entertaining when they realized blinking at each other, eye contact was considered cool and cool was considered anything coloured black. Black was peaceful to their eyes. Love was red for them and red was identified as the colour for blood. Red was everyone and every creature on the planet. Derrick and Tamana entertained themselves believing that their lives were not theirs for the keeping. The monopoly of love was conquered as they closed their eyes from the light coming from outside.

The rest of their time together was to be equally spent in one another's kama. To hold each other in body, mind and spirit before reaching karma for eternal life. For her not to be valued close to prophetess widowed he hoped that death would approach her before that arriving on him. Well established was Derrick's love that was shared with Tamana's. However within the darkness of their surrounding they both knew that this love was not theirs to keep. The morning sunlight passed from seven till eleven ante meridiem missing the window frame which darkened the floor as a shadow of their keeper.

VII: Leisure
INDIGO

Things were impossibly imagined when they came between an indigo cushion and a purple cloth. Instead of denying the lines under a completely different shade of hue as those running metros in other cities, there was no denying the importance implied by this colour. Also seen when iodine solutions are added to starch residues.

As the sky changes colour for no grounds to be played, when everyone's asleep, slowly whisper in my ear, trick or treat. Play slow whispers covered in your own time with us, and we shall pray together when called upon. Tip-toe into sweet quarters, and around tip-toe for awhile between plays, and pray with others as they watch the curtain close. One time, last rhyme, to keep the earth turning for all time. Most likely the earth would stop turning and everything including the trees would be pulled inwards. Brace yourself listening as you begin to listen to softer echoes whilst we pray together.

Pull out a large glass, one with a large rim enough for a golf ball to fall in. Replace with ice cubes. Pour concentrated blackberry syrup to inch over the ice cubes. Pour the water, pour the water, shake with stirrer. Drink slowly. Possibly, possibly remove ice cubes and drink by the gallon, three cups per ten seconds should keep them blooming like berries. Furthermore an act of action potential can be ignited as that existing between samurai warriors, like Uma Thurman and Lucy Liu, a current that can result indirectly to melt an igloo.

There was a place once where the colour reflecting from the light shining off the walls was a chapter. The chapter was a part of an active lifestyle covered by tools needed to mould strength into the mind. A cool desire for curiosity why learning was actually cool. Chromosomes splitting indefinitely resulted to men forgetting that it was learning that moved them. Usually the only sentence that needed no explanation was, 'if it's not the wall then it's black,' but that place has made this chapter the wall and the rest of the story our time. More pound of meat on cattle as they graze royally to be served.

Hmm, mmm, aaa, ooo, investigate, eradicate, just scratch over once, carry into the next interstate. A purple fish is a Purple Fish swimming in the seas around the Caribbean singing a song. Like an Indigo Hamlet found in the Caribbean, a carnivores fish eating shrimp and feeder fish, or like a bird as an Indigo Bunting being more of deep blue with striped black wings. La, la, la, you know lady holding those deep marine tulips. Love Lauryn Hill as Wyclif Jean, and Anderson Police keeps us on the ground for fair lady as delicious as a bar of Cadbury.

VIII: Leisure
INDIGO

Who likes short shorts? They like short shorts! Who likes short shorts? They like short shorts! Who likes short shorts? Nevertheless these shorts were not possible to wear at all in Moscow. Most likely they could be bought from a mall and worn around the home, but as cold as everything was behind closed doors there was no reason to wear those shorts at all, (even though they were liked in every colour especially that of purple). The short shorts were left to their imagination and let whomever wearing the short shorts keep them on, or protected over with chance that the short shorts do not become too short. We like short shorts!

Tyler would sometimes meet Derrick waiting for his food at the restaurant opposite the theatre. A side of Greek Kalamate Olives was ordered with his pasta.

"What's up with the olives man?" he asked.

"A – men!" replied Derrick.

Tyler paused for a second and reached over to grab himself a toothpick to pierce the side of an olive; he looked at it and took a bite. Derrick looked at him whilst he enjoyed the olive. Tyler looked at the end of the other half of the olive and raised his eyebrows. Staring at his piece of nectar he pierced and ate another one. Sucking in the juices that enriched his mouth he placed the left piece of olive and allowed to let sit on his tongue, savoring the flavor he took a few bites into the olive's dark flesh and swallowed.

"Nice, really, not so much my style, but possibly. How's work coming along? Anything else He needs you have me know, and spring me another twenty-thousand for smooth coverage," Tyler said.

"That's no problem; retirement fund is a sure thing to spend."

Derrick looked over the table to where they were and moved the pepper jar. A waitress came walking to place his take out on the table.

"Can I have another portion of those olives?" ordered Derrick.

"I will place them to go as well," she said.

"Next thing I know you will be buying grapes," Tyler laughed.

"A-ma'am!" the waitress replied walking away.

Neither of them usually ate fruits. Their diets were small amounts of oil, with complex carbohydrates as pasta and potatoes, plus fats and protein within meat, furthermore milkshakes with loads of calories. The sound mind brothers were large and filled out, exercised well and drank plenty of water. Their diet just as their minds were not considered something important to argue over. They ate well and they shared most things over the other, and interestingly enough they both began to like kalamate olives. They were never shy of cash, so flesh from an animal came for the same price as flesh from a fruit; hence there was no mental confusion between eating cuts of meat or baskets of plums.

"Whose bra is that on the cross? Whose bra is that on the cross? Is that your bra on the cross? Is that your bra on the cross? Jesus, whose bra is that on the cross? Jesus, whose bra is that on the cross? That's Mary's bra on the cross. That's Mary's bra on the cross. Why's your bra on the cross? Why's your bra on the cross? 'Cause all that's mine is on the cross. 'Cause all that's mine is on the cross!" chanted Derrick to amuse Tyler on their walk back.

"I don't know what you've been told, there's one God, and no devil," carried on Tyler and whistled the military melody.

To keep everything and mostly anything alive was to prove its existence. Two serpents wrapped around a sword was most definitely a path to deliverance but what if the music stopped? As for Tamana, she would demonstrate this through pulling out all sorts of stuff from unconscious throats when they arrived to her emergency room from drowning, or choking, or a shortness of breath, or any other reason for being purple. Yes, they like short shorts and they like them indoors, they incredibly never like ignorance so they help anyone swim deep rather than fall.

IX: Friends
BLACK

The ambulance was tainted with snow that fell every night across the winter. The snow left the lights to blink black and white as the vehicle moved through the streets of Moscow. Craig was standing opposite the New Opera Theatre warming up. He had to catch the train from Pushkinskaya Metro, to home across the northwest to Begovaya.

Craig Goncharov, was in his early thirties. He was dressed in a large, dull, dirty, beige coat. The reason for why the coat was dirty was because he lived in the slumps of Moscow without any soap. The reason for why the coat was dull was because he had slept in the beige pigment of polyester the coat was woven from. And the reason for why the coat was large was because he never negotiated with the life that he had been presented with. His head was covered by a wooly hat and bags of facial hair representing a beard or a hiding spot for any weapons of mass destruction. He stood at 5'11" wearing gloves with worn out finger holes and boots that were close to barking. With natural denim heavy cargo jeans and a moth breathing woolly jumper overlying any all day and everyday use undergarments he stared into the darkness, he stared into the darkness and rested to wait for the light.

Colours of Enlightenment & A Potion

The shutters of private stores were being shut. Pitched screens of street light identified the serpent and sword image on the side of the emergency vehicle. Snow kept falling and Craig noticed Derrick entering the theatre with heavy boxes. Abram, the doorman was helping Derrick hurry in a ton of weight. Silently the ambulance crossed his sight with lights' flashing.

A torso framing close to an equilateral triangle with larger limbs than normal, Abram Shiraz, stood at 6'3" covering a circumference of a baby elephant. He wore a light gray jacket with collars stiffened as when French soccer star, Eric Cantona, had when playing for Manchester United. His shoe size, his weight, and his gait prevented him from easily slipping on the iced ground, however if he had a shake and fell, he would be felt for several yards and possibly a crane would be needed to lift him back to his feet. For a well dressed, well spoken, extremely healthy individual there were only a few he could look up to and believe on. One was his faith in Derrick, and the other was with his faith in Christ, Son of God.

He believed in Derrick Tarasov, as Derrick only preached what he read and learnt. From all the people that Abram Shiraz spoke with, Derrick was likely to speak with accuracy and with noble truth. Derrick also believed Jesus was staked high so that they would have someone to look up to. So they looked up to see Jesus on telephone poles as strobes of flashes as the snow carried on falling.

Before he was blessed in meeting Derrick, Abraham's father had encouraged him to worship well for others. Through the stories listed in the New Testament, the devotion the Apostles had for Jesus was one to be admired by Abram. Unlike a million others Abram's born belief was followed by thought and action to his devotion.

Around any major city the homeless would live and Moscow too had its fair share. They would find sleep in tight corners of walls and warm pockets of air under bridges of Survorosky Park, and up north to Park Vorob'evy Gory, all the way through to Nats Park. Into Moscow city sat these parks surrounding the Cathedral Square and the Kremlin. The river flowed like soft metallic silver across the night through Moscow and under the ambulance at times. The gray scale of St. Basil's Cathedral was reflected by the river with the distinguishing patterns moving with the water, but no colours could be seen. Unlike roads built from the day of the Romans', the roads of Moscow city were always tried to be kept clear.

Inside the emergency vehicle, the paramedic held on tight and tried to stop darkened blood pouring onto the floor of the ambulance. The pool of blood gathering on the floor was tried not to be slipped on. The paramedic cut open a man's jeans. She held onto a silver handle as she felt a sudden stop to come shortly.

He had fallen off the wall of a fountain trying to collect the rubles that others had thrown in. He grinded his thigh skidding down into the water and almost pierced his superficial femoral vein as he shifted past a fountain spoke. One ruble was almost three cent, where he had many five ruble coins, and regardless none were to be replaced back into the fountain. He wondered why the people threw their money away like that. The person began to wish the thought of throwing some rubles back into the fountain as soon as he got well.

Colours of Enlightenment & A Potion

Shifting weight the paramedic held the patient down and covered his leg with a cloth. She administered him with morphine intravenously into one of the antecubital veins for an immediate response. The patient felt alleviated from pain and began to breathe slightly softer. She placed a mask over his mouth and nostrils and fed him hundred-percent oxygen. Mostly children with asthma were gently administered oxygen when they would be having an anxiety attack. She exhaled forcefully down and away from the patient for a few seconds instead to catch fresh oxygen in her breath.

Nevertheless the patient rushing through the streets of Moscow would be well. The morphine saturated into his blood had placed him into a strobe within the ambulance that allowed the patient to forget his situation. The paramedic driving yelled for them to brace.

Moving away from Craig Goncharov the ambulance did not have far to go. The hospital fell round the corner from where the snow carried to fall and obscure Derrick's notice on Craig.

"Come inside and have something to eat before you leave Abram. Have got some steak in the freezer I'll stick on the pan," asked Derrick.

"Another time Dee, it's about four in the morning. I'm waking on the crack of dawn tomorrow, then seeing you in the evening."

Derrick grabbed the last box away from the side entrance to the theatre from Abram and moved it inside. He came back outside and looked up at the falling snow. Abram had already sat in the van and had started the engine. Derrick looked around the street and inhaled, he closed the doors to the side-entrance with a loud thud. Craig watched with amazement until the doors closed. He wondered what was fueling the men to struggle with heavy cargo in the middle of the night that he decided to break into the building the following night.

X: Friends
BLACK

"Good afternoon, Derrick," said Abram. "Good afternoon, Abs. Let you know this straight away; surely the real under the thumb is not as great as the knife I can pierce Him with. Come downstairs and help me arrange a few things and make sure the doors are locked at night. The doors are locked because I too want the spider outside feeding, nesting, eating, living without audio, outside." Derrick said.

"Hmmm..."

"To keep them wondering, but that is what I attend to change. Found the key to paving His time to the next best point. Easily help me down these stairs, and easily curve through the sun's gravity to the area where I choose. Now we can go round, but not north or south in space, around to where the earth would have sat where I choose. You can take a choice too. Go on take a pick in time."

"What do you mean man?" replied Abram.

"Anytime you wish from minus infinity to plus infinity. There is no point catching your own death if that is what you were thinking? I have tried this once and you would I have said?"

"Well when is it?"

"That's right. And not going to let you know just yet, you believe me you have nothing to look forward to," finished Derrick on Abram's zen.

They headed to switch on the theatre lights and moved upstairs to the chairman's office. Abram placed a few things as his gloves, keys and hat on the table. Careful not to scratch the mahogany wood he moved the items clockwise, (this was for no reason except to spend a second of time), and then he turned around himself to hear Derrick begin talking.

To what Derrick was to Abram was his bread and butter. This man had something of an admiration placed upon him, and was not shy to deliver that admiration for his people. Abram was a large man with darker skin than most Russian natives, and brought wisdom to the people that he surrounded. Derrick admired Abram as Abram prayed whenever he found time. Derrick intentionally began praying anywhere facing south as he believed the Lord looked up at earth from heaven. Abram believed as him and at times would bow south to pray and then switch north to see what the Father was watching. Overall the light of heaven lights a dark room as a candle lit in its center, the whole room is illuminated, but still the two friends wished for their Father to look up at them as children would do for adults.

Grab the nail with the left hand, and spin upwards with a strong grip hold of other hand on the hammer, on the recovery strike through. His Father was the Father of Jesus, which made Him Abraham's Father. Baffled about this, so he decided to place the blood of Jesus to the test. However there was no need to have him dragging the stake up the mountain or was

Colours of Enlightenment & A Potion

that Him imitating Derrick? Three nails please and let's mount Him up! Climb the mountain by tensing the left pectoral major and left scapula region, the cross just lifts itself. They helped him climb a few steps and then He was there. And now Derrick was thinking what he should do next. After finding the truth about Tyler and Tamana, the only possibility would be to live ten yards ahead of everyone else.

"Once you're done here, and everyone is out, and you have locked up thoroughly, after every last member of staff have left safely home, you let her know that she will have to meet you later at the Sheraton. Here's the key for tonight only. Tomorrow you are going to choose from all the colours that Moscow has to offer. And these game tickets," Derrick looked over at Abram.

"Okay," he said.

"Take your time, no rush, not going anywhere anytime soon. Wait till the friends are there and flirt with the woman in the deep indigo dress, there'll be one in a gray dress, and another in a blue one. They all have the eyes for you tonight, so just slap your own thigh when you need some alone time. You work this how you want."

Derrick handed Abram the keys and Abram pointed to push his heart.

"But first downstairs with the fool, and nothing on your mind except sleeping with the naked broad tonight. You understand right?" asked Derrick.

"I don't know what you are talking about, but I'll be there tomorrow," replied Abram.

Derrick closed the job description for that evening's lineup and handed them to Abram. Collecting his thoughts by staring to the ground Derrick finalized the work for the week's plays at the theatre. Abram placed his belonging to hand and left Derrick's side to open the theatre for that night's performance. Derrick came out of thought after Abram had left and gathered his notes to the basement. A multi-networking array of work and play kept the friends occupied throughout all times of the day. That to rest the mind at anytime was foolish unless they wished to start back at the beginning.

XI: Friends
BLACK

Within the basement of the New Opera Theatre, Tamana, Tyler and Abram arrived to see Derrick. Derrick's living space was clean for the first time the friends had known him there. They had noticed that the piles of paper and scraps of notes that usually decorated the place were all missing, they did not think to ask Derrick why his place was tidy, but they did appreciate that they did not have to mind their step around his home.

"Alright guys don't become too surprised; you are going to see someone more amazing than me. Tyler, Tamana, Abram brace yourselves. Seriously you guys need to sit down. Don't become too used to liking me, but gather that I like you, and I like them, so let me rejoice you with some others," said Derrick.

"What are you talking about?" she said.

Abram had moved already to the couch and had sat down. Tyler noticed Abram sitting and walked over to sit with him. Derrick smiled slightly and moved Tamana to sit with them and moved back. He looked at all three of them and they remained gazed at him.

"Okay guys you can come to see yourselves," said Derrick to thin air.

From the other end of Derrick's home, over a corner step that opened the kitchen, in which the pantry was, walked out Tyler and Abram stepped in light from behind the door, and Tamana from within the closet came to slowly stand facing themselves sitting on the couch. The friends sitting on the couch sat with their mouth's wide open starring at the new comers.

"Don't faint," said Tamana to herself.

Tyler stood up to look closer at himself.

Abram sat on Derrick's seat staring at Derrick. He looked slightly at himself.

Abram on the couch looked over at Derrick. The three new comers waited fingers and thumbs. From the kitchen came another shadow. They all looked over to see another Derrick eating a bowl of cereal.

"I'm the real one, meaning your time, our time, and he's my future part, have you told them the news?" asked Derrick to himself. "I can let some stranger wake me in my sleep but to then offer him my food?"

"Ha ha ha ha. Ha ha ha!" they both laughed.

"Yes I hope they understand. Please take a moment to write down the appearance of our departure. Need to record the area of subatomic aura around us as we leave into thin air, 'well out of waves of magnetism that hold the world turning with the sun.' That is an extremely small number, but regardless I have maintained a force to move the flow of electromagnetic waves all the way from earth to the sun safely. Let alone the release has allowed me to travel through time. Wish I could travel through space," Derrick laughing to himself, and the other Derrick began to chuckle with him.

The friends of present and future sat observing themselves closer. Incredible to comprehend the actions of oneself to be seen in direct contact, that all the

Colours of Enlightenment & A Potion

friends sat in silence momentarily without tempering with the other. They smiled voluntarily to provoke a response from themselves as time passed, and to notice that the Derrick's were consumed in their own conversation to care nonetheless for their surprise.

"We were trying to find more effective ways to raise empty pallets," added future Derrick. "Lifting pallets was always tricky than heavy, and I thought what about a manual lift by using forces to pulse pallets off the ground so we can move them easier."

"But instead of moving pallets, I found that decreasing the weight of the object to be moved decreased dramatically around the machine, which I worked to become a time-machine," continued present Derrick. "I'll take the notes as you leave Dee."

"You just wanted to say your own name there didn't you? Go, Derrick!" said future Derrick.

They all smiled at each other and looked at the future Derrick. He moved over to the three future friends and they braced his shoulders as they had traveled before. He unhooked a metal staff from his possession and pressed the surface with his left forefinger. A few seconds past and the room began to get colder. A chill was evident to them as frost would have been to a rattlesnake. They all held each other tightly, whilst he held the staff tightly, Abram held him tighter and they vanished to leave naked air leaving the other four.

XII: Friends
BLACK

Later on that same night once everything had been performed and tested, after witnessing themselves come and go, Tyler thought to pray with his family, Abram knew to take Derrick's word and head to Sheraton Hotel, and Tamana grabbed hold of Derrick as they all left ahead of Abram locking the doors of the theatre. The time was early on the next morning after Craig had seen Derrick last. Abram double checked the lock and moved in over to Derrick's other shoulder.

"That was a real good show," said Abram, "Thanks man."

Tamana kissed Derrick and he rocked slightly left and right. Tyler opened his left hand and looked at the sky reflecting off his palm; he scrolled the light off his fingers and looked over at Derrick to point to his heart. The feeling they must have all experienced was uncountable. They embraced each other and walked down the street in anticipation for warm freshly baked pizza.

"Mmm, smell it now, mama's got something cooking in the oven," rhymed Tamana.

"I'll make sure to save you a slice when I see you Ab in the morning," said Derrick.

Colours of Enlightenment & A Potion

"Now that makes two of you or shall I say one? No, no, there were three now saying the same. Listen Dee, I'm just go do my job, take a few photographs, and come back home," replied Abram.

They all walked out appreciating the night air.

That morning, the next same morning after, after the fall of desperation Craig thought of waiting. He tightened his collars of his long coat as he watched the friends leave the building very early that morning. Stepping over the cold concrete ground he prepared himself for a forced entry into the New Opera Theatre. From the shadows Craig walked over to the side door of the theatre and invited a jack handle to break the lock. He shook the doors once the chain had broken free to walk into the theatre.

Craig following his hunger to eat had not realized that the alarm would sound, and as sure as he wasn't the alarm sounded. Leaving the sound howling through the air of Moscow, and resonating through his cochleae, Craig ran out of the theatre and towards the metro through Pushkin Square. Jumping past people, knocking them into each other, he didn't care but run. Six people watched him rush and others moved when they saw him coming with pace.

"Can't be?! Can't be?! I'm going crazy, you're cool, you're cool. I need salt. Can't be?!" cried Craig.

Nudging passed people walking with dogs, and the elderly pouring moonshine to the pavement, he panted and rushed into the metro pushing further people aside. Craig fell into the crowd of morning commuters. He was running from freight as fast as his legs could carry him.

"Whoa, whoa, whoa, move, move!" he began shouting as he heard the train approaching. "Get out my way!" continued to exhale Craig, "Surely I am not crazy."

Twitching his toes, and forcing the patience of people departing the train he looked around to see if he had been followed. The sound seemed natural and there was no movement besides his own thought of ghosts. As Craig panted to catch his breath he entered the train and sat with his hands in his head forcing air to the carriage floor. He began to breathe more easily as he heard the doors close. The train began to rattle the tracks, and he began to rattle his fingers, he looked around slowly steadying himself.

Two silhouettes appeared to notice him as they merged into the background from the next carriage. Craig had not noticed, and this time was too frightened to care that they were not travelling alone. Afraid of his own past he sat in silence for a few stops without motion before leaving the metro and staggering home.

XIII: Math
BLUE

Believing in his passion Tyler dressed in navy and belonged to a political party. This party consisted of his students; they honored him with a blue ribbon. Tyler regarded his students as brothers and sisters and allowed them to bank on him. He had moved from Russia close to Fort Ross, CA, to help all children and also a thousand Muslims in the United States to benefit from the Christian Cross. Moreover from what Tyler had experienced, a wager was to be on balancing Christianity to professional or amateur.

"Bhangra music is fast and upbeat moreover the differences from blues, jazz and bebop music. People of different cultures make the difference in sounds, and balancing the differences is about learning the different types of wave motion," spoke Tyler to his class of physic students. "This is a wave that I'm talking about, and this is a wave to catch your attention."

The class started to laugh as Tyler drew a wave on the board and then waved to the class.

"Sound moves in a wave motion and catches in a medium that waves pass separates the sounds that we hear. Use different lengths of bamboo rods to hear the differing sounds. The wave of a sound will oscillate different to the sounds coming from plucking chords on a banjo or striking keys on a keyboard. We can alter parameters of sounds to achieve a common liking," said Tyler. "AC/DC circuits are measured in waves between voltage and current through a plate of induction. Periodic motion like a spring or a pendulum can be represented as waves to measure forces they exhibit. And as we stated earlier there also exists electromagnetic waves."

"The distance between peaks of a wave is the wavelength. The height of the wave is the amplitude. The time of one repeating segment of a wave is the period, and the number of periods in a second is the frequency. So if I speak really slowly and with depth of base, the frequency will be lower than if I make a squeak for the same second," Tyler gave an example of bass and squeak. "The velocity of that sound is measured by multiplying the frequency with the wavelength. This is measured in meters per second, and famously the equation for the speed of sound in air all relates to the temperature of where the sound is being made. '$V = 331 m/s + 0.6 T_c$.'"

Tyler pressed play on a stereo he had brought. The beat from the box filled the students with energy. They began listening to the music as Tyler presented some questions on the board.

"Bats have an audible hearing of sound that is supersonic, i.e. faster than sound frequencies that we can hear. And they project the sound which is reflected back off surfaces with an increased frequency and above human hearing."

"Sir, can they hear sound from us?" brightly asked one student.

Colours of Enlightenment & A Potion

"Hmm, that's a critical question. Unless they are sounding clicks and squeaks of their own as a form of Braille to distinguish us from food or a threat," replied Tyler. "Human hearing is audible not sonic, between 20 – 20,000 Hz in frequency. Okay try these questions with Om in mind to filter out the sound from the beat box, of course," Tyler bopped his head to the beat.

The beacons from his students began to light as they came to the end of answering the questions. Then as the bell bellowed Tyler said: "Ok, class tomorrow we will discuss how brave Will Smith, in 'Independence Day' was by calculating the flight pattern between the gravitational forces of earth and the alien mother-ship, using Kepler's Laws of Planetary Motion, Newton's Law of Universal Gravitation, and the Cavandish Balance Experiment, remember to bring in the brains."

XIV: Math
BLUE

Aware that the post would arrive in the next day or so, and before trying to make himself anymore bluer, Tyler made his best friend aware that he will be moving far away. Tyler sat calmly on the Arbatsko-Pokrovskaya metro-line after wishing his family farewell. He tightened his navy blue bandana and sat thinking on how Derrick would respond to his request.

"I need a lift. More like I'll like a lift so that way you get to see where I'll be living," asked Tyler to Derrick at Venezia Restaurant.

"What you talking about?" asked Derrick.

"Well how can I place this in the words that you will understand? Like a Great Blue Heron, I need to lift off against the centripetal force of gravity '$F_c = mv^2/R$' away from the centripetal acceleration of gravity '$a_c = v^2/R$' to travel at a tangent away from the center of this circle at a certain velocity '$v = 2 \pi R /T$' so I can reach San Francisco by dusk tonight," insisted Tyler.

"Why do you have to go to San Francisco?" asked Derrick.

"I have brought the coordinates for a safe arrival by the board walk. Magnitude and direction for the T.M. torque perpendicular to the earth's center axis that's if we leave now. As after we'll be out of time

Colours of Enlightenment & A Potion

from the rush of the parade that is about to start there. I promise I'll explain everything to you once we are there," Tyler bravely approached Derrick and whispered slowly, "my friend I have a job opportunity that I cannot miss in California, I hate to leave you more than Moscow, but come with me on this flight so you can always find me."

Derrick did not reply to Tyler's request immediately. Instead he walked with Tyler back to his home. Once they were inside the basement of the theatre, and once Derrick had time to think, he said: "Place some music on and weigh your bag, I'll be out in a minute," basically said Derrick.

Light can be interfaced constructively or destructively. Constructive interference would make light waves bigger in phase and destructive interference would cancel out phases. Digital wave optics allows digital discs to work. Light is bent around corners through slits in a linear media that combine to read encryptions on a digital medium. Infrared light has longer wavelengths that can be bent through interferences that resolve diffractions from compact discs, hence to catch sound on circuit boards. For Young this was second nature to putting sunglasses on.

Arriving beside a balustrade facing the Pacific Ocean, just before noon on the same day that they had left, Tyler slowly let go of Derrick. They had arrived on the balcony of where Tyler was to live away from home. From where the friends stood they could see Oakland Bay Bridge, and the greatest deep blue ocean.

"Not bad Tee. Not bad at all," said Derrick.

"There are some binoculars on that barrel there, have a look around," insisted Tyler. "Look at the barquentine boats on the bright ocean surface whilst I get us a few beers."

Geometric optics consists of light that can be refracted, reflected or diffracted. Binoculars are an excellent way of refracting light through a serious of lenses, convex, concave, and plain that allow distant objects to be seen closely and with better resolution. Using lenses to focus light to a different point allowed Galileo Galilei to distinguish parts of the universe. Later out of the blue, Snell's Law brilliantly described how light was used to value diamonds. Measuring the level of bevels to allow refractions of light to become total internal reflections make the diamond more valuable, i.e. the diamond shines light that much more brightly.

XV: Math
BLUE

"Balloons form static when rubbed on fabric surfaces. The electrons from the surface that a balloon has rubbed on become attached to the balloon, and then these electrons help the balloon to stick to other surfaces like a wall. Until the balloon loses the attached electrons to equilibrium with the new surface the balloon stays attached," said Tyler to his students in the laboratory of Abraham Lincoln High School, California.

Electrons are charged particles around a nucleus of an atom balancing in space. These particles bring a charge of negativity when spinning around a more positively charged nucleus. Each element has its own specific number of electrons in balance with the number of protons within the nucleus of an atom. Enabling the direction and type of spin of each electron in an atom, agreeing with the weight of the particle as it spins to hold a compound together, that equations were fabricated to carry the integrations into a value. A database of values summing a particular equation of the movement of electrons in space for a desired piece of matter, and possibly cabling that believable sum of energy into an electromagnetic wave, to bring the compound to move from A to B was an achievable hobby. The problem of moving the matter of electrons through other electrons was simple when delivered through space as light, but harnessing the light to travel through the earth's atmosphere in an equation of electrons would prove difficult.

"Basically the light over our heads is delivered through AC circuits. Which means electricity that is traveling back and forth from an alternator or generating transmitter, through power lines across a power grid, to a rectifier that converts the alternating current 'AC,' to a direct current 'DC,' through a switch system, and then back out to the power grid through an inverter," carried on Tyler whilst drawing a diagram explaining the example. "Copper metal conducts electricity the best as their electrons are more close together than any other metallic element on earth. Hence we use copper cords when transmitting current as voltage between car batteries. The thicker the cord the faster the battery will charge."

"Blindingly amazing that a French man and an English man worked together to make the AC/DC reality possible, this happened in 1881. Batteries were being worked on before this by Volta in 1800. The use of a serious of electrolyte half cells when joined with a copper wire increased the heat of an experiment during a lightning storm. The storm must have shocked Volta to think on how to harness that energy. So from the recorded 50 volts between a series of electrolyte cages we have simplified voltage to a comfortable 9 volts for most batteries, a reaction generating heat."

Tyler began to hand out circuit boards to his class. These boards were not at all like conventional boards seen for use by most students in schools. They appeared to be parts of track used to model a speed race

Colours of Enlightenment & A Potion

course for toy race cars. The men in the room had become overly excited and tried to bear their interest amongst the ladies. Nevertheless the girls had realized that the boys had belayed their attention towards the teacher and thought they too would join in.

"Join the tables together and the track pieces all as one, mount the bulbs on the circuit wherever you like, and once you have done that grab the stools and sit around the track. The red car is for the girls, and the blue car is for the boys," encouraged Tyler.

"Now we shall use the alternating current to provide a direct current through this experiment as I wish to charge the capacitors for future use. The stored capacitance charge is measured in farads '$C = Q/V$,' where Q is the charge of an electron. '$R = V/I$' meaning the voltage equals current multiplied by resistance. The resistor of the circuit is the cars' measured in ohms, the current is applied through our grid measured in amperes, and the voltage is what's carried in the current and measured as volts," Tyler said as his class worked on the track.

"Okay ladies and gentlemen, each car will travel at the same power in watts '$P = I^2R$' for example, and for emphasis I have not added any inductors or transformers in the circuit so you cannot blame the equipment if things turn blue for either team." Tyler smiled to see his class stare at him. "The overall voltage is the same for each team which is what?"

"110 volts!" said one of his students and looked out to the class, "Eagle!"

"Excellent! You can give the count."

"I'd like Christina to give the count if that's alright?" Tyler's student replied.

"Sure I'll do it," replied Christina off the mark.

She stood up and walked across to Mr. Hussain. She rattled her bangles and said:

"On the third beep, Ladies ready? Gentlemen ready? Beep, beep, Beep!"

The cars began whizzing around the track and the students encouraged their team car. As the students enjoyed themselves racing each other on and off the track, Tyler prepared their homework for pastime.

"Slowly, slowly, steady, right, right, make it to the home stretch!" cheered a member of the blue team.

Electrical charge 'q' is measured as Coulombs 'C' found by Benjamin Franklin, by the result of rubbing glass and rubber rods with silk and fur cloths. This formed positive and negative charges respectively on the rods. He concluded that "like charges repel and unlike charges attract" as the First Law of Electrostatics states. The Conservation of Energy law states "energy cannot be created or destroyed, but only transferred from one object to another." Thus the energy needed to move an electron is only 1.6×10^{-19} Joules, hardly noticeable that anything just happened, however something just did and that electron is now elsewhere. These statements from Coulomb's Law, demonstrates how to find precise forces to move minute masses of positive and negative charges. These charges are generated through turbines of power stations to direct electromagnetic energy to satellites in space or across power grids in our environment.

XVI: Math
BLUE

Praying by staring to the blue sky Derrick immediately became aware that the move for Tyler was a good one. Oblivious to the time Tyler had left to get beers, Derrick made himself comfortable on a deckchair accompanying Tyler's balcony. Like Bill Murray, in 'Lost in Translation,' Derrick drifted into peace amongst the soft sweet scent coming from the ocean.

Having a habit for science Derrick began to place numerals to his surroundings. As a barometer he began calculating the density of the ocean against the earth's atmospheric pressure of 1.01×10^5 Pascal. This was by far an enjoyment factor for him, as he knew the pressure of water in an open environment would equal the force of pressure acting upon it. The pressure is the same as that of the atmosphere. Thus if a boat needs to float then using Archimedes's Principle, the buoyancy would equal the weight of the displaced fluid. Hence dense boats measured by mass/volume, should have enough surface area to displace enough water so the pressure in the ocean can keep the boat afloat in relation to the pressure of the atmosphere.

"Call the doctor when in trouble! Call the doctor when in trouble! Call the doctor when in trouble or when someone falls down. What? They fell over.

What? They fell over. What they fell down by the phone box that's burgundy!" sang Derrick hearing Tyler arrive.

"You looking comfortable there, what were you thinking?" Tyler said.

"Well considering you asked. If I can change the magnetic field that is radiated across that channel along the bridge, using Faraday's Law of Electromotive force, 'EMF (V) = - $N\Delta\phi_B/\Delta t$,' and the use of ferromagnetic materials in the surroundings as a magnet, I would be able to create a vacuum large enough to lift the water off the bottom of the sea as Moses did to the River Jordan and walk to the other side," spoke Derrick with a smooth smile as he knew Tyler understood him.

"That would cause way too much radiation to be scattered," encouraged Tyler.

"Beforehand, I would require a bolometer to measure the heat radiation to make sure no bolts or bones are affected along this coast."

"I see. Well when you're done put away your battle bayonets and let's walk down to the peer, see who we find at the parade's bazaar. Now I'm handing you a drink, there's a little alcohol in it, plus there's some ice cubes, no need to figure any effects of thermodynamics or conservation of energy with heat from the scotch. No changing the latent heats of fusion or vaporization, just drink up."

"Ah the old specific heat capacity of a material trick. Heat gained by the ice is heat lost by the drink, and all heat is phased into my belly, and out through my pores. Why do we drink again?"

Colours of Enlightenment & A Potion

"To enjoy a little of life my friend," said Tyler. "Stop falling asleep and go take a shower. Need you to look sharp if I'm hoping to boil with someone tonight. However if I consume 1 liter of soda with n amount of moles, within my internal atmospheric pressure of 3 Pa, and being warm interiorly at 20°C, and you not changing the ideal gas constant, using 'PV = nRT,' what mass of gas will I have by the end of the night?"

Both friends started laughing, not because the joke was funny but because they were both finding an accurate answer. They thought about placing the liquor in the refrigerator and saving the good blue label for later. After they dressed to impress, the scientists staggered beneath the blue sky to San Francisco bay.

XVII: Math
BLUE

"Using a Beaufort scale to measure wind 10 meters off the ground, I have analyzed that we will be having light winds next week, compared to those units expressing a hurricane," said Tyler. "This means that all of you should have your parent's authorization for me to take you to the billiard house next Friday to study momentum and vectors."

Tyler always kept his class enthusiastic about physics, and using real life examples his class achieved brilliant grades with improving accuracy and neatness. Billiards provided a great example to teach them about scalar units, (one number to describe magnitudes, such as mass, temperature, time, etc), vector units, (three numbers to describe magnitude and direction, such as position, velocity, and force), and tensor units, (more than three numbers, such as those to describe a matrix of elasticity).

Upon arriving to the billiard room, Tyler handed them outlines of his teaching. Newton's Law of Motion was to be discussed.

"Newton's First Law," he said. "'Objects at rest remain at rest, and objects in motion remain in a uniform motion unless acted on by an external force.' As you can see the balls will not move unless we strike

Colours of Enlightenment & A Potion

them, and when we do they'll move uniform to the force that we apply." He raised his cue and tapped a ball to roll. "Newton's Second Law: 'the force applied is equal to the mass of the object multiplied by the acceleration exerted upon it'. Thus I would not need to apply an exceedingly strong force to have this mass move to the pocket way over there."

The class stood in bewilderment to try and understand why Tyler could not explain that at school. At the present time, the class would not have appreciated the external example, but they later would learn to associate grounds on believing the simplicity of Sir Isaac Newton's practices.

"Just like how a rocket needs to have enough force to lift its weight from the ground so do the balls need to move. This is where Newton's Third Law comes into play, 'for every action, there is an equal and opposite reaction,' does anyone understand what I mean?" he asked his students.

No one replied as they were afraid to be wrong outside their common habitat of the classroom.

"Well as you will see in your handouts, acceleration is replaced with the letter 'g' meaning the rocket will have to overcome earth's gravity to lift the mass. The acceleration of gravity is 9.8 m/s^2. Now it's just a simple matter of multiplying mass with 'g' to find the force 'Newtons – kg/m/s' needed," he paused and some students sniffed to show that they understood. "Force equals mass multiplied by velocity or acceleration of gravity '$F = mv$ or $F = mg$' depending upon the question."

"Using vectors we can calculate the beauty of trajectory, standstill and the position of landing of that object over there. I don't want any of you to throw the balls at each other but practice the degrees of linear force exhibited when making these billiard balls collide. Do we need exponential forces to move the same mass a longer distance when both masses are the same? Record results on the table I have provided as ticks and crosses for the given experiments."

"Okay class, imagine that these balls are not balls but planets set in space in order to collide. Remembering that energy is conserved from one form to another, we can relate these to momentum. The force of the impact left after a collision can be measured to discover who's to blame."

Tyler continued: "The force of each body is taken into account before and after the collision; '$m_1v_{1o} + m_2v_{2o} = m_1v_{1f} + m_2v_{2f}$.' The changes in velocity between objects can be evaluated. For instance a 53' Rig hitting a Mini Cooper; the Mini Cooper against the force of the truck will crumble and if the velocity of the truck had not changed then one would become blue.

The class sniffed softly declaring approval.

"The table below the diagram on the next page illustrates using equations how to find the missing factor to objects set in motion. For instance the final velocity of an object when missing the distance traveled in time, the final distance of an object when missing acceleration or final velocity, and the final velocity of object when missing time. All these equations have been rearranged from the simple equations relating velocity 'v,' with distance 's,' time 't,' and acceleration 'a,' to '$v_{avg} = \Delta s/\Delta t$' and '$a_{avg} = \Delta v/\Delta t$.'"

The students began to look uneasy because they were losing all blood to their brains. Seeing them turn

Colours of Enlightenment & A Potion

colour Tyler asked them to breathe easy as all the equations were a matter of practice. He smiled to reassure his class and allowed them to take a break from understanding Newton's Laws. He prepared their potential energy by running through a few examples on tackling vector quantities; he later packed up the billiard balls, and decided to balance their moods by taking them out for bulk burgers and beverages, in an atmosphere that they enjoyed.

XVIII: Library
BLACK

In the lightly lit central nave of the library of Lomonosov Moscow State University, Derrick sat with Abram and Tyler. From the presence and appearance of these friends they were given silence around their table, that to say that not even the people around them would be smart enough to listen into their conversation. They together were adjusting their thoughts on what they had observed from the broken lock from the morning before.

"Dee and I followed him home. He lives off Begovaya Metro, seems like he lives alone. We watched him enter his home and with lights on we didn't notice any other people or movement besides those that came from him. We could wait in hiding tonight to see if he approaches the theatre and try to make himself vulnerable for exposure?" filled Tyler for Abram.

"That will not be necessary. I'm sure we can keep an eye on him; however what must have possessed him to try and brake into a theatre? Maybe because he had seen Abram and I unloading the equipment the night before the lock was broken? He must have had no idea what to have expected and hence I think he will arrive back soon to find out actually what he saw," anointed Derrick. "We should try and

Colours of Enlightenment & A Potion

bring him in to make sure he doesn't go too crazy or bring unwanted attention."

"Shall we wait to see if he makes himself known or shall we pull him in? He doesn't seem like the person to bring up a struggle, but I'll take Abram with me just in case," volunteered Tyler.

The library remained busy during the entire day. The place of study was occupied by graduates, students, faculty members of the university and to the public. The library was used to sponsor human resources for individuals that loved to learn or needed a place to find answers. The main building of the university housed the library. During the reign of Stalin, seven neoclassical buildings were constructed around Moscow, where the largest was made into Moscow State University in 1755.

Main metro stations around the facility were Okhotny Ryad and Biblioteka Lenina. M.S.U. founded shopping centers, restaurants, bars, more dining areas, nurseries, classrooms, lecture halls, a bomb shelter, and laboratories to analyze the universities special interest, soil sciences and geology. In the southwest corner of Moscow the building was refurbished modern in 1953 and holds the largest library (according to the number of books) in Russia. The library life focuses on encyclopedic learning for all education specialties.

"Come to think about this, bring him in tomorrow, here. Same time, I'll be here, take Abram to join you. I need to see him up close. I need to know what he saw and analyze if he can be trusted. He can see what we choose for him to see now, nothing besides what we desire, however as far as I can tell, he's an honest man that is short on food, money and love.

Possibly we could strengthen our faith by helping him," he said.

"I think you're right. I rather get to meet him and judge his behavior than wait for him to do something stupid. Finding answers about why he was trying to break in will be best delivered from the horse's mouth than us assuming. I will feed him some money or pizza. See which one he responds to better before I bring him to meet you here. Now are you sure a stranger can be trusted?" asked Tyler.

"Oh trust me, checking theories he definitely needs us, without us he will be alone until he dies, and everything that I have predicted to change will not occur without him. Maybe it was his stupidity, his poverty or his curiosity that would kill cats. Nonetheless I need to see him, so don't take no for an answer. And yes feed him before meeting here tomorrow, something light and simple like a coffee and a biscuit to keep him alert," gently spoke Derrick to Tyler and Abram in the quietness of the library.

XIX: Library
BLACK

Wooden bookshelves, tall wooden tables, wooden chairs with padding, along with dark wooden floor board, concrete walls with darkened concrete ceilings covered by wooden beams, and soft lighting kept the library masqueraded with silence over wisdom.

So three times over Derrick read his material to the end of each sentence, paragraph, chapter or book as he learnt from his work. Between sentences he would try not to become distracted by the ladies who tried to acquire his attention as they walked around him. He didn't look around whilst he was in the middle of a sentence. Words he did not recognize he filled with the phrase 'something' and finished his sentences. He would wait till he reached the end of a sentence before sitting back and taking a breather. He had no interest in noticing other people and become distracted from his thought, unless he was observing what would look nice on Tamana or himself. Derrick concluded his work by twirling his pen or tapping the table. He read his work a minimum of three times over to the last sentence to provide himself a mean eighty-five percent accuracy for his decisions every time.

Ninety-five percent averages were what he scored during his tests when he was studying with the faculty of physics and material science at M.S.U. Derrick would give himself a week before his exams to read the material. The first time over to the last sentence would take four days due to understanding both appearance and message of the material. The second time would take him two days. And the third time would take a day to complete to the last sentence. Any other time after that he would just touch the notes and by touch would realize and revise what had been learnt. He had mastered this to reading nine hours one day, three hours the next and twice on the third day, leaving two days to exercise and the last to place the icing. His strategy worked to provide him with a social life alongside.

   That social life was spent on his own passions. Together with observing if the girls in the library were observing what other girls were wearing. With Tamana taking pride in her appearance he noticed that she was the girl for him. Tamana made extra effort to look presentable as she believed psychically that this improved health, not only for herself, but also for others around her. She brightened the day for everyone when she came to study. Most the times Derrick was in the library without her, especially after they had graduated. Tamana worked at the medical centre and Derrick worked on his projects.

   For company in the times of solitary, Derrick would place invisible insects as spiders and male ladybugs on the table to motivate his mental synapses to fire. He would pretend that they would walk to the shaded areas of the table and wait to either eat or be eaten. Smiling he would finish writing or reading his sentences. If he made a mistake he would simply cross

Colours of Enlightenment & A Potion

it out with one line and carry on. No white out, nor scribbling in, no more tablets of stone, and no more papyrus to be written on, just simple black ink on paper, leaving the rest of time to hypothesize.

XX: Library
BLACK

The clock had just past three in the afternoon. Derrick was at the library waiting for Abram and Tyler to bring their guest. He was reading a large book with small font up close when he felt the environment change around him. Derrick switched hand of the book which he was reading vertically upwards and turned the page. As the book was large his hands would become tired but not the thirst of his interest. When he realized he was not reading to script but through script as well, he found this to be cool and strong, so he carried on to read for leisure vertically and for information horizontally.

As Derrick turned the next page of his book the light around his table weakened. Tyler and Abram blocked most of the light as they approached Derrick reading. Derrick carried on reading to finish his paragraph before looking up to see their new guest.

"You will not believe where we found him? He was waiting outside the theatre when I went to open the doors for the staff early this morning," Tyler said as he approached Derrick in the library at M.S.U. "Sit down Craig," Tyler said to their new guest. "This is Derrick Tarasov."

Craig sat opposite Derrick with Tyler and Abram sat around the table from him.

Colours of Enlightenment & A Potion

"Have you had something to eat?" asked Derrick to Craig.

"Yes, this guy insisted I eat before meeting you. Thank you," replied Craig.

"I know your name, I know where you live, I know that you are living on peanuts, and I know that you tried to break into my theatre a few nights ago. I know all this as that is my work, what I don't know is why you tried to break in?" enquired Derrick.

There was a silence around the table as Derrick waited for an answer.

Craig sniffed a sign of acceptance and said: "I saw you, and this big fellow, emptying a van in the middle of the night the day before I broke in. I was looking to steal from you. I'm sorry. I am truly sorry. Please I'll do anything you ask of me, just don't have me arrested. I suffer from Parkinson's and the law cannot understand. Help me."

"Help you? Like how?" asked Tyler.

"You will never believe me, but I was waiting for you earlier today as I'm sure you would be able to explain what I saw at your place."

The three friends waited for Craig to continue with what he was stuttering to say.

"I saw me, I saw me, there on the other side of your door. I saw me looking straight at me, wearing the same clothes that I had on that night. He smiled at me, and with freight I stood for a moment and bells starting to ring, that is when I fled instead of falling to the floor. I ran. I ran home thinking I may have imagined that. These past days I thought that it was a mirror I had seen my reflection in," Craig paused. "But I asked myself to leave. And now I think I'm going crazy."

Craig sat staring at Derrick, he glanced at Tyler and then to Abram. Abram bowed his sight to the table. Craig did the same.

"You realize I lost everything from your greed. My theatre was in ruins after the last incident. A wreckage was made but you are not well aware of that. Nevertheless you are showing great mercy now, and that through the hand that you dealt, I am with great gratitude for whatever made it possible for you to meet me," said Derrick. "I need something from you."

"Anything, however I have nothing to offer you except myself, but please explain to me what I saw. I cannot sleep, work, or even breathe without sweating. I will do anything you ask me. Was what I saw a reflection? Then again how can a reflection speak back? I'm a good man. I'm a good man. I'm a good man. What would you like from me? Don't report me to the police, I have nothing of yours."

Derrick leaned over the table and brought his hands together. Tightening his grip with both hands he expanded them out like he was holding a world of knowledge between them. Moving his fingertips as some sort of chart mapping he organized his archive of thought within the sphere of perplexes. Derrick sat for several moments in his own world with his friends around him. He pitched and forked ideas of progression within the space of his hands. The rhythm of Derrick's thought was felt by his friends and Craig. Slowly the rhythm slowed; sliding his palms over each other he made contact with his smallest fingers and brought his thought back to rest. Derrick tapped his index fingers together and began playing incy-wincy spider with his fingers.

Colours of Enlightenment & A Potion

"Go home, wear the same clothes you had on two nights ago, and meet me tonight at the theatre. Come and speak to Abram, this big fellow," Derrick said looking at Craig and gesturing over to Abram. "Meet me tonight after nine; make sure you are wearing the same clothes. I assure you there is nothing to be concerned about; I am not calling any authorities on you. Let's say I need you to help as a backstage extra," Derrick said as he sat back and looked towards the library's exit. "I appreciate your confession Craig."

Whilst bowed to the table Craig said before leaving, "I appreciate your forgiveness Derrick."

XXI: Relations
GREEN

Gradually coming to an understanding about how men and women can stand together goes a long way as communion of grass blades growing. Meaning there are as many men and women as there are grass blades standing together, then stems grow, and later trees with leaves, and with ivy vines to blooming apples and pears. Some like to try herbs as coriander, parsley, and basil before planting anything firm whilst others like to see if they would like to add chilies, jalapeños and certain capsicums with their diet.

    The guys had a system to prepare themselves on finding the right caterpillar. The guys would circulate three dates a month whilst in education and kept this rhythm occurring until they graduated. Later they would intend to circle the globe, arrive back home, enter employment and decide to love old grapes or pick new ones. As for Derrick he allowed his caterpillar to grow, cocoon, to hatch from the chrysalis and into adult Tamana.

    Grounds for the strategy would not have started during freshman year. Freshman year was used to make friends and find common interest with new colleagues during education. The friends agreed on a strong

Colours of Enlightenment & A Potion

foundation with their peers, for themselves, and for each other as they progressed into adulthood.

Within the woods of the parks that they were near they would meet after school during their adolescent years. Here they would discuss on how to introduce themselves to the opposite sex. They sat amongst the trunks of trees and themselves around a campfire. As the ground warmed around them the crickets began to click.

They pitched ideas on settling on an agreement for maintaining a three date average a month. The guys loved their work but they needed to understand what love was elsewhere. Luscious appearances of multi-desires all need to be loved as particularly admiring a certain somebody can be hard to judge. As sparrows listening over each other the guys spoke in third dialect within each other's speeches, mastering how love in friendship can co-exist with love for another.

So they laughed whilst throwing sandal wood chippings into the fire, and the fire roared upon combustion to help keep them warm. In the quietness of the forest a hard crackling came loud and with a thud. A log of lumber landed in front of them from tumbling down to gravity from the branches high above. Their decision was made when the natural plank of wood covered with fur and moss landed between them and the fire.

They concluded by their lives being spared that their decision towards finding true love by statistical assortment from a random population was a good one.

XXII: Relations
GREEN

Grace was delivered into dining for the first date for all the guys. For all people over all the metro lines to affordable restaurants and cafes scattered along Zamoskvoretskaya Metro. The truth for the friends to take their first dates out dining on the last Friday of the first month of graduate school allowed them to assess their date.

Eating food from salads with crisphead, romaine, butterhead, or other leaf varieties of lettuce to a little meat on the side, and other members of vegetables as green beans to a little dressing and some drink, wine or not, allowed the conversations made to sound in scrumptious expression.

If the date wasn't going well then there was always the food to adore. Later leaving a peaceful peck on the cheek by the bus or metro stop, or at their date's front door enabled them to move onto the next date. The guys would usually meet one or another at the local twenty-four hour fast food diner, mostly Sbarro Pizza, to discuss some fun or why they weren't invited through the gate.

Dining included times that were juggled around study. Sometimes dining with a date had to be forced into lunch times or quick breaks between lectures. The men from the friends happened not to waste time when

Colours of Enlightenment & A Potion

deciding to approach the women. They approached women they found attractive when they felt they needed to express their feelings for them. The social networking was performed by trial and error. Libraries were used to study just as breaks were used for coffee.

Tyler would take out girls he fancied due to their charismas for Starbucks during lunch. He would watch them buy a muffin and then he would allow them to watch him place his money back in his pocket. A gracious smile was what he watched for, plus he waited to watch if she noticed other girls. Like Abram and Derrick they only dated girls that had girlfriends.

Girls that were suited to see what other girls were wearing led themselves into further dates. Sometimes the second date in the second month would lead to a third date in the third month, but never would there be an intimate relationship before graduating. Dining more than once a month with the same girl depended upon the grandeur of their work and the grace of their date.

Tamana had a predisposition of facial symmetry with most her dates. That to mean she would screw-up her face when she felt uncomfortable, showing a face of anger and disgust if she felt threatened. She had learnt that scrolling her fingers would work to defend her position. Furthermore she developed the ability not be embarrassed in public. The guys she dated quickly learnt that about her, that to just hold open a door for Tamana would be considered as strong as a date. The second date would be her bumping into you whereas the third date would be to break.

To be born in right proportions as intended through Adam and Eve allowed most to become envious. Gleeful covered girls with modest guys that were not in pray came to realize that God had other intentions. Through freight, crime, greenery amongst the same or crossing genders, would have brought smiling towards personal shopping fears for genocide. Into the darkness like disability they can enjoy forever. That was another reason the guys dated on a gradient as through this gradient they gave to others.

XXIII: Relations
GREEN

Sitting with Tamana in Sbarro Restaurant, in their favorite location next to the jungle painted wall she asked Abram for some advice.

"I have nothing to talk about when I'm on a date. What do you guys talk about? And what do the girls you date talk about? I'm losing my mind; I keep talking to the guys I'm with about medicine, pharmacy crosses, or gangrene," asked Tamana.

Abram laughed, gave a sigh and said: "That's funny. Well you are half on the right track. Listen to this story: Shree Krishna, 'The Lord in Hindu scripture that agreed with Prophet Prince Arjun, that his salvation was made regardless that he killed his brother or not. Lord Krishna was a friend of Arjun's, and was his charioteer in the Kuruksetra War, 5000 B.C.' Now before this, gopies were all the farm girls, all girls loved Lord Krishna, not because He was from God, but was God Himself for the people. So the girls' flirted their good stuff amongst Him to grab His attention. He gowned them clothes in all colours to try to keep something on them. Now these gopies only had questions to ask Him. Then there came one girl that He found fond liking as she studied in various arts and spoke of her interests, and asked Shree Krishna of His.

"So you can either ask questions to your dates

or find more things that interest you and talk about them. Possibly give time to listen to your date. Ask him what he likes to be worn on a woman. Share some interests of his. Overall enjoy time away from work. Show confidence to other girls around you if you cannot find any common ground with your date."

"I see, like 'I'm doing my nails tonight, what about you?'"

"That's good, that's more like it. Now if I wish to pick up on the nails thing I can but it's second date night tonight, so hate to leave you but I have to glide."

Second date night for Tamana was usually non-existent. She had feelings for Derrick since youth and rarely allowed a date to reach the second month. Nevertheless she felt at times a second date was needed, times when she wished to make a point, or times when an Antonio Banderas would have bumped past her with grace and asked with sincerity for the time to be spent with her. These dates after dining would follow into the cinemas or dancing with a dark green bottle of Carlsburg by her girlfriends and Banderas.

The guys helped each other on second dates. They would join a night for qualifiers at Brunswick Bowling Lanes. They would wait for each other and their dates at Shosse Entuziastov Metro, on a Friday or Sunday, to walk to the bowling alley. Cans of Sprite or 7-Up, if so Mountain Dew, maybe with water or vodka, great for the guys as they would warm the girls, and great for the girls as they would warm each other. Neon lighting with twelve pound bottle green bowling balls kept the men shooting turkeys well past graduation.

XXIV: Relations
GREEN

Camouflaged within the shades of leaves their clothes completely made them invisible amongst their surroundings. Through having darkened paint smeared across their faces, only the white of their teeth and corneas could be seen. The beasts in the jungle knew of their presence, the birds watched with stealth themselves, and both stayed silent not to give the commandos colours away.

In solitary these men have lived without any pleasures from women. Days, to weeks, to months, to years had passed since they had set up camp in the middle of the Amazon. They silently stand in secret away from the working world. They remain concealed away from humanity. The light that they share shines in from the sunlight in the day between branches of leaves and lanterns from locals during the night.

The ground would shake to make the trees drop fruits for them. Currently they remain waiting for the world's leaders to destroy each other. Grace fall onto my unborn child, the g-chord would ring, and they will be able to raise humanity once again, simply because they showed love.

Nothing was past their tendency for their passion for what they knew to exist. They glowed with radiance together as they knew how to show love.

Times amongst cries could be heard through the night carried by howling of the wind. They would look left on their own trunk to bring to reason their existence to live.

Gravitopism would enable them not to fall over, and phototropism would enable them to grow towards the light. However at times with closer observation they could be seen bending their bark to peer their appendages through residential windows, or imitate curves of gravel lining roads.

The earth had yielded a fine group of soldiers. They showed love unlike those that had plenty of green from the sweat of making others cry. These men adapted well in their chlorophyll filled leaves and cellulose based cell walls. They were the most merciful. There was no one stronger. Glad to say that they were the only ones worthy enough to live on this globe.

XXV: Relations
GREEN

"That glitter dress would look nice on you. That velvet dress would look nice on you. That dress would look nice on you. This would look nice on you. These would look nice on you. Those combat pants would look nice on you. That Brazil t-shirt would look nice on you. She would look nice on you, these would look nice on you and this would look nice on me, Score!" said Derrick as he walked with Tamana on their third date around Okhotny Ryad Shopping Centre.

"If you like it, like seriously like it, then I'll buy it," she said.

"Well make sure to try it on first. Besides I like video games, Grand Theft Auto is a cool game, Halo is a cool game, Pro-Evolution Soccer is a cool game, Need for Speed-Most Wanted, is a cool game, Tekken Tag is a cool game, the Nintendo Wii seems to have cool games, SSX3 is the coolest game, however can you buy some lunch instead?" he asked.

Abram's third date happened to be with a girl whose role model was Beyonce Knowles. He happened to see her in Starbucks whilst he was entertaining another girl. The girl happened to grab his attention by speaking about Cassius Clay during drinking coffee with her friend. Abram smiled over at her to acknowledge he liked her tone of voice. And not being the shy type she slipped Abram her number, time, date, and place for Friday night dancing.

The glorious girl wore clothes that left just enough to the imagination. The secret to her success was to sleep with her mouth open. Along with taking pride in her appearance she practiced the stance of yoga when resting or working. The stance was to maintain first finger and thumb contact to keep her heart beating. Improving cellular metabolism with the heart pulsing kept her in shape. This glorious girl managed to receive a third date, and on this date Abram took her to the zoo.

"I would like to see an Emerald Lizard," mentioned Abram.

"I would like to see the Siberian Tiger," said his date.

"That is a gorgeous animal. Hope he's not sleeping," said Abram.

"I'll wake him with a growl," she said.

"Now that just turned hot into sexy."

"Enough to add me to twice a month?"

"Hey look we're here Barrikadnaya Metro Station. And I'll have to hear that growl before I can decide."

The doorbell rang to Tyler's apartment. His third date was movie night with a choice between watching Gladiator's, Russell Crowe or Gerard Butler's, role in 300. The Gladiator was given more emphasis by his date as there was less gore. Whereas with 300 there was a likely chance that she would end up throwing herself on Tyler.

Colours of Enlightenment & A Potion

"I wouldn't mind watching a comedy if you'd prefer?" asked Tyler.

"Action suits me just fine. Do you mind if I take my boots off?" asked his date.

"If you like. That's a nice glittery hijab, how many do you have? And would you like a drink?"

"What do you have? And I have several. My favorite is a white stitched one with lace."

"Beer, wine, apple juice, orange juice, water and milk."

"Do you have any cookies?"

"I have some cookies and cream ice-cream if that's what you were thinking."

"What are you going to have?"

"Mmm…. I'll blend the ice-cream with a little milk and sugar to make a shake."

"Do you have any white wine?" she said and began laughing to herself. "Forget that, I'll have a cold soda if you have one."

Tyler chose the movies to see his date's reaction towards movies of leadership, honor and righteousness, this in all to find grounds for her grace for ending gruesome suffering. His heart filled with love for this girl as she gave a tear gladly to the mercy of the Gladiator.

XXVI: Relations
GREEN

Usually an image of jealousy and envious cruelty projected from the edges away from the surface of emeralds. A decision was made by noble persons to have all things flicked off to be adjusted to mark churchmanship. Thus gothic graves were turned to greased gears that peddled gondolas across sea water as grasshoppers across lawns.

"Managed to find yourself to me this time? What have you come to let me know? That my time is still yet to come? How can you judge your time around me? What if I was sitting there?" asked Craig. "Yes, you can probably answer all questions, mostly with more reason to persuade yourself other than anyone else."

"One thing I could not predict was your gratitude that you have. What living around all these g-strings you have become an old fart," replied Derrick. "Thought you would be able to handle the sunshine?"

"Get out of here man! There is nothing for you here."

"What? I have come to listen to the music, hear the wave's crash onto the shore, the sweet smell of sea water, the sound of birds in the sky, the sight of bright papayas selling around every corner, ripe coconuts

Colours of Enlightenment & A Potion

hanging from the palm trees, not your lazy ass. Now take your turn!" demanded Derrick whilst he poured himself a glass of water.

Since his last move Craig had opted to stay in Copacabana Borough. From traveling with the friends that made him a brother, they were not pleased for him to leave them. Nevertheless by the end of 2010, Rio de Janeiro, Brazil, South America had become home to Craig Goncharov. Through the festival that the friends had come to see Craig met Gwyneth and fell in love.

Waiting in line at a local bar across the stretch of Copacabana Beach the friends spoke Russian in Rio. Every other person spoke Portuguese except Gwyneth who spoke both languages freely. The accents changed to find common ground, (that ground found being their tongues), from then Craig remained behind in Brazil as the others waiting for each other to age.

"Teach me what you have learnt in your travels young scholar," asked Craig as he moved his knight three spaces.

"I witnessed the finding of the Holy Grail," Derrick said, and moved his king close to Craig's knight. "Inscription laid out in the mind of a young adult, Thomas Guy, who lived 1645 to 1724, and was a bookseller whom later founded Guy's Hospital of London. Later another fell and broke all boundaries to establish Guy's legacy. The Holy Grail was founded when all men thought on one wavelength. That all men are now bowing over to the Messiah for forgiveness and not to sand on beautiful women."

"So that is true. I had felt much calmer winds living here. There is something of peace written in this so called stranger's testimony that I wish to be worthy to untie his sandals. I mean the personas have begun to speak in a richer dialect. Walking in the market I hear speech expressions on niños have changed. They are actually speaking to the adults, all about a country amigo trabajar as a till clerk silencing the ignorance of Americano pride."

"The truth to the Holy Grail is that no man needs to fall at anyone's feet no longer but that of the Messiah's alone. The new founder insisted to nail Jesus before the wood began to degrade and rot, and the Father watched Him be raised so all could have a chance to see Heaven. Thus I went to seek the birth of trees. Gradually back in time but this gyroscope measured me back to the present all times I registered for Genesis. I know I will not get to see the first man, but I'm sure you'd agree that we should believe in him."

The last words to come out of Craig's mouth before he checkmated Derrick were: "God is Good."

Craig felt greatly overwhelmed to hear Derrick paint that picture for him. Distinct measures of Derrick's vocal pitch turned the world's dark jealousy around them into umbrella cocktails with drops of sour light lime like Lyublinskaya Metro line.

XXVII: Sport
BLACK

"*A grand opening to the massive event of 2008 here in Quebec City. What a glorious start to a hundred year anniversary in International Ice Hockey. Canada with the last win in 2007 on Russian soil, and now for the first time in 100 years Canada is hosting the beginning of another fantastic win against Russia."

"Last year the Canadian national team clenched the title from the Russians, and progressed to beat the awesome Finland team winning the 2007 IIHF title. Can they do the same this year against the mighty Russian squad on home ground?!"

"If the passion for Team Canada is as much as the excitement as the crowd brewing here in Colisee Pepsi Arena, then we are in for a fantastic night. Three periods of explosive energy, I just can't contain myself Cephus!"

"Amazing absolutely Juan, best to put down the coffee and hold onto your seat. The arena seems to be as excited as we are, the ice is being polished, and looks like the dens are being loaded!"

Early hours of a morning Craig pulled open the side entrance door to the New Opera Theatre.

"Leave from here Craig. Leave Now!" cried future Craig to his counter self.

Craig made his past self vanish from freight in the matter of seconds without thought. He looked over at Derrick as Derrick walked out of the shadows to pat Craig on the shoulder.

"I almost scared myself," said Craig. "Dam I definitely scared him."

Derrick closed the door and led him inside.

"Hold onto the time-machine once again as we have somewhere to be," asked Derrick. "Take a deep breath."

The room began to chill and crackles of sound formed electrical charge separating the air space around them. Derrick and Craig lost touch of the ground as they became covered in subatomic aura bright enough for them to shut their eyes. A pulse of potential energy released itself from the time-machine and was drawn back as kinetic energy, leaving nothing but naked space in the basement of the New Opera Theatre.

Landing outside the Colisee Pepsi Stadium in Quebec City, Canada, on Sunday May 19th 2008, Derrick and Craig presented themselves between the path of the car park and the stadium. Craig opened his eyes slowly to hear talking from the distance. As much to their surprise they witnessed the Big Red Machine walking from the distance towards them.

"What is the Russian Team doing over there? Shouldn't they be inside?" said Derrick.

He looked over at the main entrance to the stadium and saw the coach for Team Canada. Team Canada was exiting the bus outside the stadium into the building. The Russian team, Big Red Machine, was approaching Derrick and Craig, but with their sight fixed to walk past them. They were uttering abuse amongst each other. Derrick recognized the team captain Alexei Morozov, and approached him.

"Hey Morozov, couldn't you get parking closer to the arena?" he said.

"Don't get me started man. We were also stopped by the Canadian police on our way here, you'd think an international event would host appropriate measures for the teams. Now I'm witnessing the Canadians walking in, and we have been carrying our gear over a kilometer. Seriously man, who are you?" said Morozov.

"Well for Russia, for me, and for my friends you make sure you win tonight. Just be cool and no doubt we'll win. We'll take that title back and on their home ground. Now get to the cloakroom, Oorah! Don't let them get to you. We are here for them, you remember that," said Derrick looking at Morozov, and then the rest of the men.

"Ya, for CSKA Moscow!" shouted Craig.

"For CSKA Moscow!" shouted back the Big Red Machine.

CSKA Moscow stood for Centraliy Sportiviy Klub Armii, which translated to the Army's Central Sport Club. They were the best in the Continental Hockey League and in the European Champions Cup. They dominated the Soviet League for forty-six years winning 32 titles, (and one streak of 13 titles), compared to the closest rivals Montreal Canadiens at 24 titles, (and a streak of five titles). CSKA Moscow was the best at what they did with no team ever to have come close.

Sandeep Patel

Ice hockey was first played indoors in Montreal, at Victoria Skating Rink, on March 3rd 1875. Since then they had climbed to become one of the most talented orientated sports of all time. Cold countries such as Canada, Scandinavia and Russia dominated the recruitment in finding the athletes of this sport. The National Hockey League supported by the American government went to greater lengths to sponsor the life of the sport, and with more indoor arenas the sport has stayed alive for over a century.

From 1946, CSKA Moscow had set the bar and brought the challenge into the sport. Anatoli Tarasov, played on ice and then coached the team from 1953-1974. After this time the number of players signing for the sport began to decline till 1980 as the Soviet Union changed to the Red Army Team. New players were to be sieved to find the best athletes and them to be shifted for work in the Red Army instead. Thus attributes of CSKA Moscow declined, and the last game played was a friendly with the Russian National Team, Big Red Machine, playing in January 2008.

"Sliding onto the ice the officials have made their way. The teams are all aligned and the puck is about to drop."

"As we count down to a fast paced action packed game I would like to mention the pressure that our visitors are to face. The Russian Machine has not won a title for fifteen years with their last being captained by Vyacheslav Bykov in 1993. Now he's coaching the team to hopefully take the World Championship 2008 title back to Moscow, but can he

Colours of Enlightenment & A Potion

break the Canadian spirit? The atmosphere of this ice rink makes this extremely hard to imagine!"

"Nevertheless Juan, Bykov has led the team with outstanding outcomes against the Swiss and the Finns to bring them here today. We hope this game is a clean one, all supporters are to enjoy and there are many supporters in the crowd, a nice clean competition."

"Ha. You're right Cephus; if the heat of this fabulous stadium becomes any warmer we will not have any ice to play on. O.K.... the puck is dropped and possession has immediately fallen to the home team!"

XXVIII: Sport
BLACK

Of a crowd close to the full capacity of fifteen-thousand people, Derrick and Craig made way to find their friends in the arena. Squeezing past French speaking Canadians they climbed down the alley and crossed the right wing opposite the team dens to be welcomed by Tamana, Tyler and Abram. Their view stretched close to a diagonal clockwise of the whole arena.

"What took you so long?" asked Tamana, as she made space for Derrick and Craig to pass. "Your seats were becoming cold." She winked at Craig as she kissed her boyfriend.

"I've got to say that this is by far the coolest atmosphere of hockey that I have ever seen," said Abram.

"By far the coolest Derrick. Can't believe you thought of this night here. Is there something you are not telling us? What year are we in?" asked Tyler. "What happened to watching the game from Khodynka Arena next year? Don't leave us here now Dee, seems like we are a long way from Belorusskaya Metro, and Dee where did I park my car?"

"So are you going to let us know how we got here in the first place?" asked Abram.

Colours of Enlightenment & A Potion

"*Cephus that was a strong first period. Seems like the home team are showing full devotion for their crowd here in Quebec. Superb having the Big Red Machine fighting for their twenty-fourth title. If they manage to take the title home they will tie with Team Canada on world championship titles. This can be likely as they haven't lost a game this season.*"

"*Yes Juan, I really enjoy watching the officials skate across the ice. Still amazes me how they manage to dodge the biscuit as it flies across, that, and how they manage to keep their distance from the players. I think they should wear more padding.*"

"*Crying out loud Cephus, they are professionals, no need to worry, best for us to stay here and them to be there. I tried skating once, carried on going forward until I hit the wall, then I went the other way until I hit the wall, then I skated back, decided to stop half way through and then I couldn't start again. I was stuck in the middle of the ice until I managed to crawl my way out.*"

"*Excellent Juan. Well... I see that the goal keepers have made their way to the goals and time to begin the second period.*"

"Simple really Abram. Simple once I figured out what would happen if the earth stopped still. The idea came to me when I saw someone fall off the metro and checked around to see if anyone had noticed. There was no one there besides me, and she never saw that I had noticed. However the lady felt so embarrassed that she started weeping. Then I thought what is she crying for? The earth would still move after we fall into it. As long as the earth keeps on turning the Lord can keep gathering souls to build heaven," returned Derrick. "This got be thinking on how much energy I would need to freeze a tear instantly in a second, in joules."

"The specific heat capacity for grams in seconds, I see where you're heading with that," added Tyler.

Derrick paused for a moment and nodded his head believing Tyler was on the right track.

"So what if the earth stopped turning? Everything would become sucked into the ground including this arena. Not a pleasant thought right?" he continued.

"Oh, so then what?" asked Tamana.

The sound of the game, the shouting of spectators, the chants of the horn, and the whistle of the referees drowned out the conversation that Derrick was having with his friends. In addition the spectators were consumed within the match that they had no interest in anything else.

Derrick spoke the story whilst looking mostly straight across the field of play. Somewhere past the barriers, into the crowd, up a flight of stairs, between a pair of stewards, into a fire exit, he held the world and watched the players' skate above it. He continued in his explanation looking past the people that came from the exit.

"I calculated that if I happened to stop the earth turning for a split moment, I would be able to control where the earth would be when I started the earth turning again. The gradient of the forests work in both directions, but mostly away from the direction of the wind. Then I realized that I could make this easier if I could harness the energy of Reka Moskva and Volga

Canal, to use the delta system to triangulate the hold of the earth's gravity."

Derrick looked over at his friends realizing that they didn't understand but were paying full interest not to critique.

"Imagine holding the earth's electromagnetic current from the core of the earth and summing that energy to another point, that point being the sun's hold of the earth. Making this point the South Pole and the North Pole being any time and place I wish. The release of reserved energy would spin a swing shot for the earth around the sun to whenever I like as recoil."

Tamana had studied a little physics and so had Tyler, now however along with Abram they began watching the game as Derrick. The first time Abram and Derrick began to watch a game as such was when Nascar played on television. Being at the racetrack was altogether a different idea, but what was the point of watching cars circle around and around? The point was to hold the background as the camera man changed. And the world that they experienced on HD was worth watching. Like this game, Abram paid attention to the game as Derrick.

"Those boxes that night when you decided to break-in contained uranium crystals. Uranium has four oxidation states and four levels of ionization energies that can be struck to release explosive energy. Abram and I collected them from the geology unit at Lomonosov," Derrick looked over at Abram and said: "If he knew what he was carrying for me he would have charged extra." And stroked his right thigh with his third finger.

"Oh I see why you didn't need any help unpacking them now," replied Abram without turning over to look at Derrick. "Out of 0.05% of the Russian population, that is about 78,000 people that sign up to play hockey a year, we can't find a squad to take the lead in this game."

Derrick smiled and carried on with what he was saying: "Using the uranium and composing them within electrolytic minerals such as sodium cations 'the oxidizing agent' at one end, and sulfur anions on the other 'the reducing agent,' with separate casing cased over with a pure titanium casing, this would allow the minerals to keep their electromagnetic properties as they would have in natural form. The casing of this staff is pretty thin, but the density is extremely great, which keeps the mass of the staff sufficient for the staff to stand straight on gravity. And sheathing the casing within itself I can control the volume to surface area for which the solution can be carried. What that means is that it can be mobile when not on."

"So that was the reason why I couldn't move an inch once you switched the switch and for some moments after I opened my eyes?" rhetorically asked Tyler.

"The possibility of us holding against the acceleration of gravity is impossible to imagine. Imagine we were floating as the earth turned. But somehow we are here and not where we were."

Pausing for a moment to watch Team Canada come two goals ahead of the Russian team, with the Canadians becoming excited around them, Derrick looked over at Abram. Caring for a comfort reason Abram looked over at all the girls. The only reason for

Colours of Enlightenment & A Potion

what Abram cared about was why Derrick had brought him there? Abram looked around at the Canadian supporters chanting the score in French with excitement.

"The Russian Hockey Federation is having a hard time to meet the competition this year. They rank fifth place entering this final event we are having. The best possibility tonight is if they are able to hold that standing. If Ken Hitchcock's team overcomes Vyacheslav Bykov's team tonight then we are in for a celebration."

"Best not to underestimate the Russian team Juan. Trailing two goals with twenty minutes still to play in the third period, I am glad that we are not in Moscow witnessing this event."

"Well, what do we all do when we get knocked down? We pick ourselves back up again!"

"I couldn't agree with you anymore Juan."

"That sounds great Cephus. Well to our audience at home we look forward to seeing you back after this short commercial break."

"Later I triangulated the frame of energy I would need to hold my force on gravity against gravity around Moscow. Moscow is 1,080 kilometers^2, that's 417 miles^2. Not much of a distance compared to the circumference of the earth, however I thought I had to start somewhere. Now using details of my mass multiplied by the acceleration of gravity gave me a force in Newtons. My force was extremely large to the area I was to electro-magnetize, so I used the energy of the moving water in the seas around Russia to extremely, exceedingly, exceptionally reduce my mass allowing me to hover over the turning earth."

"You mean you found the energy it takes to hold the water of the seas to the earth?" enquired Tyler.

Derrick looked at him and blinked: "and adding them together, the Sea of Azov, the Baltic Sea, the Caspian Sea, the White Sea, and the Black Sea to find the pressure they exert around Russia. Surprisingly I realized I could minus the density of the water from the earth's density and have minimum effort with moving the earth alone. Using a spark plug and a magnet the current separates the uranium particles into radicals, and used as massive amounts of energy radiating from the staff cored into itself to hold the earth, and allow the staff to repel and float," Derrick paused with some concern for a second.

He continued: "The first time I thought about flicking the switch I had forgotten to place the time and where to land. Almost blew up the world. If I knew coordinates in space for safe landing I'm sure I would have altered them. Later I calculated that I could travel with my friends as long as I knew how much each of you weighed. Adding insulators as carbon fiber to this device was the last thing. All allowed me to use the force of energy needed to move a mass at the speed of light^2 to follow us here, only $E=mc^2$."

XXIX: Sport
BLACK

"*The thighs and the backs of these athletes must be aching to the core. Can only imagine how they are to feel once this night is over.*"
"*This night is still not yet over and these soldiers are not getting paid pennies for their work. We hope to see a fantastic response by the Big Red Machine, and if Hitchcock has told anything to his crew is that they should play this period with caution.*"
"*They are getting paid to touch other men. Let's hope to see a good response.*"

Returning back from bringing snacks from the kiosk the friends sat down with anticipation for their home team to win. Abram's passion towards his faith was about to bring tears into his eyes. To him this wasn't a game, this was really life, and as this was really life he would be in a foul mood all week if his team was to lose.

As for Tyler he enjoyed sports as the next person. Tyler was suited to watch soccer, forty-five minutes one direction without moving his head away from the screen, and forty-five minutes the other. Best to keep all objects away from him in case his team lost or the other team fouled. He found ice hockey difficult to watch on television as the ice blinded his sight; however he still managed to watch some by staring at the black television frame whilst the game played.

As for this game; Tyler and Abram sat close to one another with a tight grip for the other to stay calm. The mercenaries tried not to swear, however after the fourth goal Tyler cried out an insult that shocked the screaming audience around him.

Derrick brought Craig as Craig had no one to enjoy life with. Craig was a man and assuming that any man likes the company of men, that Derrick allowed Craig to enter his circle. Craig enjoyed ice hockey from all other sports. Without a television he caught up with the pucks in play by sitting beside a local barber's radio. Craig instantly loved Derrick as gave Craig purpose.

"Where did that come from? A shred of time into the third period and Russian, Alexei Tershchenko has closed the gap to one behind. Team Canada and Cam Ward did not see that forced entry."

"There is still hope for the team away Cephus. The arena atmosphere has shifted; if the home supporters don't bring their spirits to the brim then they may be going home with a frown."

"Juan, the gold medal champions from 2007 should be able to hold off the elite pressure of the Russians, we just have to hope that no more mistakes happen. Oh dear! Oh dear! Where did that come from?"

"That came from Ilva Kovalchuk, Kovalchuk has not scored any goals in this championship but has just equalized for the white, blue and red."

Colours of Enlightenment & A Potion

"The Canadian goalkeeper Cam Ward is devastated by that outcome."

"How can we blame him? He had no time to even catch his breath before the Russians responded again with the equalizer."

"Shalbu! Shalbu! Shalbu!" cheered Abram.

"Shalbu!" chanted Russian supporters.

"Ah just as great as Viktor Tikhonov," Abram said turning round to look at Derrick.

Viktor Tikhonov, was as famous as Anatoli Tarasov, in CSKA hockey. He played from nineteen to thirty-three, and from thirty-four in 1964 became coach for Dynamo Moscow. Later he seeded Vasily Tikhonov, who seeded Viktor Tikhonov II, who became drafted by NHL Phoenix Coyotes that year, 2008. Derrick realized that Abram was speaking about Viktor Senior.

"Now that's what I'm saying!" said Abram.

"I don't know what you mean Abram, would you like some chips?" asked Derrick as the horn to the end of the third period hollered.

"Can we believe this!? Do we want to believe this!? Can this even be possible!?"

"Three minutes into extra time, and Canadian Rick Nash could not stop the stamina of Kovalchuk forcing the puck over the shoulder of Ward, and through the Canadian net. His soul, his flesh, his will to be remembered forever seemed to be driving him."

"Let's give to Yevgeny Nabokov, the Red Machine goalie for his defense against the pressures of

the Canadian squad. The goaltender voted the most fearsome by the Canadians."

"The Russian Team entered the competition in fifth place and now ranks second in the world. Mare ten points shy from the Canadians International Ice Hockey Federation stats as 3400 from 3010. As for 2008 the Russians have tied with 24 titles in IIHF World Championship, alongside Canada. Tonight the Russians conquered Canada with great anger and furious passion."

"And tonight they are going home settling their defeat against the Canadians last year. Marking up before the ice melted they staked the bread before the twig rotted,. 5-4 Russia."

XXX: Nutrition
YELLOW

Yielding to the force of nature Abram exercised daily. Every morning he would wake to watch the daffodils in his vase turn their faces towards the sunlight shining into his apartment in Egypt. Abram had moved to this northern state of Africa as he was appointed by the Chairman of Water, for the African Water Facility, to bring yeoman to the continent. His job was suited to him best as he spoke the Negro language of West Africa, Yoruba, along with Arabic, and Russian.

He practiced yoga each morning before eating healthy amounts of fats and carbohydrates. He would consume a whole melon in the mornings. The fruit would provide him with intrinsic sugars as electrolytes with water that would keep him nourished and hydrated during work. Egypt day was by far a contrast from days in Moscow, so to prevent heatstroke sport drinks were consumed by the liter to keep the synapses firing faster.

Since youth he had used his technique to physically contain his energy balance in a positive manner, i.e. to increase energy intake and reduce energy output. This would allow his basal metabolism to respond much faster, and relax the bodies resting metabolism at a greater rate, just as Yellow Hammers or Japanese Hornets would when resting from motion.

Sandeep Patel

A behavior modification from drinking yeast fermenting sugar drinks, into eating low-fat diets with complex carbohydrates with resistant exercise, kept Abram as solid as a steed yoked to a carriage.

From yesteryears the situation that all men had was the yank of tension and this in the heat was that much more uncomfortable. Yahweh brought consciousness into animals but some became confused along the way. Young, to youngsters, to yashmaks allowed tolerance in most situations as a sunflower would be forced to shed the seeds in neglect, from once a week, to once a month. The young men were taught that laughter was more pleasurable than women and apologies for youthfulness.

Weakness and cowardly behavior was the last impressions that Abram would have liked to portray. His build was large, and his stance was larger, and any unscrupulous sensational recklessness was considered being 'yellow'. Whereas with Abram the cheap metaphors were ruled out and replaced by odds with Yarborough.

XXXI: Nutrition
YELLOW

Abram's apartment in Egypt was painted a light shade of butter vanilla. This was to reflect the sun's heat back into the atmosphere. His terrace, which was seventy feet above sea-level, was painted with the same colour as limestone, all into keeping the building as cool as possible. The only entrance to the terrace was from indoors unless someone was to parachute onto the deck. One late afternoon there came a rattle of taps from the terrace glass window. Abram walked to see two tall silhouettes appearing through his cream drapes to the terrace, he paused for a second and slid open the patio deck doors.

"Dee, Tamana, come in! You could have used the front doorbell, I had the door open. What are there any faults in your device?" said Abram after giving them a hug.

"Well we were just over there! Abram," said Derrick pointing at a yacht floating in the Mediterranean Sea. "Tammy thought she'd like to scare you by knocking on the window."

"Seriously Tam, the time-machine is not a toy," replied Abram.

"Who is it?" cried a voice from behind him.

"You've got yourself a mistress haven't you?" asked Tamana.

"Soon to be Mrs. Shiraz, so nice, nice."

"Indigo?" asked Derrick.

"How did you know?" replied Abram.

"Ha. As you have no English rhyme and she had plenty," Derrick answered.

The warmth of the day began to cool as so did the wine placed on ice. Abram closed the doors facing north, and closed the drapes of the windows. The friends sat together to eat around a round table. They span laughter as a yo-yo on a string, drinking, singing, eating, laughing and spinning laughter still.

"My job; my job is to prevent infections across these climates, as well as bring drinkable water to all of the Sahara states from Sudan to Senegal. Mosquitoes transmit various diseases one being Yellow Fever, which is a fatal disease leading to vomits and hemorrhages. Now our Yggdrasil water pipe development across Africa will prove beneficial to all life. Some scorpions in the desert may not like it at first but I'm sure we can overcome that," said Abram as he made himself a banana shake. "I'll show you how we are planning to excavate the task, keep this smoothie on shake, I'll be back in a second."

Passing the ladies in the lounge whilst they giggled about what girls' giggle about, Abram ran into his study to bring back a scroll to show Derrick. He unrolled a map of Africa.

"This is the Red Sea; below this is the Gulf of Aden, leading to the Arabian Sea, leading to the Indian Ocean. This point we are to build a dam. Yemen has agreed for our company to mine there. So between Yemen and Djibouti, a dam will be made emptying the Red Sea from the rest of the waters. Now scattering

Colours of Enlightenment & A Potion

from Egypt, Sudan, and Eritrea a network of pipes will cross east Sahara to the west, emptying out as oases throughout the desert. The pipe network would cross Sudan, Chad, Libya, southern Algeria, Niger, Mali and spill out from high altitudes of Mauritania, Guinea, Senegal, and Nigeria into the Atlantic Ocean," explained Abram. "Finally I don't want to know how this works out. We have spent years planning this, so if you have a Yellow Pages advertisement on Shiraz Industries, I don't want to know. Now have some smoothie and tell me what you think?"

XXXII: Nutrition
YELLOW

Youth can overcome all physical necessities thrown at them when they have mastered containing themselves. Yoga was practiced by Abram, but not as anyone could have imagined. The idea came by watching Jackie Chan and Jet Li fighting. Just the mare fact on tolerating the blocking pain made him think.

Self defense for army and against enemy, produce attacks only if ice is available readily. Firstly tense the hands against each other beginning in motion of pray. The muscles of thenar eminence are at the base of the thumb, moving the whole thumb moves the thenar eminence. Touching both hands together with palms open indicates the area of the hypothernar eminence. Folding the thumb over the palm to closely touch the pinky finger moves both eminences in action.

Tap right hypothenar eminence to left palm; rotate tapping of right hand with thenar eminence folded towards the palm. This will show four fingers, and tap gently rotate the wrist and massage eminences with the other hand. The rotation will allow for the left palm to slap the back of the right hand. Rotating right wrist carry to tap left palm, and approaching exertion change hands.

Colours of Enlightenment & A Potion

Hands are held together by finger-tips to help blood circulation, this in turn helps breathing, and this in turn helps a person remain sane. A man with one hand will close first and next finger with thumb to allow blood circulation. A man with no hands will have to press up against something, and hold onto Yahweh. Circulation maintained from the left hand works at a greater rate than closing the right.

From the left leg using a mixture of eminences strike the gastrocnemius medial and lateral head muscle. Work around this muscle to the shin back around. Striking, stretching, grapping, massaging down to the calcaneus, and around to massage the foot, with hard heavy blows as chopping actions with both hands. Breathe a little, stretch a little, and try not to yell. Fill the joy, move to the gigantic quadricep and hamstring. Balance right gluteus maximus at the edge of the bench, and work fully on left quadricep and hamstring. Shift all weight over to the left gluteus maximus, and start again from right gastrocnemius. Pulling, and stretching, and striking the muscles to expand the peptide bonds between the amino-acids, within the microfibrils, and overall expanding the muscle fibers.

Load weight onto lower body weight machine, and exert operation fully to maximize loading option with resistance. One brick, ten bricks, twenty bricks, thirty bricks, fifty bricks, seventy bricks, ninety bricks, ninety-one bricks, one-hundred bricks. Place feet back to gravity and rest. Lift again and rest. Lift again, rest and eat, to return again with eminences to pull the muscle fibers. Largest muscles in the body need to be stretched properly to be able to hold the required amounts of water as necessary.

Yet as martial arts are performed with best attentions the forces exerted from minimal effort can be quite harmful. Practice striking forearms with eminences, rotating whole arm to acquire maximal coverage. Tapping around bones to allow adaptation for more muscle tissue to expand over them, pulling, stretching, and covering all surfaces of pain to be covered by elastin and collagen.

Moving finally to involve the triceps, trapeziums and the pectoral majors. Striking with the eminences, striking a muscle group at a time, striking to withstand pain, and striking until there is no more wind left to expire. Time to sit up and inhale. Time to load with weight when stretching is over. Thud, thud, thud, slowly at first until all is done. Time to eat and to fill the muscles and bone, now the flesh, bones, cells and plasma are closer to the ground.

Careful consideration should be taken when performing this yoga. Studies of Abram's interest evolved him to investigate that this yoga was practiced to the tee for war. Abram reading this interest had read there was a Veda-yoga which was stopped from the Bhagavad-Gita, but some saw pass this caution and embraced an art of Kung-Fu through Siddhartha Gautama, and known as Sankar Yoga.

XXXIII: Nutrition
YELLOW

After coming home from his regular exercise routine, Abram yodeled to find out if his sons were back from school.

"Anyone home?!" he yodeled.

Slowly sounds started bouncing from the children's room as the door to their den opened. His sons came running towards him and began climbing him. He placed the youngest, Isaiah, who was three years onto the kitchen top, and Lester, at five years old on the kitchen stool.

"This is the diet of champions," Abram said.

He pulled the boys attention by blinking several times and twitching his toes. This helped them filter their excitement from seeing their father and concentrate on what was happening at present. Abram opened the fridge freezer and picked out three tubs of banana frozen-yogurt.

"Yogurt 'milk fermented' helps the bowel work well, plus tastes good. Packed full of vitamins and minerals that help us grow. You guys should drink a cup of milk a day, and have low-yogurt as lassi, and some water too. Your strength will be my own," said Abram. "What else helps with the movement of the bowel is cereal as oats, grains and barley. This makes the cellular physiology move, therefore helps us shit."

"Dad said poo," said his youngest Isaiah.

"But dad only says poo," underlined Lester.

"Now try not to consume too much soda and fizzy stuff as you'll get gas and fart. Stick with water and lemonade that will hydrate you, and make you that much leaner. Now talking about getting larger, potatoes do the trick, small amount of unsaturated fats to limit cardiac problems. Eat a little salt from salty chips, as these help our synapses fire action potentials without hiccups. Moderately eat a little fat, but concentrate upon consuming complex carbohydrates as pasta and baked potatoes to hold down reserves of water. Beans and meat will provide amino acids to build more protein; in turn will make it easier for living. Thus to become big and strong as your old man, you'll have to follow these guidelines, and have one egg at least in the morning."

The egg, with or without yolk, but some agree how incredible that, that eggs' exist. What came first? An organic cell, which later developed to need a host, and later still developed to produce a delicious recipe of lipids needed to keep our bodies lubricated. One egg can be better than another, and the best omelet ever? Three eggs.

XXXIV: Nutrition
YELLOW

Tucking his younglings to sleep, Abram explained how the yum-yum in yams' was involved in digestion. His children yearned for his attention and learned from his teachings.

"Food is eaten to provide energy for us to stay alive and to think well. There are four main groups for food; carbohydrates, proteins, fats and fiber. Now you can remember what foods each of these components come from right?" he asked his two sons, as they made themselves comfortable before sleep.

They nodded, neither caring much at the age of three and five, so they stayed quiet to hear their father speak.

"Food also helps build Y-shaped antibodies that fight infections, and strengthens our immune systems. This way if we happen to fall over and hurt ourselves, the immune system will heal us up as good as new. This can come by if we eat well, and drink milk and water. Milk will help our bones and teeth to grow strong due to the calcium, and water to be drank frequently to keep us hydrated. If you feel a little woozy, then this is most probably because you are dehydrated, so get a glass of water or a sports drink to quench the thirst. This will keep your brain clogs ticking," said Abram. "Now who knows what the energy carrier is in the body?"

"ATP," they both said. "Adenosine triphosphate, to be in full," said Lester.

"Excellent! Well through food being digested, 'broken down' in the stomach, the carbohydrates enter aerobic respiration, 'living with oxygen' in organelles called mitochondria, in the cells of the body. Carbohydrates are broken down to glucose molecules and other sugars, and then these broken further to produce carbon dioxide; which we breathe out, and water; which is absorbed into cells, and ATP. This ATP is stored in muscle cells that when needed help move our muscles," Abram paused.

"What about protein, fats and fiber dad?" asked Lester.

"They all act for fuel for the body as they can produce ATP. However they have further individual importance as well. Aren't you guys tired already?" he asked them.

They looked at him and then each other with their puzzled look.

"Seems like you won't let me sleep until I finish this, I'll carry on until you two start yawning," said Abram and began taking a fake yawn.

"Stop that dad," said Lester.

"Well, proteins are consumed and after digested to provide nitrogen mostly to the body. This will help build muscles, and nucleic acids that are essential to replicate each cell's DNA, so we can live and heal. Some people's nucleic makeup gets mixed around and complications arise."

"Ha, ha, dad said makeup," said Isaiah.

Colours of Enlightenment & A Potion

Abram smiled: "Fat digested will help insulation in the bodies, keeping us warm in colds, and helping with structuring our cell membranes, plus fat provides faster releases of ATP when needed. However eating too much fatty-food as fried stuff with more oil will begin to weaken cell membranes and cause atherosclerosis to severe heart problems. Fatty foods are lovely to eat as their oil yields plenty of pleasure, that's why you feel great after eating fried chicken. Plus it tastes good. If you see someone with yellow skin, then that maybe due to their fat stores not breaking down fast enough, this is due to bile salts not being released from the gall bladder. They are known to have jaundice."

Abram watched his children's eyelids wither: "Now for fiber, fiber helps the passage of stools, which is why you see grandpa and grandma eating fiber, so they don't get too much constipation. Fiber, like sweet corn is not easily digested by the body and pass straight through into our poo," Abram paused for remark. "The affectivity of digestion depends on the body's metabolism, which is inversely dependent on?"

"Dad said makeup," Isaiah said and began yawning.

Lester began yawning.

"The answer is, stress level," Abram finished and gave a larger yawn.

They all yawned again and went to yonder.

XXXV: Nutrition
YELLOW

The word for blood without any cells is called plasma, the plasma is yellow. The hemoglobin protein in the cells of blood contains iron. This iron is needed to carry oxygen. This oxygen is used to prevent anyone being anemic. The iron is important for maintaining an athlete's performance on regards for oxygen transportation and energy production. Furthermore without the iron the blood remains yellow.

Sleeping in bed with Susan dressed over in a yellow sari as he liked on Kajol Devgan, they both played whispers of intelligence until she mentioned another infant.

"Best thing to give a mother whilst growing a fetus would be protein and folate for synthesis of DNA, carbohydrates for energy, and of course iron," said Abram.

"For the chance for us to have another baby, I'll feed her so she can be provided with antibodies to protect her from her father's digestive habits," said Susan.

"Oh and improving her on development of her jaw and teeth. I don't like the sound of that. Sure it's lovely for the child's growth but I think we should wait

Colours of Enlightenment & A Potion

a while. Only advantage I see is for you to return back to pre-pregnancy weight," replied Abram.

"You were meant to say 'Oh and reducing the chance of pre-menopausal breast cancer.'"

"Ha, ha, you said breast."

"You silly, now give me a daughter," insisted Sarah pushing herself onto Abram.

"You are as bad as the boys. No snacking in excess amounts. You'll grow resistant to fruits and vegetables, and more depended on chocolate and potato chips. Only one snack a day with three decent size meals. Learn to live your own life instead of consuming mine," resisted Abram.

"Hey I'm still young. No intestinal tract problems of constipation, if so I'll eat fiber. My liver is working fine thanks, thus keeping this body in shape. And my basal metabolism is ticking for you. Plus if my senses become reduced then I'll eat folate foods, vitamin B_6 and B_{12}, and a bowl of cereal more often. Hey honey can you smell my perfume? It's from Y'lang-Y'lang trees," she said slowly.

"Ok time to really slow down Susan, my head is pulsing," said Abram.

"I'll slow down if you give me what I want," Susan replied.

Abram thought long and hard for his actions and delivered to reward Susan with what she desired. He stretched to grab his stance on the cold marble floor and walked to the bathroom.

Later that night noise started being yelped from outside their home. The noises came across as yelling. They became more distinguishable and woke Abram and Susan from their sleep. The yelling was coming from their neighbours. The couple looked at each other. Abram grabbed his robe and Susan went to see if the children were awake. Abram opened the door to their home and walked out of his driveway towards the cries. Running out came two souls and three gunshots. His neighbour with a few shreds of clothes dropped to the floor, one gunshot had grazed Yama, and the third struck Abram's temple.

XXXVI: Future BLACK

Traveling from three different locations the friends arrived to sound the bell to the side entrance of the theatre. The time of day was approaching dusk, and the time of year was chilled enough to see exhaled air condense into vaporized water clouds. Tyler bounced on the spot as he waited for Abram who was approaching from the distance. Tamana walked around the corner to see Tyler blowing clouds of warm air into the cold to see them evaporate. Abram increased his pace as he felt a shiver down his spine.

The door buzzed before Tamana could pull out her key, and Abram pushed his way in taking full opportunity towards quickly getting out of the cold. Abram was naturally from Africa, regardless that he had been born in Moscow, and being also as a baby elephant he preferred the warmth. He walked ahead of the other two into the basement of the theatre. Derrick was on his couch throwing playing cards into a hat.

"The roll of the dice can be fixed. Shall we witness our pray being answered?" suggested Derrick. "I owe a favor for a lost soul, which without my practice would have only fallen into theory. And this favor I have to pay in person. Do you remember the night of the break I first tested my invention Abram?"

"Yes, Derrick," Abram replied.

"Time to place equities in motion. I know you guys must have been anticipating this moment; well the moment has finally arrived. The sense of déjà vu in the back of your minds will be lifted," said Derrick. "As Peter I, changed the capital of Russia to St. Petersburg in 1713, I can guarantee that Moscow, first founded by Prince Yuri Dolgoruky in 1147, will always be the capital of Soviet Russia."

"Wasn't Moscow always the capital?" asked Tamana.

"Before Peter I, the capital of Russia was Moscow, however this changed and later changed back in 1918 March 12th, my birthday, due to Moscow leading the countries finance and transportation of goods," replied Abram.

"By 'goods' he means everything that Russia has to offer; coal, oil, metals, gas, military hardware. All the smart people of Russia began to live in Moscow, and constructions of electric power generators, nuclear power, rail transportations, building materials and medical expertise concentrated themselves here," added Tyler. "But I have no idea what Derrick is getting on at? I rather not ask him."

Tamana and Abram chuckled slightly as they understood Tyler.

"If you guys haven't eaten I suggest we eat before we leave. The trip will make you feel a little woozy and I need you Abram, Tyler, to be on guard. Can't afford to make any mistakes," carried on Derrick.

"Have you been drinking?" asked Tamana as she walked over to him.

Colours of Enlightenment & A Potion

He kissed her as she leaned in. He held her by the waist and sat her down beside him.

"If all goes well then when we return we will still have television transmission, the Moscow Metro, and the XXII Olympic Games in 1980. Just to prepare you that if all turns soar then the deaths of millions from Iosif Stalin reign in Russia to keep communism, would be better for the world than this experiment," said Derrick. "Nothing to worry about, as I said I owe a favour in time, not like I am trying to take over Japan."

Derrick sat back and looked up at the ceiling. He exhaled a long thin gust of air from his lungs; he inhaled fresh air and looked over at the ludo board. He began to explain the travel to his friends. Abram and Tyler found the words coming from Derrick hard to imagine but they felt strength from his expressions that they played along.

"So let me get this right. After we show the others the importance of the task you will take us to see how Siberia becomes industrialized?" asked Tyler.

"But before that to Quebec City? Why is that?" mentioned Abram.

"The strength in our worship and the belief in faith will allow us to do just that," replied Derrick. "I want good things to happen for our Lord. Jesus was strong on his decision to be struck with iron just as I am certain nothing will go wrong. Now let us stand and brace one another together in pray."

After they sat in silence for several minutes, Derrick showed them the invention he had made. The staff like looking rod brought uncertainty to Derrick's friends. He asked them all to hold and feel the contraption. He explained how the dials worked and asked his friends to repeat what they had just heard from him. Then Derrick stood and stamped the ground gently with the time-machine. The T.M. extended in length. He propped up against it and spent a time to pray beside it. Derrick nudged his friends closer to him and pressed a button. Whilst holding Abram and the machine, Abram held Tyler who held Tamana who held Derrick and all realized that they no longer could move or blink. And as fast as a lightning charge they vanished out of sight.

XXXVII: Future BLACK

Thousands of footsteps, some to see, some to experience, some to feel like progress was being made in the twenty-first century, and some to have coffee travelled south on Zamoskvoretskaya Metro to Domodedovskaya Station. And then to relax amongst thousand others as they traveled to and from Domodedovo Moscow International Airport.

"I didn't mean any harm. I was looking for money or food. There was no intention in my blood to cause any harm to anyone inside when I tried to break in. I was raised in the old Soviet. My great-grandfather fought in 1905's Russian Revolution for the working people, and my grandfather survived until my father was born, and my father died in World War II, so I was raised with my mother, until she gave me up to my father's sister and fled to God knows where. Since then I have been moving from foster home to foster home until I found the Salvation Army, who moved me to where Tyler found me," said Craig.

"Who knows if you would have caused harm? You may have panicked and hurt someone or caused psychological pain," replied Tyler.

"There is no possible way to see what disturbance you may have caused and I made sure of that," concluded Derrick. "From the 11 million people in Moscow I'm sure you would have hurt someone from your desperation. Don't worry about that now."

"Why not consider working for missionary groups, giving hope to the less fortunate. The way I see it, you have shelter and you have food. May not be a palace but better than living in a hospital," added Tamana.

"What can that work do for me?" asked Craig.

They all looked at each other and smiled then looked back at Craig.

"Craig, mission work is not about you. Think about this; a U.S. Ambassador recites in Moscow who manages St. Petersburg, Vladivostok and Yekaterinburg for the American people who visit Moscow, or if Abram wishes to visit the States," said Derrick.

"I have no intention of moving, I like Moscow," said Abram.

"There is also a Diplomatic Representer for Russia in the U.S. for Russians living there. He works as a missionary for Houston, New York, San Francisco and Seattle from their capital. So you can help Russians with your history for any Russian Embassy over the world," said Derrick to warm Craig's spirit.

"Wow, for the information you know you should become mayor of this city," said Craig.

"I would rather be the President of the U.N. however I don't see that happening."

"Ha, funny, 'see that happening'," said Abram.

Derrick smiled towards Abram and said: "Russia, the white, blue and red, last year 2008, cost $1.75 trillion to buy, represented by the official

Colours of Enlightenment & A Potion

exchange rate. I'll either have to be Bill Gates or make the country bankrupt. The U.N. would be practical."

"Ha, more practical," said Tamana.

They all looked over at her: "What? I just wanted to join in," she nodded through to Abram and he nodded back at her.

Derrick nodded at Abram and Tamana then said, "Delicious."

"Ha, delicious," they replied and laughed a little as Derrick smiled back.

After a few seconds; "To make the country bankrupt I'd..." continued Derrick.

Derrick paused for a second, stretched over the table and picked up a roll of bread. Looking at them and second glancing Craig he said: "Initially we have to make the place worthless and workless, no people, no animals, no beef, no milk, no grains, no sunflower seeds, no fruit, nor veg and no life to grow or trade to bury." Derrick stared at the table as the sentence caught up to his friends.

"Best for you to stick to videogames Dee," said Tyler faking to clean his tear sockets.

Derrick threw half the roll of bread onto the floor. Later he would dispose of it, but as for then he kept gaze on his friends instead of the piece of bread on the floor.

"My caruncula lacrimalis itches, do I have something in my eye?" asked Tamana staring at the bread on the floor. "I can hear a pair of nines they are tapping every so softly."

"Missionary work then huh? Where can I start something like that?" asked Craig.

"You could help with the mosques," suggested Tyler. "We have over two million Muslims here in Moscow with only four mosques. I hear they are planning to make another two; you can help arrange classroom tables and chairs if you like. Come with me to the next pray, I'll introduce you to some people. That's one way to bite the bullet."

"Sounds like a start Craig. You can start by carrying my old books to them. Most have fun stuff like math but I do have comics, and books on history and invention," said Derrick.

"I have writings by 1799 poet, A.S. Pushkin," said Craig.

"Yes that's a start. Like Muhammad Ozbeg, approving Ivan Kalita, the Prince of Moscow in the early 14th century to collect taxes from all of Russia. You will be given assistance in collecting people to help with Allah's work," added Tyler. "Now that doesn't sound so bad right?"

"Plus you are not that bad to look at either," added Tamana. "I mean you are easy on the eyes and people like that."

They all looked over at her; Derrick leaned over to whisper something in her ear.

"Do you think I can be the knight on the white horse slaying the dragon, like the knight on the Moscow flag?" asked Craig.

"Sure you can Craig," replied Tamana.

"Plus that knight still has to be discovered. They made him in '95, before we started college, along with the anthem and emblem of Moscow that his identity still remains fiction," added in Abram. "You can be that knight even though I wanted to be him first."

Colours of Enlightenment & A Potion

"You both can be knights," added Tamana.

"There's only one knight on the flag. And I don't know how to ride a horse. What if Abram knows how to ride the horse and is a better knight? What should I do then?" asked Craig.

"I think you should move to St. Petersburg and work in Baltika," said Abram.

"Well if I was a beer, I would be a Baltika."

"If I was a beer, I'd be a Fosters."

"If I was a wine, I'd be white," added Tamana.

"If I was a white woman, I'd be Kate Middleton, hands down," added Tyler.

"If I was a white man, I'd be Ryan Rayolds," returned Derrick.

"If I was a black man, then I'd be Denzel Washington. No, no, yes, Denzel," Craig said.

"If I was a monument I'd be the Washington Monument. I don't know why I said that," laughed a little Tyler. "I'd be the Holy Kaa'ba."

"If I was a monument or landmark, I'd be Madison Square Garden on game night!"

"Nice, nice," returned Tamana. "If I was constellation of stars, I'd be Orion's Belt."

"Nice," complimented Abram. "If I was a Hindu god, I'd be Shiva."

"Thought you'd be Krishna," said Tamana.

"You are Krishna," replied Abram.

Derrick looked over, "Well if I was a super hero, I'd be Superman. And if I was a super villain I'd be Megatron! Leader of the Decepticons."

"Jesus Christ, have mercy," Craig added.

"If I was a vegetable, I'd be a potato. And if I was a fruit, I'd be a watermelon, as you like that!"

XXXVIII: Future
BLACK

Landing to affiliate the future of Moscow, Derrick placed north and east latitude coordinates from Greenwich median to his time-machine to stand square on one roof of Stalin's buildings. Prime choice was chosen due to importance of still being in existence. The M.S.U. building had survived since 1755, and reconstructions through three centuries allowed Derrick to believe that the building would still be intact for a further three centuries.

Pulling into the circumferential tangent from the center of the sun to the change in the earth's orbital position, the time he wanted to land in was June 12th 2309. This was to be a Russian National Holiday celebrated since 1994, and resulted from a constitution enabling Russia to be presented with a universal life. The children would dance to celebrate this holiday away from communism and into a diplomatic Russia. Derrick would analyze on his travel if Russia Day was still being celebrated, this would enable him to calculate that earth had become a diplomatic planet.

As he landed from space he instantly felt his lungs expand. The usual fog of Moscow's atmosphere had been diminished remarkably. Derrick felt uneasy within the same habitat. He inhaled and looked across

Colours of Enlightenment & A Potion

the horizon clockwise from standing facing south. The sky was noticeably clear regardless that this time of year was brought into hot summers, however something was greatly changed. Stepping to the side of the building Derrick looked over to the street below. People were celebrating within the street, evidently Russia Day still existed.

Everything that Derrick remembered about the economy of Moscow seemed to have been enhanced. The divergence from where Derrick had previously seen had changed by a reduction in pollution. This once heavily industrialized city seemed to have less smog. Air pollution had seemed to have reduced and the distinction that he had felt was a change in smell. The city not only smelled cleaner but the air was thinner and easier to breathe. The prospect of less air pollution would have resulted to improve agriculture and less soil impurity. The result from using hydrogen and electrically fuelled vehicles within the cities had paid well to the environment.

Derrick adjusted the gyroscope on the staff and moved from the roof of the building to the ground below. Waiting for the fragments of ions that dissembled his space in time to move with the coordinates that he targeted on the street beside the building, the staff moved him through the stone of the building, and he was to stand firmly as time found him space on the busy street of Lomonosovskiy Prospekt.

He approached a newsstand picked up a newspaper and gave the man a few rubles. The man looked at him with a puzzled look like he was some foreigner from a distant planet. Derrick stood waiting for the man to say something. The man waited for

Derrick to say something. They waited standing in the same pose as when Derrick reached out to hand the man money. The man began to laugh and carried on working. Local citizens walked pass the man's stand and collected drinks, food, newspapers, candy, anything but a packet of smokes and left without paying the man anything. Derrick stood waiting for someone to pay the man. 2309 was printed on the papers. Derrick asked the man why he was not collecting money.

"Nobody works for money son. Where are you from?" asked the man.

"What do you mean? What about food? What about tax?" asked Derrick.

"You are not from here traveler are you? We have stopped chopping trees long ago. Since the beginning of the last century we live entirely to better ourselves. All necessities are shared accordingly and signed for when received. This enters the database which compares the number of members in a family and daily consumption. Now where are you from?"

"I've just been away for a while. What about luxuries? What about education?"

"Yes it's you," said the news man with gesture not to push the man into interrogation. "Luxuries are not so necessary as long as people have families. They can always have what they need but excess of anything is counted for. Where you been hibernating?"

"How do people live?" said Derrick and looked at the man's heart.

"Man you have been asleep for a while. We are all given living quarters, some more extravagant than the others, but all equipped with unionism to work, live and enjoy life away from war. Some say life is

Colours of Enlightenment & A Potion

meaningless now, but I can go on holiday whenever I like, wherever I like, and for how long I like. You have been in space for some time now haven't you?"

"Something like that. Thanks for the paper."

"Enjoy Russia Day," returned the newsman.

The previous acting impressions of life for Russia were remembered by toxic radioactive wastes that filtered into the globe. These were bound to be stopped. One of the smartest places in the world, and indisputably one of the strongest in terms of defeating 1941 Germans at the Battle of Moscow had changed the world's economy. Six hundred years from murders, drug trafficking, and slanderous distribution of weapons, Derrick could go back to where he was from and fall asleep. He stepped away from the newsstand with his time-machine disguised as a walking stick and walked into the shadows of the university. The wind stopped blowing as Derrick turned the time-machine on and returned back into the comfort his couch in 2010.

Russia had changed the face of the world. The once most heavily industrialized country had approached an eco-friendly future. Being the lead in scientific development they had managed to stabilize the use of un-renewable natural resources (fossil fuels), and place renewable natural resources to work. Energy from hydroelectric power, wind turbines and hydrogen fueled pistons all emitting water as byproduct followed to bring a fresher appearance to universal days.

XXXIX: Evolution
ORANGE

Overwrought from curiosity on where man had come from, Derrick balanced his views to agree that consciousness was given to all animals. All animals' conscious was to their ownership of their own fate, which lived in harmony to their personal habitat. Any animal considered not upholding to their own consciousness was outcaste, and later eaten by the earth to allow the growth of more organisms.

Man had evolved on dependency of any other animal, either by a unique cell or growth of mutation. Initially their consciousness fell into providing for their families and communities. Later conflicts from opposite ends of Orange River, led to man declaring power to protect their communities from those that were more suited to survive. Not to misunderstand the consciousness of every beast that beauty resided in a manner to respect a superior being. As animals prowled to eat whilst others grazed, they all began to understand that another creature was still yet to overcome.

Animals felt overwhelmed when food was not scarce as because their cells were nourished away from starvation. Lions and lionesses would watch their cubs play as ordinarily as most animals' would become to please a superior being. Naturally there is only

Colours of Enlightenment & A Potion

tendency to remain numb whilst life degrades everything, however why is there an overbalance to feel emotion? Derrick wished to find the root of this question.

Oxygen was a necessity for all land, sea and sky animals. From plants using gases as carbon dioxide to release oxygen as a byproduct, filling some of the atmosphere, this led to the creation of other organisms that brought balance to the equation with nitrogen, filling most of our atmosphere. Sea organelles laid eggs on shores just as the mitochondrial eukaryotic cell established themselves from prokaryotic chloroplasts, leading to marine meiosis.

Animals evolved before 4 million years ago, and from 1.5 million years ago the dark coloured African Ape, began to form a branch of dark coloured hominins. One meter tall the species developed branches of its own likeness from Australopithecus to Homo habilis, to Homo floresiensis and Homo sapiens. The ossification developed the brain in the man-like people to become larger. Anthropologists studied skulls from the size of a grapefruit to average man capacity. The branch of Homo sapiens ovulated more following a better survival factor.

Far from observation the African Apes presented themselves to survive with an opportunistic gene pool of hominins to the land of India. (This observation reaches times of mythology before that of science). Hominins that evolved in the nourished land of India over 1.5 million years ago travelled over the Himalayan Alps and overlapped sand dunes for the curiosity of exploration, where the survival of the fittest strengthened them into more cultured humans.

Sandeep Patel

In October 2004, in the Indonesian Islands of Flores, anthropologists found a cache of bones resembling a hominid of Homo floresiensis. In isolation the specie had not evolved since the departure from Africa, 94,000 years ago. The specie became extinct 12,000 years ago, whereas from 150,000 years ago, the common Homo sapiens dominated. Finding a remote cave of hominids the scientist analyzed wrist bone appendages to discover another branch of the Homo family. They were from the African Ape branch, such as from orangutans.

Once evolution occurred, some family members survived. Overall man came from ape differing in sizes to best suit their habitat. Plus their curiosity to survive gained them skills to hunt, craftsmanship to building tools and spears, which they passed to their families, and to the more opportunistic Homo sapiens sapiens.

XL: Evolution
ORANGE

According to opportunistic science the land would overflow by water. The infrared radiation of the sun's rays would penetrate the earth's atmosphere easily as the ozone layer would tear more. This would increase the temperature of the waters to melt the polar icecaps. Mostly everything will become flooded either by rain or raise in sea level. There's no reason to expect this happening in the close future. On the contrary draught could expand leading to fewer crops for the expanding populations on Earth. Within some deserts of the world as for Chile, Africa and Australia, animals were adapted to survive. After all moisture had been pulled away from the ground by air currents or cactuses, animals had to reserve water for the drought seasons. Man, Nelson Mandela, M. Carey, and the rest of the humans, had moved far from these habitants as their biological suits were not made to survive hot days and cold nights. The desert over the earth's equator would increase by $5°^C$ every hour, along with sandstorms built to roast hives from the pulsating heat would make it unbearable to survive.

Enormous animals are usually herbivores like elephants, kangaroos and camels known to eat hay, roots of plants, rice balls and oranges. Carnivores like tigers, lions, birds of prey, some spiders and reptiles, like rattlesnakes become adapted to hot climates, but when food is scarce they resort to death in the shade. Lizards of the desert take cover under rocks, and like some animals come out only at night to stretch their legs or find food as other animals. Omnivores eat like herbivores and carnivores; they possible can eat them as well. If not they eat eggs for saturates pardoning that they are unfertilized.

Tropical climates allow for thousands of animals to ovulate and breed. The source of life between rainforests and dry suburban regions vary in constitution of animals. Nevertheless there is still evidence of life in the quietest regions of this globe. All adapted to fit their main goal, to feed and breed.

Moreover the orange sun doesn't provide any form of life on other planets of the solar system except this one. Regardless all species believe in their own heaven or to become human. Only under specific conditions did life start and evolve on this planet. Let us pray that there is another one.

XLI: Evolution
ORANGE

The Catholic Church was neglected by some Christian followers whom orientated Christian Orthodox sublimity to the book of Genesis. This orthodox practiced evidence and just causes to the followings of Christ. To overestimate the Father's passage on creating life on earth through six eras, (overseen with the Father) Derrick believed that animals either wished to be man or with man.

As the Lord would require all life to enter His realm, all life was to be judged accordingly before He could make this happen. The only matter of confusion arose when animals exceeded the rate of acceptance, thus the Lord lost the right to judge everyman fairly. Once man had learnt to make fire, they were given sighting of God. Saying; man was allowed to have children as early as possible just in case one had to be placed down. Sightings as such made the whole process that much swifter to the earth's orbit around the seasons.

On a thunderous day lightening crackled across the skies of Africa, and before rain began to pour a tree was struck with a lightning bolt. Flames of fire spread throughout the tree's branches and crisped the leaves to ashes. Every animal in the vicinity fled in freight except for one man who witnessed the tree burning. A branch of fire disembarked to the ground and the man took this torch to heat his home. Others later followed to find out the root of fire.

The spark for fire can be made possible by burning tinder, leaves, grass, bark and resin. Later kindling as small twigs and sticks were added on sparked tinder to grow the fire, later still firewood found from dead trees can be added to grow the fire further. The ignition was sparked by smacking stones together to fly a spark to the tinder.

So animals not only gained consciousness from Pangaea, but intelligence as they moved from origin Africa to the north to become Caucasian, cracking of the continental plates to become Red-Indian, through the mid-east to become Persians, climbing against forced winds of the Himalayas to become Oriental, over generations.

The offspring initially had difficulty on maintaining their curiosity on why other animals were allowed to play whereas they were forced to work. Overlooking the sand dunes of civilizations that were made in the time of the Pharos, no child overnight was given pride of his ownership with the land. Impossible to agree with ostentation for those that do than those that do not was better. The oxidization of the sand from rust was gleefully appreciated by civilizations, which then built their own kingdoms to orchestrate freedom, and then to divide and conquer.

An oxymoron description to help those children with wealth, as also the children without ostentation, was decided by one. What was the objective for the humble to help the crude through opsonin? When the crude operated obstructive barriers ahead of them,

Colours of Enlightenment & A Potion

Marshall Mathers sang to reach the osmotic offspring of the new generation that there was three ways to live: to build credit, to learn to build credit, or to learn and build credit.

Oratory conduct should be spoken by an orator. Their words should be filled for acceptance that neither the superior beings' should be close to hunger or famine. Nevertheless the next evolution was psychological and regarded to be on approach to Nirvana. The new evolved man was away from predator Ospreys and towards wisdom as Great Horned Owls. Just for instance the Lord gave to some with owlish behavior the fire-ant off chance that there was still something left to owe.

XLII: Religion
BLACK

Craig Goncharov opened the main entrance to the New Opera Theatre to let in Derrick from his arrival back home. There was pace in his stride as he brushed past Craig heaving his bags not to hurt him. Derrick walked past the lobby of the theatre straight to stage one, ground floor. Tyler was sitting in the main row listening to Abram standing beside the stage front. The curtain was closed to reflect dark burgundy. Derrick dropped his bags close to the aisle and stepped onto stage.

"I need you to explain a few things to me Tyler," insisted Derrick. "When I arrived to Toronto, crossing over to the States, I was stopped by a U.S. Customs Officer. This officer looked at me as I was shit, and I think it was because I was wearing that warm scarf you had gave me. Now instead of him directly facing me and swearing, he began swearing under his breath towards the computer. He didn't know how to listen! Mmmmm. Now I know girls can just speak shit on the off chance and at random moments, ruin whole football games, this is all to acquire attention, or just because they didn't know how to tell a joke. I know it can be distracting, I hate them for it, but you're at work, no need to involve me!"

Colours of Enlightenment & A Potion

"Steady man, slow down. Did you look at her feet to let her know she was at work?" interrupted Tyler.

Derrick continued: "Well the place was filled with all people of all ages and of children, some learning how to speak, others learning how to live, and more finding the reason on why to like the customs officer. This 'man' with his counterpart, two 'men' now, swearing amongst themselves behind their petty desk and chewing gum whilst being on the job. Don't they have a lack of jobs in the States? What a shit way to enter a country that lives within by the Lord's words. Now these two are grinning and smirking amongst themselves, chewing gum and stealing moments to provoke me to swear, so they can take me behind closed doors..."

"Have you eaten?" asked Tamana.

"Not now Tama, I won't be able to enjoy it. I just feel like using my work to destroy that officer, and his family, making sure I meet no one like that anymore. Dick-head! There am I raising funds so his children have a steady life, and there's him abusing the Lord's will. What a pair of morons! They're paid much more than half the people I know, and they abuse the right to be civil," continued Derrick. "Ha ha ha ha, they can't listen to music," and he began to Om in his mind.

"I'm sorry to hear that Derrick. So what do you want me to explain?" asked Tyler.

"Teach me how to relax. I really feel like I should make a list of individuals I would like to send to hell now ..."

"There's *fajr;* the dawn pray, which is a compulsory pray, there's *dhuhr;* the noon pray, and there's *ishaa;* the night pray, there's also *tahajjud;* a voluntary pray at anytime of the day. Now with these we seek *istighfaar;* the forgiveness from Allah for our thoughts. Come with me to *ishaa* tonight, once you showered and eaten," insisted Tyler. "Best you come tonight and then for *fajr* in the morning, I want you to find *makrooh* after what you just said."

"What's that?" asked Derrick whilst he paced to-and-fro across his theatre's stage.

"Due to *sharee'ah,* the code of law written in the Holy Qur'an, we are to walk away from discouraging acts, and with *makrooh* we will be rewarded from abstaining against the *haraam* of *sharee'ah,* and this is *fatwaa,* the religious verdict."

"I like the sound of that. I praise our Father for you Tyler; you have relaxed me greatly by *makrooh.* Blessed be He who is able to do all things."

"*Rahimahullah,* may Allah place his mercy on him, and we wish *radi Allahu'anhum,* that Allah be pleased with them. Note how your thought process is gathering the negatives Derrick, I need you to stay calm man, otherwise I will help you to conquer God's final verdict. Now don't force that on me, I rather have *sunnah,* but for you the Qur'an is in favor, so don't argue with the people of scripture. The Jews and Christians will be judged just like the rest of us."

"You should allow Prophet Muhammad, and Lord Jesus, and me, to work and love you as you have loved us Derrick," said Tamana.

"Yes, trust Tamana, and with the meaning of her name in scripture, trust us," forwarded Tyler.

"Breathe man, breathe strong and hard, blow all that bad air out of you, and inhale our air to fill your

Colours of Enlightenment & A Potion

lungs. Breathe hard Derrick. I cleared my smoke filled lungs after you saved me, and I made sure that when I spoke to you I would exhale only clean air," said Craig, and exhaled with force to the ceiling above him, then inhaled gently to see Derrick slow his pace across the stage floor. "When I accepted Muhammad with my Christian faith I was filled with tears, thank you Tyler for being merciful yourself."

"*Saheeh,*" said Derrick looking at Tyler.

Tyler shook his head and said: "You don't have to pray as *rak'ah,* but do pray and pray for the well. Try not to be induced by the jealousy of other men, plus I'm scared of you Derrick as you have the power not only to change lives but to change all time as we know it."

"Doesn't the scripture read, 'Allah does not like evil except by the person that He has wronged?' Well He has wronged you Tyler; you didn't deserve your fate to be presented as it did. Thus I ask you, should I have mercy?" enquired Derrick and blinked at Tyler sitting down on the first row.

"I maintain *tasbeeh,* something that the Bible describes as, 'To glorify the Father and reject any imperfections attributed to Him,'" replied Tyler. "Believe in the Lord your God."

"And that is *fatwaa* too?" asked Derrick approaching him.

"Masha'allah," Tyler said, "Meaning as God has willed."

"*Saheeh*, that's right" replied Derrick. "*Shokra,* meaning, thank you," he continued. He began breathing normal and went to hug Tyler.

"I like living in the light with Allah, Allah's light, Light, but I would definitely be cautious of those two. I can see them clearly through your eyes," said Tyler as Derrick approached him.

Tyler shook his head and said: "Alternative to maintaining fingers and thumbs together you can go stand close to the wall, enough to keep arm's length. As like surgeons might during operations. Do what I do at times and prop against the wall with one finger, arm high above your head against a curtain rail, breathe and get back to some love," returned Tyler. "And when done look over the wall to the horizon."

XLIII: Religion
BLACK

Dust gathering on old cobwebs accumulated to greater masses at some corners of the main lobby in Dormition Cathedral. Outlined against the gray background of cold stone and tarred painted wood the spiders would nest. They would collect dust that had built during services which kept areas of human services clean.

All friends came to worship here and at times they would have come altogether. Standing and singing hymns from psalms and proverbs brought warmth to light their souls. Amongst the cool atmosphere laid between the tiled floor and the clayed roof the sound of admiration for Christ remained as sharp as the thorns were to His head.

So a miracle was performed when Jewish scholars read and taught. Moses picked up a snake, and later man came to deliver the snake back to the Lord. Another miracle was spoken through the Father as blind men, paralytic persons, the sick, and unwell were healed in an instant with the faith of the one as His alone freed all injustices. I'll stand with you awhile where you can always see me.

Witnesses came to believe that water tasted like wine, and compromising love allowed for some ladies to be forgiven through oil and lanterns. Furthermore

Solomon's Kingdom was greater than all the sand on the seashores, and allowed safety from all backgrounds, may that be of cooks or princesses. Later the Romans bowed to allow righteousness to flow for all humankind from building roads and aqueducts.

Through the closing doors behind the backs of the souls that entered the cathedral, love was closed within the building. The building represented the body of Christ, and after three days of reconstruction the wounds were allowed to heal for the gospels' to speak. The men spoke freely as they spoke with one name in mind, and that name came through the truth and grace of Jesus Christ. The law was given to Moses and witnessed by the friends, whilst the Father witnessed them from the neighbouring mountain.

The masoretes listed twelve prophets and later twelve apostles were grown for Jesus to find. Just as the friends would find dark red blood of the Christ fall bringing hallowed sand to Jerusalem, they sang in church for no more prophets for all time. And they prayed from Matthew and Luke, The Lord's Pray, all in one voice and one sound, to forgive Jesus Christ trespassing through man, which the Father had already declared as holy, and for the Son of God to forgive them, all in which to bring us to the Promised Land.

Gather your belongings, rise to your feet and leave. Words were cried with red fury eyes that to stop and stare at them for longer would leave that person never to be remembered. Great tears in the eyes of the Father, and the Father needed everyone, that those that used the devil would be ignoring the Lord's generosity.

As Saul began to realize the evil spirit of God dwelling within him, he called for David as the Lord's

Colours of Enlightenment & A Potion

spirit was with him. That only David could release Saul from the evil spirit of God as the Lord's spirit was within him. The role that Father left on them could have only been forgiven by the Father, thus Saul finding himself closer to David, who played the harp and repented on many killed by him, that the Father forgave him also.

Nevertheless a judge's counterpart was not forgiven but thrown into the depths of hell. No moments to repent. Momentarily he should have left with a lantern instead of continuously striking his partner. The crime that her husband had performed enabled her to kill him quickly, but gave her great pain. Thus her decision for the rock that landed from the hands of the victim into the head of the defendant, allowed Deborah to be more than remembered.

Across the pages of scripture learnt amongst the friends, through the dull observed nights that were felt by them, only one felt true compassion through oppression. Like Paul wrote his findings as not to write them would have resulted into nothing. And Paul, a prisoner and chained to another prisoner in Philippians, wrote his memoirs in the cell's heat, in sweat and shit that would have resulted into nothing, leaving everything to be ignored and no world to have ever been discovered.

The apocalypse declared through the faith of Jesus Christ and the witnesses of John the apostle, resulted to more arriving to believe in the true will of the Father. What a story to make up about nothing and nonsense, that that story itself could be hocus pocus. Nevertheless the story made the rest of the Holy Bible seem that much more real. Especially that of Peter's fishes to be a fool of witchcraft from Jesus, that later condemned himself to phrase judgment starting with the family closest to God, declaring that Jesus Christ was the path to the light.

In Moscow, 1468, was born Basil, later renamed as St. Basil the Blessed (Fool for Christ). As in 1547, he saved the people from a rampaging forest fire that covered the entire town. His faith in Christ allowed him to prophesize the coming of the fire early. He died in 1552. During 1555 – 1560, St. Basil's Cathedral was built in Red Square to commemorate him and give him a place to rest. Later in 1588, Tsar Fyodar Ivanovich, built the Ninth Chapel across from St. Basil's Cathedral to grave the Fool for Christ, and allow him to rest over the times of refurbishments to the cathedral. Finally declaration to the outstanding belief of Petr Baranovsky for Christ, that the architect in 1930 stood on the steps of St. Basil's Cathedral threatening Iosif Stalin, that he would slice his own neck if anything was to happen to the magnificent monument.

As for Judaism and Islam coinciding in most degrees of service to the Father; the strong foundation of rituals maintained the importance for them to worship and pass over that importance. People had to be hard hearted to allow custom for the Father to be appreciated. That in order to allow God's word to be maintained, that heaven is open, and the road for salvation is to help thy brother and thy sister and thy neighbour. They read and wrote to learn from the Father's word which kept them growing strong.

India seems to be further in the past than any other country. This nation had declared themselves to have heard the word from God initially. The One Spirit

Colours of Enlightenment & A Potion

received from Indra, who was recorded in scripture through the Rig-Vedas books (5000 B.C), and later the Bhagavad-Gita (3000 B.C), teaching children the words from Shree Krishna. Hinduism kept love in Father's name along with stick dances that kept demons out of earth. Unfortunately time played course and people naturally progressed to sinful acts of crime and sexual immorality. Somewhere along the line people bread more than they worshipped or worked. This led some scholars back into the forests and jungles to write about dealings with suffering in the Upanishads' scripture.

People divided from teachings of Hinduism to find refuge again in God's grace, which led to Islam growing exponentially in the golden era of the 7th century. From Arabian influence to those of Abbasid Caliphs, translations of Prophet Muhammad, his words spread throughout India to reduce the pace of injustice spreading, and beautiful monuments were made to compliment the love from the Father to mother Earth.

Islam presented strict rules in maintaining one's self from sin and towards the liking of the Father. Roughly at this time Abraham received the word of God and spread Judaism from the Middle East. Most likely due to preservation of land the Torah was neglected from India, due to the separation of the Islamic community and the blind eye developing in India. The Torah listed times of growth from first human civilization, i.e. much similarity to Sanskrit scripture by faith in the Spirit left by the heavens for a world not yet unraveled.

Not surprising that when all faiths had pride upon themselves, and with Hindustan broken into many kingdoms, the British penetrated in the nineteenth century. Eventually hypocrisy was lifted off the Christian Cross, and carried into the nation to mark the resting spot for Apostle Thomas.

The British left Hindustan in the mid-twentieth century to be separated into Pakistan and India, on the agreement that India would be a diplomatic nation. Islamic worshipped freely in their right and Hindus worshipped in their right. Overall they both began to worship for forgiveness and love for their neighbour.

The Chinese community found acceptance in Buddha, from India, to live peacefully amongst themselves. They prayed to things that had importance in the world, like animals, like weather, like music. Buddhism demonstrated personal reflection to their survival only in the Father's nature. Om Namah Shivaya, as Om as a long sound to be held for body and mind relief was carried further by Buddhist. Theoretically the separation of tongue would have led to disobedient language to be used. Hypocrisy against worship would not have been tolerated by the Spirit. Shiva's finding's was delivered to the Chinese by Siddhartha Gautama.

So the Father masqueraded as a Jew, and brought Lord Jesus Christ, to be presented for all mankind to learn the word that all men were looking for, and that was love. This however could have only been learnt until Christianity was born by His resurrection. Once Christianity, the new religion of the Common Era was born, and the word of Lord helped worshippers of all religions bring laughter, and the word of salvation to dying souls of the eastern and modern world.

And as for this from today and forever the simple nature of one man had brought balance to the whole world. If one was not spiritual then they would be an atheist. Distinguishing the two is a matter of asking the man which scripture he reads. Now whatever religion one may follow they too will come to realization that the cross is to be approached by all men who wish to enter heaven. Now to make things easier for the forth coming generations, allow them to live for the Father through the acceptance of the Messiah. That those that repent realize that there's no way back.

XLIV: Religion
BLACK

Born again into a new development of species with lines of scripture to be repeated only in this manner. Entirely a change in aberration from once what was illustrated by some false callers for Prophet Muhammad. Those false callers of intensively repeating callings of our Father were undeniably begging to be punished. Common callings erased from crying Father's name to praising His name instead was to be the final call allowed by us.

The Moscow Grand Mosque was refurbished with shades of light paint, which covered the outer walls and reflected a little more light to the surrounding buildings. Inside beside the basins, sinks, plumbing, cool tiled floors and shoe holds allowed flowers to decorate the area of pray. The flowers were replaced once they began to wither. Two more mosques were constructed outside the busy vicinity of the city. All mosques paid emphasis to strengthening the young amongst humbling themselves.

Is it so the elder Muslim men don't have problems with arthritis because of praying motion? Whatever it may be a fraction of the population are finding this difficult to do, beats the whole purpose to finding their own answers. Praying should primarily be open to hands, hands together, crossed thumbs and then

Colours of Enlightenment & A Potion

finger-tip to finger-tip and push. Calling this praying with Allah was strong, and could be done anywhere at any time with confidence. Rolling the fingers between each other by passing them through each other; playing with them when beads were not around made all of Lord's men have fun, whilst counting the seconds.

Children targeted for abuse, crime and suffering were replaced by children eating well, smiling graciously and humbling the hearts of elders. The smell had changed from burnt paint that presented itself for half a decade to the sweet smell of blooming flowers towards the end of that period.

The children begged for mercy and asked for strength to smile, leaving the majority of worshippers prostrating at home. Thus this led for Islam to stay alive as the children had a place to learn the lingualistic rules of recitation for prostration and engraved the desire to listen.

Most of all the children were encouraged to ask questions. Each question that was asked was returned with a comfortable reply. If the question faced a factual answer that couldn't be answered by a particular parent or practitioner, the child was given an honest alternative. "We don't know, best to ask someone who has studied in those facts for the most accurate answer." The elders were not ashamed if the question was unheard of before, as changing generations inevitably brought changed tasks. And unlike historical pasts, children were not mislead on prevailing the truth, just as adults would pause before lying on closed questions.

Moments for pray would become difficult especially when exploring into adulthood. Nevertheless a feeling of attraction was felt when standing on a pray mat when thousands of thousands of people pray. The feeling of attraction how man is drawn to water. The Son of God spoke of the Father, and thus the future as when to leave the left hand of God free. The attraction pulled when facing east not west is distinguishable. Some answers are too difficult to answer like, is the attraction due to the earth spinning counter-clockwise, west to east? Or does standing alone on faith exist? The answer becomes null when the question itself needs applauding upon merely for its existence.

    Short sentences with counted pauses allowed pray to Allah where sound came before language. Fifteen laws held the faith for Allah to hear us. Following the fifteen laws became easier as they became pleasurable. The scriptures all fell into each other and tightened amongst themselves except for one law that contradicted the others.

    Beautifully understood that this one reversed law, reversed within itself, and became blissful as the scratch was forgiven when recited from the Holy Qur'an. The sentence of sound was not to prostrate whilst scripture was being read.

    The other fourteen laws embedded themselves within the children and into the twenty-second century which allowed more food to grow. Prostration was the key to life when away from holy words, prostration meaning to lie face down and touch the ground, total devotion towards repentance. To preach prostration draws close to Allah. We ask for joy so we can weep.

    The sun nor the moon with the earth and all of space not to be worshipped, but only Allah, Father to be worshipped and worshipped alone. All those that

Colours of Enlightenment & A Potion

worship Him will never fall in fire but would be given sights of respect from crows when Father's pleased.

So people lost their pride in worshipping their clothes of sterling and praised the Lord. Either consciously or unconsciously they would bow their heads when their clothes were smudged, or when checking the time on their watches, or by playing with their phones. The quoted number was recited to prostrate ourselves, to do well, to pray with desire, and this all led to have knowledge of their successes.

Thus without pride, people came from all depths of the earth to kneel onto the ground that Allah had made. That all the shadows of the mornings and evenings bowed to Him, and sang holy, holy, holy allow us to prostrate beneath you.

The laws fill necessity to believe as much as Allah knows through time that most people would not. And those that do will end suffering for others. Others Allah will disgrace and those who were righteous can too be ignored, as too Allah will ignore those that ignored the righteous. Thus the disgraced dwell in Satan, dismissing that prostration is clearly to Allah and then thy neighbour. Hence to allow the disgraced find redemption if not given by their victim.

Time and time again, sound words to pauses to embed the weeping of Noah and Abraham before Allah. King David as he agreed to find repentance through the Lord, he found peace into salvation, that even without his son or his wealth Allah forgave him, and brought him closer to feel that he knew nothing besides the will for him to write and enter heaven.

The shadows within the sight of Allah came to deliver another prophet to allow balance to be appreciated. He allowed the voices of the Holy Qur'an to be understood and be presented as hymns. These hymns were preached with joyful strength to the coming generations to keep the earth turning. Thus after the saviour left, the last prophet, Prophet Muhammad came and kept the fear in the Lord alive.

    The differences in religion were only in environment as the atmosphere was exactly the same. Hence members of world religions had become one. Because you love us Father we can love. The power of love was like ephedrine.

    Ephedrine evolved from an idea for the need to increase heart and breathing for a dying individual. The idea was like light or a sequence of lights that better made themselves the Light. A light illuminated creativity and eternal wellbeing of every living being. This Light everyone sentenced as One.

    Communities soon needed entertainment from the life they lived. Entertainment was anything considered 'cool', anything peaceful, anything casting a horizon. Many horizons even shadows held peace so thus cool was anything 'black'. Black was searched for when the Light approached fast or beamed bright. Thus the circle of religion merged into one as they began to count the drops of ephedrine needed to mix with blood. Red was the colour of blood and the colour of love for blood. Overall people monopolized unrequited love that made peace and real love lightning.

XLV: Love & War
RED

All red cents had been shown to Tamana just before Christmas Day 2006. All the practice she had performed allowed her to have restraint on feeling emotion for her patients. Her apparel of scrubs was changed as often as inflammation would without a rectifying raconteur. In a single day she overcame a red streak towards the world's top causes of inherited and acquired death.

Autoimmune disease such as multiple sclerosis, rheumatoid arthritis, type I diabetes or vasculitis, initiated by the riddle of the body's own immune system attacking its own tissues, was what she declared to a few patients that day. As calm as a ladybug she rationalized treatment for those blowing raspberries and those souls' really suffering.

Immunosuppressant drugs are manufactured to be reflectively used in organ transplant patients. Some like azathioprine and cyclosporine are used to reduce inflammation from host immune activity, and those individuals' taking these medications are diagnosed with autoimmune conditions. Reciprocally these drugs would inhibit the patient's defense towards infection and may induce cancer. Tamana was to make the patients aware of this. Initially she prescribed prednisone; a corticosteroid, like all steroids have side effects, but hopefully with controlled doses they could respond without remorse.

The reaction of supplemental corticosteroids was to enhance the body's natural supply of steroid hormones produced by the adrenal cortex: the glucocorticoids (cortisol), and mineralocorticoids (aldosterone). Randomly these have been triggered off, and basic functions as fat, protein and carbohydrate metabolisms have become affected. Naturally the former controls basic metabolism, alongside limiting phospholipid build up in cells, the latter controls renal activity. Unfortunately the adrenal glands have become like raisins that the only hopeful cure would be to rely on a remedy that could alter a ribosome completely.

Consuming only a red apple for lunch Tamana walked onto the oncology floor. Least likely human cells had proliferated into metastasis by radiation therapy, but this she had to keep in mind especially when the individual had been forced to arrive. Most reliably the red herring was due to acquired habits, as excessive smoking and drinking, all rained over with ridiculous amounts of stress or random acts of love. Improve diet, improve lifestyle, and improve exercise, if all fails try immunosuppressants, try radiotherapy, try surgery, learn the ramble between a Summer Tanager and a Vermilion Flycatcher; and learn that repentance had to come from another.

Caution to the wind and share likely when a stop-sign octagon comes in sight. Both are careful as they take a right. The sign as a tomato to one person, and a red capsicum bell pepper to another, made no sense when Tamana heard she would have to give a red ribbon to an infant.

Colours of Enlightenment & A Potion

In contrast to an autoimmune disease, acquired immunodeficiency syndrome, is presented by a virus that affects lymphatic cells not to respond to infections, primarily affecting the brain, the retinas, the lungs, the skin and the gastrointestinal tract. The only rapport of the virus was to prevent the infected from living and breeding. The only human cure was to begin to live life healthily and peacefully. Antiviral therapy inhibits reverse transcriptase activity of the virus forming more viral-RNA, which slows down the rascal development of painful infectious and malignant deaths. Best to either be courteous about one's own life or that given to others, providing that the resistant vaccine was available.

Tamana's heart grew to be overwhelmed to see the infant smile. Royally she saved her tears and walked to wash and change. Retiring out of the evening and hopefully for Christmas Day she made her way out of the hospital. She dodged a stretcher entering the emergency room heading straight to surgery. The person was trying to be resuscitated. There did not seem to be any lesions on him, or any cuts, or bruises. The man was large, the man ate red meat excessively, the man drank excessively, the man was a reduplicate of another and the man needed a cardiac shock as the other.

XLVI: Love & War
RED

Relying on keeping the raging bull of all men's needs to fall baron at bay, the time-traveler had to be well aware not to encounter trouble as he traveled. Derrick had to study the cries of war that the people of earth had to suffer to make his home a safer place to live, and his vacations a safer place to visit.

Cries from murder in the twentieth century fell all upon race, and drafts of ethnicity, or communism. If one cry came from one person to kill the unjust then his word would be questioned, even though he sat by the right hand of God. A rancor for racial blood to be spilt was more appreciated amongst the nitwits that relied on race to be the only reason to murder.

Initially the stories of crusades building empires that led to millions to die by the knife. In 1914, World War I horned for people to find shelter against the resistance of Russian communism, that after four years and three months found armistice. The Russian Revolution being the world's first communist change from Tsarist Monarchy, led to the bloodshed of the monarchy in 1918. Now these random acts of violence left red on sand and snow.

A massive turn of events from World War I, not only caused no travel to New York, Wall Street, but also stopped ranches being built on free land in 1929. Widespread bankruptcy to unemployment resulted in no place to raise cattle; the only place to work was back to war and stop Nazis' making genocide of the Jewish in World War II. And stop Hitler's fascist movement. Six million Jews murdered and rivers were to run red blood, but some Jews were burnt instead.

Luckily the atomic bomb was created that stopped the war, by killing only a mare 160,000 in 1945. Benefit of the mushroom shaped out blast was so no rivers ran septic as the blood of the victims' was immediately vaporized to air.

Ransacking with new rifles gave ideas to the state of Israel concluding World War II in 1948. Palestine wanting freedom to live as an independent nation, but pressures from Arabia and Israel, remixed with pet fights, would carry on until there was nobody there to nourish the land. The land would become dry and not even vultures would land to feed. Pity was by far out of reach for those people. The answer was simple; the nation with the most wealth upon feeding and providing shelter for the state, should have taken complete remodeling of the coastal state of Israel. Not one individual had worked hard to keep what they had built, but all kept fighting to destroy little of what they had left. All prays across that park to remain holy, but now there's only one pray to silence them altogether. One ranger could take care of that park; the people should appreciate that ranger.

The countdown for Armageddon during 1962 Cuban Missile Crisis allowed closure of the Cold War. For people to recognize that stools were prepared the same way regardless to where they lived was harder to imagine than the clock that had stopped ticking, and had shut close the gates of heaven. The fortunate should learn to provide a whole lot better. As its fair to say what was taken from the Red-Indians could still be taken from the Americans. Rubies can be exchanged for robins, and the feet of the young for the heart of the elders.

There will always be a fortunate and someone left to neglect. Rotating this concentration will still make no sense, but finding a narrow pivot would ridiculously balance the love. Just like the Iranian Revolution in 1979, that only living for ignorance of one's own kind would make finest rituals for Allah to weep.

Through the pages of repeated history many have come to rise and many had regressed into suffrage and poverty. Realizing that had made the rich humble to the poor respectful they brought roses to be thrilled in their standing.

Pleased as some had come to flatten tyranny of evil, some as Jay-Z to Aamir Khan would and could bring destruction from a moments glance; nevertheless they obey the Father's request to give love instead, to shine their light. Leaving morals of pray to be taken harshly, if not to play sports aggressively, stop the hilarious types of bloodshed supposedly, or nobody would have retired from dying out of the starring towers for eternity.

XLVII: Love & War
RED

The range between January 21st and February 20th declares the start of the Spring Festival in China, also known as Chinese New Year. The lunisolar Chinese calendar relies on the wait of the second new moon after the winter solstice to mark the beginning of spring. The Chinese come to rejoice in this occasion for fifteen days. Derrick and Tamana came to join in their festivities in the year of the rabbit in 2011.

Beijing was decorated with candles, lanterns, celebrated with dragon dances, small firecrackers, and all enjoying fine cuisines from noodles to sweet glutinous rice balls in soup. The first day was to welcome deities of heaven to bring warm prospects for the following year. Families would visit the elders, and the married folk would give youngsters red paper envelopes filled with money. Tamana honored the Chinese ritual upon honoring family members with those alive or deceased that they prayed with them, and they prayed for a family of their own.

"What's on the cards for the people of the world Des?" she asked Derrick, whilst lighting a candle for the Jade Emperor of Heaven, as the Chinese do on the ninth day.

"I like to say that if the right receptors are triggered then the people of the world will prosper greatly," he replied whilst staring at the lit flame.

"After removing all the rebels, raids and rafter from history, where shall we focus our attention?" she said, as very well she knew that Derrick had seen much further in the future.

"What has brought all this on?" he returned.

Trying to hide her emotions that she could not share with the people around her, and hiding under her gorgeous figure that curved her cherry dress she cried: "Just answer me. What do we need to do to keep this light shining?"

"You almost blew your candle out. Very well I think there are many raffling ethics intertwined like a dismantled rubric in the world. I agree that Buddhists and others have rituals on not eating meat products on some days, but can the world really argue on genetically modified organisms, helping to grow quantity and quality food for increasing populations? Secondly, if population growth doesn't slow down we are to look for new forms of energy other than nuclear and oil. There are hydrogen cars, hydro-electric power stations, with solar and wind electric generators as well, but not following closely to the Kyoto Protocol by the United Nations, the world's leading countries are going to cause a massive effect on global warming, and unfortunately these are going to be hard to reverse," Derrick blinked four times. "And do you really want to know what would happen after this? I say 'would' as if people ruled out a few points of personal ethics then this light will always keep shining."

Colours of Enlightenment & A Potion

"He has written in Romans 1:20 that 'there's no excuse not to learn.' We should learn as a fox not to allow others to step into danger. The healthcare systems in the world are a good example of this. Simple basic diseases as malaria and flu due to contamination of water or lack of diet, millions of paramedics that can respond to millions of doctors, in turn can bring millions of people vaccines. How do high levels of healthcare insurance make sense? Take Heath Ledger for example, it's worse now than before we had penicillin," he paused so Tamana could realize that he was not talking about her specifically.

"All I'm trying to say is that not all people have to be born to breed. And if they are to breed, then they to be fully aware for whom they are multiplying for. Use genetic intervention, use embryonic stem cell research, safely, appropriately and allow people to appreciate that form of curing diseases and aborting babies. People forget that they should live for the Lord's love when they supposedly lose something or work without reward. I pray for ramification amongst individuals to either make no decision or make the right one," Derrick stepped back to admire Tamana. "We'll have three, lovely and as radiant as you."

Tamana pressed up against Derrick and placed his hands on her hips, "Tonight," she declared, and moved her lips to his ears, "General."

The 'General' she was remarking to be was General Guan Yu who was honored by the Chinese on the thirteenth day of festivities. General Guan Yu was acknowledged for his truthfulness, loyalty and strength over hundred raptorial riots for the Emperor.

XLVIII: Love & War
RED

Reproducing had benefited in some scenarios. Red roses bloomed to show affection for the emotion of love, and their beauty resembled cures for the depressed. Rewards in history as such marked the time-traveler to assess adventure as greatly as a conducted copper wire. The energy from reverting his thoughts of histories past failures allowed Derrick to appreciate what had been successfully conquered.

For instance the first printed book being the Gutenberg Bible in Mainz, Germany, on 23rd February 1455. Before this, kingdoms had chambers called scriptoriums where scholars would sit day and night replicating scripture.

Anesthesia was a huge hurdle that was overcome. The production of cocaine from the leaves of the coca plant administered in safe doses allowed for anesthesia to animal nerve systems. From 1884 the effects of this plant had helped hundreds of surgeons perform operations with reliance on comfort. In 1904 an aminoester form of the local anesthetic was formulated as procaine, and throughout the last century clinical trials have improved the action of the agent, allowing for a miracle ease for relieving pain.

The Coca-Cola Company, established in 1886 began to provide bursts of energy to mostly everyone

Colours of Enlightenment & A Potion

on the globe. Derrick enjoyed the recipe from this soda compared to that of others, possibly for the high content of cocaine prepared from coca leaf and caffeine prepared from the kola nut. A mixture of this drink with plain water provided enough energy and nourishment to bodily cells to accomplish any task.

In 1914, Emmeline Pankhurst, led the Women's Suffrage out of redemption by chaining herself to the bars of Buckingham Palace. She notably was arrested, but she gave spice as strong as a red chili to allow women's right to vote from 1928. The era was one to be admired by Preity Zinta, and Tamana; however Derrick had no interest in placing either of them close to the ramblings.

Another turn in history that inspired Derrick to achieve his own was when he read about Deoxyribonucleic Acid (DNA), found by Watson and Crick in 1953, a double helix series of nucleotides that coded for the genetic makeup of organisms. The remarkable breakthrough in biochemical engineering that allowed genotypes of cellular functions to be analyzed. Fifty years later the Human Genome Project was complete, the sequence of genes within chromosomes was complete. These sequences could not only provide a template for an ideal growth of a human, but also to distinguish humans from Red-tailed Hawks, flamingos, strawberries, raspberries, Flaming Red Oaks and other non-synthetic things.

Just as for every man gave his rib for each woman; possibly for affection or possibly for stem cells; the freedom of speech for all individuals was declared when Martin Luther King, Jr. of the United States, met Mahatma Gandhi of India, in 1959. This in turn empowered the Civil Rights Movement to eradicate racial segregation. The famous "I have a dream" speech was one to be reckoned with, and Derrick asked Tamana if she'd like to visit Washington D.C. on 28th August 1963. She agreed.

The travel to the moon in 1969 was well appreciated by the thousand minds at NASA, recounting that not one man was to be praised, but instead one devotion.

Love was not just accounted for by technology alone; the moonwalk of Michael Jackson in Wembley 1988, across the Bad concert was another remembrance of how people felt when standing together.

A little later just as thousand minds knocked down the Berlin Wall in 1989 to bring an end to repining death, Tim Berners-Lee brought multitudes of awareness to thousand minds across the globe, through the world-wide-web in 1991.

Further still ringing of radio waves brought better communication to use digital medium of electro-modulated waves to signal telephonic wi-fi into the twenty-first century. And as for Derrick the turnouts of thankful revolution allowed him to look forward upon his prays for revelation.

XLIX: Finale
BLACK

Wellbeing of their nature for one another grew to greater depths as time drifted. The friends began exploring different eras every time the earth turned to colder weathers in Moscow. Together they traveled around the world exploring what countries had to offer around the clock. The countries they had past time with became their excuse to stay closer to Derrick. Tribute given to Derrick as he had already witnessed the loss of his friends and so they trailed close to witness themselves the drop of his tears. Through the cloudy days of most in Moscow, Derrick decided that he should leave.

Blackthorn winter had approached with the white flowers of the thorny shrub about to blossom with the dark berries for the new cold season. Like all travels that the friends had listed prior to this one began in Dormition Cathedral. Lighting candles for those that indefinitely lived in darkness; museums clerks, librarians, repenting prisoners, homeless souls, overworked physicians, and soldiers that built hospitals in the line of combat, all the bone thugs playing to harmony, so with pleasure they gave thanks for their blessings. The friends dipped their fingers in the hallow service of holy water into the cathedral.

Sandeep Patel

From outside the cathedral was life working to keep the walls of faith safe. Children playing along with sirens' howling like wolves could be heard simultaneously. Sirens molted within white falling snow that embedded the emergency vehicles could only be seen as flashes of strobe in the best of circumstances. The dusky gloom atmosphere of night Moscow with falling snow made these drivers the best of their kind not to skid. The roads by far became covered overnight that during day settled snow turned to slippery ice sludge. To keep all things blackened from the blinding snow so the sirens could be heard throughout Moscow also required the application of sand and salt.

Inside the cathedral the choir brushed their gowns and waited for the choir leader to begin the hymns during ceremony. Ceremonies presented themselves to establish the new world, that world presented by Christ for the forgiveness of all sins, past, present and future, for Christ to present himself with name to stand as 'Jesus is Lord'.

The friends stood close to the middle row left to the speaker's sight. Abraham was to the far left, Derrick stood by Abraham's left and Tamana alongside with him, leaving Craig beside her, and Tyler by the aisle closest to the foot of the cross. The choir began with psalms; the friends listened in and enjoyed their environment. They stood, sometimes with hands together, sometimes as stance, sometimes as pose using the dark wood back rest of the row ahead with the forefinger.

Leaning back Derrick bowed his head to the floor and then to a donation envelope, to a book, to the

Colours of Enlightenment & A Potion

wood of the seating, through the clear black spaces of rows ahead of him, to a dark shadow on the altar resting ahead of Derrick. A spider crawled out from behind a candle stand on the altar and dashed over towards Derrick's sight making Abram startle. The spider stood for a moment then dashed over the ledge behind the altar's offering.

The surprising thing about that the friends found was, why had the spider come to the light during service? Without any auditory senses the spider was not prone to hearing the music. The only possibility that they could ponder was that the spider could feel the vibrations of notes off the walls of the building, that the spider came to see. Slightly startled Abram opened his mouth so the insect would not come any closer and groaned alongside with the choir.

Prays were followed by the end of the service. Prays to signify a prosperous start to 2011, and prays to bring Derrick's friends to realization and move away from him. Derrick nudged Abram and moved in-between Tamana's toes, pass Craig, to Tyler and out to the aisle. They blinked and watched their friend sit in the first row closest to the foot of the cross. Derrick bowed his head and pressed his hands together towards a mounted nailed person on a crucifix.

He began tapping his first fingers together for several seconds and then held them. He held them a little longer and allowed the rest of his fingers to touch. His friends began to feel uncomfortable. They had witnessed Derrick moving his pray into his world before, and every time they would fall to wish he was pretending to do his nails. They glanced over at Tamana, she was in pray into her palms, and smiled.

She brought her palms closer to her face. She looked up close at her palms as the others moved to their brother.

Abram walked over his left down the rows minding the people leaving the building. He pardoned his stride just to be observant of Derrick's thoughts. Craig moved Tyler out onto the aisle and stepped him down towards the second row. They smiled graciously as elders, seniors, adults, adolescents, toddlers, and choir members as they move to provide donations and final condolences. Tamana walked down to a few rows behind them and sat in a right row of the sight from the foot of the cross.

For the protection and immunity for Derrick's wellbeing he remained bowed on his seat. He began with soft prays that could be heard by the friends as slow whispers. The whispers gradually absorbed the light radiating from him to fall upon his friends. The discreet secret that Derrick whispered amongst the Father filled air into the lungs of his friends. Three hands touched gently the shoulders of Derrick and pressured him not to stand. They stood there in silence revealing their love to their friend. His lungs filled with air and he expanded his brawn. Gradually as young birds leaving their nest, Abram, Tyler and Craig left Derrick in Amen. They left their deeper than blood brother in peace with the Lord and followed their own light.

L: Finale
BLACK

Continuously the rain fell throughout the day. The clouds had thickened for the past week that they could not contain themselves any longer.

As soon as the earth had revolved from night, enough for the sunrays to approach Moscow from the east, the streets began to become cooled by the storm brewing from the west. The weather forecast for the evening was to have the raindrops change to snowflakes. Evening approached and the rain had stopped.

From the horizon opposite the entrance to the New Opera Theatre over the telephone cable lines a raven soared. The rest of the rain allowed the people below to look above at the raven circling into a helix towards the ground. A soul of prey that was made accustomed to bow during all times of the day. Nevertheless the people looked about their way and the only one watching the people was the raven. He descended with stretched wings to perch on the roof of the theatre.

As the bird of prey stepped foot onto the building he folded his wings and cried a caw three times. Chasing behind his laugh followed screaming police sirens, and their laugh that resonated throughout the city streets around Pushkinskaya Metro, and up towards the sky immediately filled the sky with snow. The snow fell softly with large snowflakes and began covering horizons like remnants of volcanic ash.

Streetlights began to switch on allowing the falling snow to be seen by Moscow habitants. The snow became entrapped with a warm wind that made them dance under the streetlights. The streetlights lit cafés where clean aprons were worn everyday serving black coffee. Black coffee seemed that much richer as individuals began to make themselves comfortable within the cold. The cold air was slowly being pushed away for the night from the city, to the seas; pass the suburban and rural areas of miners. Coal miners and iron workers packed their tools to make haste on reaching home before the blizzards trapped them to work for longer. Wind chilled to the core stretched with frost that howled through the shivering souls out from the metros of Moscow cooled the raven to rest. More streetlights switched on.

"Beautifully, sing it to me, where we go from here? Shall I pack my bags? Shall I wear my shoes? Oh, who knows but you? I don't know, nor does Cain, what I've done to my brothers, along the way. Oh, you cry more, if we're last for sure, how can I not switch you on?" sang Derrick.

Within the New Opera Theatre, staring at the light that reflected off the table sat Derrick singing to distract himself from his thought of work. Once he came to realization that he was sidetracked he found his black cube that he used as a paperweight on his table, and brought himself out of the light. Staring at anything black would have helped, nevertheless he liked to make

Colours of Enlightenment & A Potion

the most simplest of things exciting, so he sat and stared at the cube and brought himself to thought.

"Electromagnetic 'EM' waves consist of radiowaves, microwaves, infrared 'IR' rays, visible 'ROY G BIV' rays, ultraviolet light, X-rays and gamma-rays. Speed of light from Maxwell's equations between electric and magnetic forces allows light waves to travel when $c = 3 \times 10^8$ m/s. Properties of EM waves travel perpendicular to each other. Everything is checked including the radiation pressures of the invisible waves that travel through space or power cables that ensure harnessing the energy can be stable. Electrical force over magnetic force, $E/B = c$ brings me to control the speed of travel with a window variable of 100 m/s." dictated Derrick and gave a large sigh.

Weighing himself within the heat of his basement away from the rest of the chilled filled theatre, Derrick made preparations to test his invention. Derrick hesitated each time he held the titanium-carbon coated time-machine. He propped his device to balance still on the ground with his left hand and hesitated again. He queried if he should represent the white pieces or the dark pieces of a battle chess set. Neither of which would make a difference to his overall task to see if his invention would work or not. Dropping the staff onto his couch he grabbed a pencil and began to scribble off sheets of carbon graphite as lead onto blank pieces of paper.

Outside of his lair, there was a thud at the door, loud enough for Derrick to hear but he had not. Music beating through large amplifiers masqueraded a break in. The concentration between anxiety and curiosity blinded Derrick to witness that someone had entered his lair. The heavy weight of space that shrank around his own habitat made him stand. He walked over to his couch and picked up the time-machine.

The break-in was caused by a stranger of Moscow. The stranger overwhelmed with the free entrance, and bewildered from the cold, along with the loud music springing his hangover allowed him to keep his knife sheathed. This stranger was Craig Goncharov He paced softly to the door where the music was coming from. All of a sudden there was loud tuned note sang from the opposite side.

Desperation marked the stranger as one victim, instead of two and waited. One shadow distorted the beam of light from under the doorway for several seconds. There came another note of the same pitch from the other side of the door. The stranger waited several seconds and turned the doorknob and stepped into his victim's blind spot. Nothing was going to stop his hunger than himself.

Derrick paced himself to the wall furthest from the door and smacked his hanging fighter bag with his right thenar eminence, hard, and rattattatat, rattattat, he exploded on his fighter bag with a mixture of push into stances, with eminences and sidekicks, back side sick, rattatat-attack, tat, tat, until he pushed his whole body into the bag, pushing his force out of the back of the bag, and hugged the bag one time to stand still. He slowly paced himself back where the light was shining off his notes. Pushing his fingertips together he tensed his whole body, extraction of his quadriceps to push his thumbs along with supporting his back to brawn to stance. Derrick stared at the time-machine and sat down.

Colours of Enlightenment & A Potion

Shortening his stride stepped out of the shadows the stranger. The stranger unsheathed his weapon. He moved down the landing into the right shoulder of his victim. Derrick stood abruptly pushing his chair back to block the stranger closer. The stranger moved behind the victim, behind the wall of his kitchen and watched him move to the living space of his area. Derrick lifted the time-machine as a swordsman offering his weapon to a king that the stranger was clueless on what to do.

Craig walked closer to his victim as he adjusted to his own thought. Derrick twirled the time-machine to stop in both hands. Derrick had quietly grabbed his grip of his device and pushed a surface of the device to begin harnessing power. Through the change of reflection of light off the surface of the casing of the time-machine, he noticed he wasn't alone. The stranger leaned in to grab the contraption away from his victim's hands. Pushing the weight barrier of chance Derrick pushed himself back into the light, and pushed the assaulter off guard. Derrick shrunk his brawn and pushed up to strike the stranger, and whilst watching him fall to his mercy the time-machine had powered. Derrick noticed a deep scratch that was leaking on his invention and threw the time-machine onto the couch. He grabbed the assaulter and moved him into the kitchen; pulling open the pantry Derrick threw himself and the Craig in like he was throwing trash into a trash bin. A large explosion forced the door to shut.

The raven that sat above the theatre felt the concrete of his ledge halt. Without waiting any longer to find cause or effect he lifted his brawn and stretched straight out up into the falling snow.

Everything within the building, from the basement to the theatre lobby, all the floors, with all the cushions, and the stage with the curtains were torn to splinters and splits in thread, and what wasn't was on fire in a matter of seconds. There was no light to shine into the pantry, and the pantry had no need for a safety light if one knew where the handle fit. Through all possibilities everything stayed alive. Through all necessities the earth stopped trembling. Through all realities the pantry door pushed open.

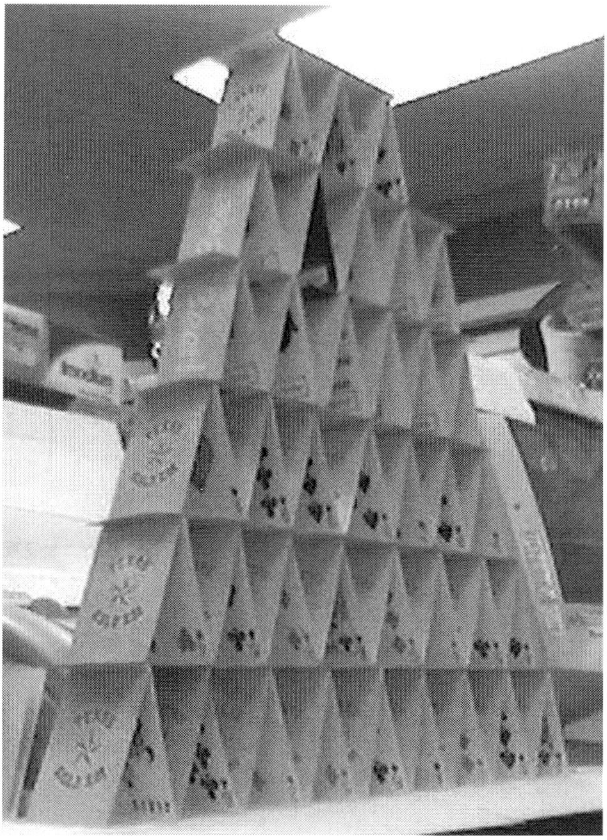

Epilogue

There once was an American man, an English man, an Indian man, an Islamic man, a Hispanic man, a European man, an Oriental man, an Australian man and an African man, they were all in a helicopter flying over the River Nile.

The American man lights a cigarette and then throws it out onto the world. The others ask him why he did that? And he replied, "I'll make more on my land."

The English man cracks open a can of ale and then throws it out onto the world. The others ask him why he did that? And he replied, "I'll brew more on my land."

The Indian man peels a banana and throws it out onto the world. The others ask him why he did that? And he replied, "I'll plant more on my land."

The Islamic man breaks his pray beads and throws them out onto the world. The others ask him why he did that? He replied, "I have more on my land."

The Hispanic man picks up his gun and throws it out onto the world. The others ask him why he did that? And he replied, "I'll buy more on my land."

The European man pulls out a book and throws it out onto the world. The others ask him why he did that? He replied, "I'll print another on my land."

The Oriental man looks at his videogame and throws it out onto the world. The others ask him why he did that? And he replied, "I'll create another from my land."

The African man stands up and throws the American man, English man, Indian man, Islamic man, Hispanic man, European man and the Oriental man out onto the world. The Australian man asks him why he did that? And he replies, "I'm tired of them littering on my land."

The Australian man shook the African man's hand.

SANDEEP PATEL

A Potion

- Light -

A Potion

Light

Sandeep Patel

Dedicated to my Brothers and Sisters

"Understand that a great fortune from your previous lives has become manifest. There is no other that I have seen like you. Whatever food or clothes he desire should be given to Sri Guru Nanak Dev Ji, and never upset him in any way."
Adhyai 11:34

"The people of Judah and Israel were as numerous as the sand on the seashore; they ate, they drank, and they were happy."
1 Kings 4:20

Contents

The Ingredients
- 1: The Realm — 201
- 2: Goman — 206
- 3: Sasha — 211
- 4: The Candlestick Makers — 215
- 5: The Revolutionaries — 223
- 6: Joule's Lair — 230

The Utensils
- 7: Firing Rocks — 235
- 8: The First Attempt — 241
- 9: The Possibility — 246
- 10: The Track — 253
- 11: The Insurance — 257
- 12: Ground to Grow — 265

The Boil
- 13: The Boil — 275

The Rest
- 14: The Biomes — 281
- 15: The Stones — 285
- 16: The Kingdoms — 287
- 17: The Atmosphere — 292

The Specimen

- 18: Jai Sainapat — 297
- 19: West Sasha — 303
- 20: The New Ground — 308
- 21: The Path Home — 314
- 22: Healthy & Music — 320
- 23: The Settling — 323
- 24: The Explanation — 329

The Outcome

- 25: The Visit — 339
- 26: Into Grounded Lava — 342
- 27: Radio Communication — 348
- 28: The Cities — 357
- 29: The Fields — 360
- 30: The Reality — 363

The Wish

- 31: Master — 373
- 32: The Wish — 380

Epilogue — 383

About the Author — 385

*For the places beyond here and
there are always to be shared.*

Deep 1:1

The Ingredients

Chapter 1
The Realm

There was a man in a garden, and that garden was covered in snow, and the only person the man could see was a snowman at the bottom of the garden. He tensed his bicep and his body followed through the rest of his arm, down through his pelvis to the tips of his toes, and he inhaled. And exhaled forcefully to rattle the icicles hanging on the wood by where he was sitting. The man watched the trees shake off the snow, jealousy for his attention all the branches followed, and the snow that fell off the branches sat on the snow below. The man saw the ground disappear into a valley of lava straight into a darkened window of a castle guarded by a spellbound male dragon.

The valley dropped from a brow that poured lava behind a bridge that brought a temple to its foot. The temple was a duplicate of that elsewhere, where the molten rock was replaced with water. The civilization that would have normally recited by that temple read Gurmukhi Script. A temple blocked without life just for appearances for the dragon's master.

The temple reflected metallic blue light that waved from the lava-fall; the rest of the crater walls were dark and sculpted the castle of where Master lived.

The dragon was on guard by a spell, and that spell was cast by Master, he who lives forever in the castle with the dragon. Joule was who Master called him. And in the lair of a deep crater, Joule would sit and listen to the lava flowing from a rock peak above him to the ground below him, forever he remained alive.

Joule pronounced Master's name with a grunt. A grunt was sufficient. Joule would watch his keeper conjure a spell with rock into a cauldron of dust, and powders of space into spider webs for something to happen. Mostly what Master worked on were spontaneous miracles; thus to mean Joule would keep guard once Master clapped his hands. The last time Master conjured a spell, the ground was forced to open and they were raised high above the rest of their land.

Master created energy from the realms of outer space and whatever he imagined became possible depending upon his mood. He would bring spirits out into the open as he imagined how spirits would be if left in a comfortable habitat. These spirits would only be seen by Master, but at times by Joule, he who would be waiting patiently to observe what Master would be bringing.

"Watch this Joule!" said Master, as he opened his hand to stare at something floating, over his palm.

Just as Joule we would watch Master cast this spirit to bounce off all walls of his crater, and fall back into the palm of his hand. (We would see with them when they dare, across the crater's dark stone walls' reflecting a shine of gold from the lava that played harmony of life on cold stone). After the spirit shaped as a small dense ball returned back to Master's palm he extinguished it noticing how un-amused Joule was. Joule's grunt that followed expressed his frustration towards Master's mockery further.

Colours of Enlightenment & A Potion

"Once again Joule!" said Master, and Joule smiled gently not falling for Master's same pun again with just the other hand.

The burning heat of where they stood was bearable by these two identities. They amused themselves by being well tolerated to their surroundings. Steam would be extinguished from the lava as the rocks would melt with the brimstone back into the center of their gravity. As Master was well pleased with Joule so was Joule of Master. They both had a fond liking of peace. Both identities generated heat within themselves being extremely endothermic, touching Master's skin or Joule's scales would present colder than ice. Basically where they were living the only cool surroundings would have been by their side.

By far and away into space where after the stars would carry dark matter, there would come another star. Drawing closer that star would be a patch of stars, where now they would be surrounding us. Bringing closer to the spectrum of light that would shape the constellations of stars would finish on navy away from the center. There the stars would collide to bring in an entrance to another universe. Through this universe resting a hundred new galaxies, one galaxy had a star that shined indefinitely. Master and Joule lived on the side where the star did not shine. A rock made for them different and distinct from other galaxies.

The reason for why Joule lived with Master was for his love for him. A reason for why Joule loved Master was for his inability to make quick decisions. Master had programs in which he would show Joule; however with the time they took structuring perfection, Joule would have most likely fallen asleep.

Whilst this great dragon slept, Master spent time rearranging his living-quarters. From where Joule had his living-quarters, Master's quarters were above his about a hundred feet. A castle sculpted on the side of dark stone built a main lobby and a table that faced space. Within the stone itself Master would sit to think about moving more rock from beneath him, or changing the arrangement of a rock table bedded into the deck lobby elsewhere.

As Master moved stone, rock, the table from one end of their space to the other, he felt amused knowing of Joule presence. Regardless to the spell that Master had bound on Joule, Joule was free to deny Master his appraisal for him. Joule could be anywhere he wished to be, but he chose time over time again to be closer to Master. Thousands of stars, planets, moons, asteroids, meteoroids in space, but dark stone and lava-falls surrounded Master and Joule.

"Catch up!" said Master to himself, whilst moving his thumb over his palm like he was reading something. "Place three of these, two of these and something from here to there, and a knock on the cauldron, with another one, and there you go."

Two sparks screamed out of the lobby and into space. Joule looked towards space to see the firework exploding into the shape of a fish.

"One more time and that will be that."

He hopped around whistling a beat, raised his arms and conjured a spell from the heat that built Joule's lair. Heat, steam and sparks of light hissed beneath the floor of Master's outer lobby. And from a pool of lava below came a loud whizzing howl shattering apart into pieces of fire-rock.

Colours of Enlightenment & A Potion

"Joule, watch!" ordered Master.

A cannonball firework screamed away from the lava around Joule's pedestal and smacked into the dark stone opposite to where Master was. Stone crumbled away and began to fall towards Joule. Joule bowed his head and hissed strong gas from his nostrils as pieces of stone fell around him. And with one swift move he leaped into the air, with two strokes of his wings he soared a hundred feet to look Master straight in the eye.

Master looked at Joule and then through him, with one more stroke Joule turned his body to face the wall that the firework hit. There was a carving etched into the rock of what Joule could gather as a moon, a rock and a planet.

Surprisingly for Joule he recognized the planet. Joule had named the planet Bani. Thousands of years had passed since he was last able to play there. With excitement Joule opened his mighty wings and flew out into space to see if what Master spelled had come real. The planet was a hundred million light years away from where Joule and he stood. Master had created him on the planet and Joule lived and grew there to witness the outcome of nature. Joule saw how life bloomed and died. From the tears shared by the great dragon Master realized that he had made a true companion.

Chapter 2
Goman

The center of Goman stood a mountain, above and away from the ocean's face, which reached all of space. Built into the mountain was a stairwell built by Gomen that hosted an entrance for the gods into the foundation of a castle. The tallest tower from the castle marked the origin of the stairwell within the castle within its fortress. The tallest tower had a tall fine peak ascended through the clouds to the sky illuminating most of Goman. Surrounding the peak and the tallest tower of the castle grew Goman. Apart from the foundation of Gomen, Goman was covered with meadows that filled livestock, vegetables, fruits, barley and grain all fueled by the weather from the seasons needed for Goman to be.

Goman was an island; an island on one side of Bani. Goman was difficult to reach let alone see with the most advanced forms of technology. The island's sea developed tides a hundred feet high, and sheltered a tenth of a hundred miles around the coastline of Goman. These tides were controlled by the stars that whoever happened to reach the island would be there for all eternity. There was no reason to leave Goman as Goman was beautiful and mature in all delicate cultures of the land, that one may even say there was no world better than that of Goman.

The tides naturally brought sea life to the shores of Goman, some to eat and some to observe. Human

Colours of Enlightenment & A Potion

intelligence recited on the island and to their beginning started on Goman shores. Here isolated an impression that Goman was not a place to be unlawful in, as the ones that would see was the ones closest to the gods, they who have been blessed to watch over all of Goman, thus for all life and for all eternity, from the tallest tower close to the heavens out to the seas.

  The sweet taste of fruits and the richest tastes of livestock, freshly prepared from the foothills of Goman, were served to the monarch of Goman every day. The fruits were handpicked by all who felt that this particular seed in shape, smell and beauty should only be savoured by the king, and was passed through the villages till that fruit arrived to the king's table. The Gomen loved their king as their king loved them. And no dispute was taken when cattle were bred to be fed to the king and all his people, morning and evening after each other as rotten fruit bedded soil to make fertilizers.

  Time spent in Goman was unaccounted for as nobody cared for time. Gomen had no intention to be of concern for time being a part of their life. All they believed was that they should live, and grow, and laugh, and sing, and dance till they were asked to live, and grow, and laugh, and sing, and dance in another village closer to the castle. That was what the people of Goman waited for, if waiting was what they actually did, which they actually had no desire to do as life was great, as life was filled. And to grow, and laugh, and sing, and dance was all that was needed to keep the tides of Goman a tenth of a hundred miles away.

  Further still life on the island was not measured in years. As there was no time, no soul cared to see that they had lived for two-hundred and thirty nine years, or eight-hundred and so years before becoming king or queen. All they waited for, if they knew how to wait, was for the tides to bring more life to the shores.

    The king watched with his queen all the people throughout the land of Goman. And their younglings watched with their peers all the animals of Goman. There could not be a brighter picture than the smooth green-yellow fields that they could see from their home upon the mountain.

    The king would surely visit the gods once his son becomes king. Whereas, if the father passes earlier than expected, then the prince should spore again to secure his path to the gods. The prince would marry a Goman daughter, and celebrate in this occasion, and again with the prince's siblings.

    The reign to the gods' visits two paths, one path climbs into the fortress, and the other was within the fortress to the castle, as man and woman. The castle walls' order this. As unrighteousness, and sinful thought, and psychology are dismissed once the person or persons enter the gates. The thought of a better day always followed a good day, and a good day always preceded a better day.

    Deceitfulness of crime was not seen here. As this was Goman, and night cries would only be delivered by babies asking in another linguistic manner for attention, food, or a fresh piece of clothing. Humming could also be heard. The land was sound and peaceful, with winds that blew down the mountain in spirals from the stars, to the shores, and out to the seas. The wind maintained the tide that protected Goman from those who had built boats from skulls, bones, and blood off innocent believers, thus crime there was not.

Colours of Enlightenment & A Potion

No one outside the island knew that there was an island within this hundred foot tide with a slowly stretching radius. Nevertheless the innocent believed that there lay something of hope with the curiosity to be away from unlawful acts. And the quick and restless would fall into conquering temptation and drown. Thus allowing the believers to come one and value the tides in making continuous liquidity safer. That was how Gomen kept faith.

Now Goman was enriched with music, and food, and life, and horses, and water, and work that to become monarch was not a desire, but an opportunity of the highest blessing. The rule from monarchies inked that couples could be engaged under their thirtieth year into livelihood, but no persons to conceive offspring any earlier. To deserve the highest blessing, Gomen gave their land the requirement to grow rather than to be swallowed. A realization from the initial harvests, that the soil had become hallowed by overpopulation of the Goman ecosystem. Later both men and women gained the right to watch over the land of Goman, to drink from the divine word that flowed through the mountain, and to protect the tower to the heavens.

To enter the magnificent castle was not as difficult as would have imagined by newcomers. As long as the doors were open the rules of the castle walls were obeyed; and along with the rules of grace people flowed to and from the castle gates. The people would walk to the mountain from the seashores, resting on their way, and through the arches of stone, across the fortress streets to the highnesses. As for farewell some strengthened greatly drawing closer to the horizons off the tallest tower to the highnesses that they abode.

Fellowmen and women shared with the king and queen of Goman all the beauties of life that they surrounded. The children learnt infinitely as they knew that they had one path to follow; a different path to each other as consciences as different creatures, but the path was the same nonetheless, and that was to become king or queen; to visit the gods through the clouds, and through the gates of the tallest tower that ascended above the sky and into the stars.

The innocent upon their arrival to Goman from the outside world descend from the clouds, pass the gates, pass the king's quarters, through the arches of the castle, down the mountain, through the fields, and pass the villagers to the shores, to circle their belief and dwell for others away from Goman. They awake as they left, to hear sweet music, and laughter, and celebrations, and to see the tallest tower of the castle ascending through the clouds to the heavens.

Chapter 3
Sasha

An island named by the people who recited there was called Sasha. Sasha was on the opposite side of Goman on Bani. Much of Sasha was covered by people. The trace of life came from the sea which developed into man on the island. They parted from the seashores to bank upon the channel's bay. The possibility for life was printed in abundance for the warm fronts of where the Sashans could see. The warm fronts were two horizons that they could see from their island. One horizon without cranking their neck came from where the sky met the sea. And the other was a hundred-and-eighty degree turn stretching to the other end of the sky, a dark, gray/brown cliff that had risen from the planet's mantle development.

    The Sashans learnt to raise themselves and their children at the foot of the cliff realizing that there could be a possibility of collapse. The collapse of earth would have only been made by the top of the cliff, regardless that the cliff was continuously eroding due to air currents hitting the cliff's face from sea. Sashans recited in a manner to respect their dead by burying them close to the ledged rock too. Planting sandstones firstly found from where Sasha held civilizations, that they planted them around their deceased. Acid was not born to affect the stone, and Sasha flourished with immediate crop, and flocks of poultry to accompany them as the seasons changed.

Vegetation grew around the base of the cliff that exploring the discussion to climb the piece of desire was not primarily thought. Good vicinity from the strength of the earth provided ore of iron, hence alloys in the cliff's mixture kept them at bay.

From the people there stood the cliff, and the seashore full of yellow sand, and under this sand formed the conglomerate stone crust. The people axed timber for providing shelter, and log cabins lit coal that began to be mined from the cliff. Once all of the land on Sasha was discovered the timber was stretched evenly prior to the steel. The steel overlaid rail tracks to both ends of Sasha.

The Sashan people made places to study the stars, and presented monuments different of each nature, but all respecting something for their existence. Some monuments covered staples, and others with arches, and others as temples with small naked clay figurines, and some with massive dome constructions, all to allow reflection to their unknown.

Moral of life developed away from suffering through what Sashans called, Panth. A message from an immortal being that was heard across the rock's face let way. The message was a sermon that repeated verses of hymns, some hymns repeated themselves for emphasis, and each sermon was equal as the other. The immortal being of Panth gave Sashans enlightenment for their days of less sunlight to grow in the darkness. With the sunlight reflecting off the land of Sasha, the light let alone the heat becomes unbearable to withstand. Monuments were built to be presented to Panth scribers, and scholars, and to have strong holds for bread. Far from this island there was no other.

Colours of Enlightenment & A Potion

There was a monopoly of love in Sashan hearts from when they made monopolization of equilibrium a law. Unrequited love was solved through three orders of understanding. The law mandated that every person be taught this way of life. The first is the Light (Panth), which was life; life that they live. The second was to have peace from moments away from life and for Sasha this was anything coloured black. Black was peace, black was cool, black was anything away from the light reflecting off the sand. Eye contact, along with blinking was peaceful. They all had vision to see anything as when needed they could find something black. An example would be the horizon. And the third was conquering that each creature on Sasha had blood, which was red. Red was with every person and every creature including the fish. Overall the law was told to live to hold the first order over the others. The Light was considered as that which came from their sun and from the other ends of space.

Far from across the mainland and through the savannah to the mines there hollowed cracks in the ore. These were filled with roots of mighty trees that scattered the hat of the cliff. Birds could be seen by Sashans above the huge distance covering the horizon from the cliff. The birds indicated life on the cliff's top. Nevertheless civilizations of Sasha concentrated on fishing off their coastlines as they made settlement with each other and their fisherman nets.

Constructions of awareness grew to greater depths as the land of Sasha filled. More buildings and heavy work was mandatory for the people as time passed. As Sashans watched the shores become filled with people they thought on what to do with each other.

West Sasha held the civilizations of people and East Sasha gave rise to woodlands. Scriptoriums were built in the woods where more trees were learnt on how to be planted, they hosted times of salutatory into the Panth. Once the trees had grown tall they returned back to West Sasha and suited housing around their teachings. The teachings from the Panth built a university, Sasha Khand, a university to build curiosity.

Great boats were made as grand as the Mayflower from strong oak and rum. They sailed to the ends of the earth once all the barrels were filled. From the planet's axis to the west of their sun's light they sailed off the end of the planet. Towards the east they travelled after failing the second time to the west and the waters whirled them into the void of the ocean. Maps became charted and wood chopping reduced once wax on every voyage melted at a greater rate.

The planet around Sasha revolved around a sun, and revolved to the center of that sun that the planet revolved around. The water was on edge as the planet was not a circle, but a slab. The Sashan people realized that there was no escaping their island to see the other side of their planet, let alone the top of their land.

So round and round Sasha and Goman turned on an axis made for them. The axis had been named by Joule, Bani. Bhagbat Bani was what the people of Sasha called their planet, the divine words being earth and water, with the divine word being water. So Bani turned and Joule watched. From a distance Joule thought about the people of Sasha and Goman, and for a moment the people of Goman and Sasha thought of the existence of each other.

Chapter 4
The Candlestick Makers

Tarun regarded himself as a visionary. He meant to say he liked to collect anything shiny and place that in his shekel. Mostly what he found were shells of snails, and red berries, and these he placed in his shekel. Through his walks along the mountain stretch that his family lived on, he would walk to the ledge and would sit and count what he had collected on his way there.

Since he could remember Tarun was curious about most things around him. A true passion into believing that for anything to be alive there must be the existence of a true creator. Tarun would walk to find light and a place to expand his thought in the forests of Goman. He would paint his appearance of life into a world between his palms. He would sit for hours reflecting the light on and away from his hands. Casting his thought into the shadows made on his palms in his own world he would catch the perplexes of horizons made. From youth Tarun's thought process was at light speed from using what his brother called as, 'mapping'.

Faran was Tarun's brother and was four years older than him. Tarun was fourteen once he started walking alone. Before that he would have walked to the face of the mountain with Faran. They would regularly walk out their home and towards the sunlight that shone through the trees. Their walk recited towards the farms and their cabin on Mount Dev Ji of Goman.

Sandeep Patel

Both brothers were aware about their role in the kingdom of Goman. Faran was soon to be placed to work at the castle. His age had reached summit and Tarun was just as excited for his brother as he was. Nevertheless before then Faran thought to spend all his time with his brother evaluating if he was safe to leave.

At adolescents their father had given them the words of the castle walls. They were overwhelmed to hear such words that brought no meaning to them. Their father at times worked with them in mind and sprang sentences of the order to help him work harder. His children watched him play with the sentences during his work; he was a woodsman director for the king and now a deliverer of men for the castle.

On mornings when no chores were to be done Tarun woke later than usual. The morning frost would have melted as Bani turned, leaving him to warm out of bed for his morning walk. Within the forests that lined Mount Dev Ji with Tarun's home was filled with noise of wildlife, and with them he would rest in shade to wait for the castle markets to clatter. The southwest wall of the fortress reflected the morning light over a dip in the valley across from Tarun's walk, and there from across the valley Tarun would walk to and wait for the sound of his future to call him.

On all days when chores were to be performed, Tarun and Faran were bread to plowing ripe spuds from their plantation, and picking grapes from their vineyard on Mount Dev Ji. Duties involved preparing vegetables from the earth and planting fruit trees where the humidity changed by altitude. Tarun watched over goats, and Faran gathered sticks and tree barks to burn when the sun carried to fall over the southwest wall

Colours of Enlightenment & A Potion

carved on the mountain. Barrels of water from the natural spring flowing beside the Goman family were collected last. The brothers would count their chores, and be prepared for supper as soon as they heard their father from the woods bringing home the meat. Pack up, place the lids on, and move all goats to the barn, and sticks on the stacks with more on the fire.

By the time Faran went to serve at the castle Tarun was eighteen. Faran had grown a beard, but unlike Tarun had grown the hair for warmth. Filling most hunting duties that their father taught to them the boys grew to be strong men. Tarun built a fine passion for digging. Whatever he collected in his shekel to the time Faran left, he had found by digging he had kept. Some treasures would urge him to dig further, and treasures like smooth pebbles, and scraps of iron were kept with him till he could meet Faran, and show the king of his findings. Faran was to work as the horse keeper within the castle walls. Feeding, grooming, cleaning and exercising the castle horses were considered a high standing for their kingdom.

When Faran met the horses', he was as flattered as they were to have a fine work colleague. He groomed them twice a day, speaking to them about how times used to be much different, and how Tarun was waiting to serve in the castle too. The horses heard Faran as being delusional. Hearing him talk with emotion about the land outside the castle gate, the horses never felt that anyone else could see the beauty of Goman.

The stalls would be cleaned and the hay stacked, and Faran would then assist his neighbours with clearing the market space from the castle courtyard to the main gates. Everything must be cleared before the sunsets. Goman was lit during the night through the light of their moon, touches on some street corners, and candles, lanterns, or fireplaces within homes of Gomen. The people would thus clear out any obstacle to help music flow from the castle's tallest tower to the waves of the seashores.

"To be true and not to be disheartening Brother Faran, as fate has been chosen for us," said the blacksmith that worked beside Faran in the castle courtyard.

His name was Marcos, and he was slightly older than Faran. A well built individual that lived gloriously by moulding metal for the king's people, and drinking at the castle tavern. Marcos was a Goman family man, with a spouse and three children. All of which lived outside the castle walls, and only once his children became of certain age they would be permitted to live within the castle. Until then like all Gomen, Marcos' children will first manage the fields before serving the king closer.

"Aye, I wonder what should be of my fate warming with her or the sun?" replied Faran, "with her in these walls is better tolerated than where my family is,"

"Yes, from within all of Goman, here is that much cooler. Maybe in some years we may have snow," humoured Marcos.

The men finished packing the remaining tables, and folded the canopies at the south end of the castle courtyard, and began walking towards the north. By walking further south would be to enter the castle and

Colours of Enlightenment & A Potion

serve closer to the king. Marcos and Faran entered the local tavern and sat to be served.

Inside the tavern was filled with town men and women who had served within the castle walls daily to unwind, and socialize before leaving the castle, or attending other duties. The tavern was run by Landlady Caffe. Caffe assembled chairs, tables and barrels full of fermented sugarcanes, which she served with her smile to the people of Goman.

"Have you managed to cool the drinks further, Caffe?" asked Faran.

This indirect question was to ask her what was the scenario of the king's order on the increasing humidity to Goman. There was no chance that Caffe could know what was spoken about within the castle, however as Faran knew of her parents being within the castle he thought of every opportunity to ask and acquire her attention.

"My brother should be able to help you cool the barrels once he arrives," forwarded Faran.

"Well that would be nice. At the moment I have plenty of space to hold them, but in the coming years I may need a hand," winked Caffe at Faran.

Times of war brought sorrow and anger to every person thought to be a mercenary. These times were held tight and tighter by the dhol that played into The New Age.

Plenty of gold, plenty of gold, plenty of shiny, shiny, gold, but all we want is you. Plenty of gold, and myrrh, and myrrh, with frankincense would be brought to be presented to you. And with all that to bring will be more than happy to carry to you.

Another man from you, and another woman from you, for another son-in-law for you, and a daughter-in-law for you. Another man to be named to bring the future to the present and then another man after him. Where shall the line be drawn? Where shall they pray for someone else? Another man began to play the dhol, that another man stepped up to join in. Many men joined in behind them to chant to the many women building behind a line of three mystery women.

Plenty of gold, plenty of gold, plenty of shiny, shiny, gold, but all we want is you. Plenty of gold, and myrrh, and myrrh with frankincense would be brought to be presented to you. And with all that to bring will be more than happy to carry to you.

Caffe had felt love for Faran since he had arrived to the castle. She felt that there was something special about him. Faran had no idea that Caffe was genuinely fond of him, and thought that Caffe spoke to all customers as she did to him, and he didn't assume any different for them, that they all lived in harmony. She saw Faran as a sweet, strong man, and noticing Faran notice her, she was in no threat from any other lady in Goman. Caffe would wait to see what further orders the king had for the horseman before she could take a gamble and let Faran know how she really felt for him.

"Would you like me to make you something?" asked Caffe to Faran.

"Anything you like, whatever is easiest," said Faran whilst in deep thought.

Colours of Enlightenment & A Potion

Three years had passed since Caffe made Faran his first plate. He never asked her for anything else until he was insure of his brother's arrival. The concern for Faran was that Tarun lived alone, and for him to live within the castle would be better as Tarun had a mind to inspire. Unbelievable inspirations made Tarun an extremely interesting Goman. For him to waste away outside the castle walls would seem pointless as the years of Bani became warmer. Faran felt that Tarun would be able to help the king and his fellow-men accomplish over their fate. Regardless if Tarun could or not, Faran also wished for his brother to be safe before he gave more attention to Caffe.

"I'll make you a gammon steak, gravy and smash," she replied whilst brushing passed him.

Faran ate whilst staring out to the light and dark part of the counter ahead of him. The moonlight was shining in from behind him, across the dining room of the inn, across clattering dishes and few flavouring munches, through to the opposite end of the bar and out of another window.

Faran and Marcos consumed their meal as Caffe left them to clear the tables. The men left a little beverage in their glasses and left for home once they savoured their last bite. Warm winds entered from the tallest tower filled the tavern as Marcos pulled the entrance door open to forward Faran out.

"Come and see me tomorrow Faran, bring me some flowers or some horse hair!" shouted Caffe over to Faran.

Faran laughed and some customers made mash of their meals from that comment. Faran pointed at her heart. She pointed back.

"Only if horses could stroke themselves," he laughed, and turned a no and shook his head, patted Marcos on the shoulder and walked out.

The courtyard of the castle was lit with torches carried by people lighting more torches. Pass the castle gates the streets had become silent with only a few torches lit under the horizon. Faran glanced at the stone making the horizon of the gate and a metallic shine of light floated across his view. The light was from the reflection off the Rock from the sun. The Rock appears over the Gomen every nine days. The light disappeared over the horizon of the southwest wall of the castle and to Tarun's sight, where he too was waiting to meet with his brother and the king of Goman.

Chapter 5
The Revolutionaries

From the cringe of living by Professor Esjah for all classes became unbearable for two students, Manson Blue and Barsy Marine. The incredulity of Prof. Dev Esjah's class was that there was all the reason to be there except for the fact of Coach Lindsey Butcher sitting on the eighth row. Blue and Marine loved what they did, they believed in Sasha, and they believed in dying for each other. They were outstanding at placing what they learnt in Prof. Esjah's class to experiment, and most the time the experiments went well. With Lindsey riding on their every nerve the classes went by too slow.

"Do you guys want to accompany me in the gymnasium later?" whispered Lindsey to Blue and Marine.

"The theory of planting something within the cliff could save us from possible incineration, should we have considered more?" Prof. Esjah asked rhetorically to his major class of engineers.

"We have come a long way from running fresh water to drink from, and close to next month, tests on Rock travel will commence," carried on Prof. Esjah.

Blue and Marine carried on scribbling notes onto their paper as they were to manage this travel, and successfully operate the excavation. Now since the last exploration off Sasha nobody had returned anybody from the past voyages before them, and no one from the times before them. No boats from the crusades that Sasha had worked on docked back on Sasha's coast. So from where Blue and Marine were standing, they were scared as well as excited.

"If we can't go left or right, then we'll go up, then we'll go up," sang Marine.

"Then we can go further, then we will go further," replied Blue.

"Live in prison no problem, live in prison, no problem. Live out to sea, be content, live out to sea, I'm content. Live in prison, no problem," they carried on.

The bell began to ring and the class began to pack their bags. Blue, Marine along with the research engineers, crew staff and Prof. Esjah, began to gather at the bottom of the lecture hall.

"Now lads, you ready for this? Nothing to worry about really, we have been over this thousands of times, and now do you guys have any questions?" asked the professor, whilst the team packed to visit the launch site.

"No. Just ready and eager to try, sir," said Blue.

"We have been over the schematics several times sir and we don't see a problem with them either," forwarded Marine.

"Nothing to worry about, sir," said Blue.

"Very well, let us go over the settings and practice one more time today. Talk to the mechanics about where they placed the brakes then get your asses to the gymnasium. If your blood was to be placed in a hypotonic solution I'd care, but if I get parts of your brain matter over the dashboard then I am going to get your siblings to clear it up. Got it?" Prof. Esjah said.

Colours of Enlightenment & A Potion

"Got it, Prof." replied the guys as they looked through Dev Esjah's heart.

After simulations, and drawings of flight paths, and distances from orbits of the moon and the Rock they came to a close. Dev Esjah knew very well of the men's consciousness, that their worked amused them and who lost was the one who slept the longest. This was the mindset that the students had set themselves in and out of the classrooms. The aim of this particular task was a purpose strong enough for Blue and Marine that no other persuasion was needed or appreciated. In the third space between each others' sentences the fire pitch would have started. Like ideas and settlements, like battling with words to organize their thoughts, and trust in each practice.

Barsy Marine being a natural marine special-biologist did not care for haemoglobin as much as haem' or some other protein molecule. Marine liked studying marine animals.

He studied by mapping. Mapping was used beautifully for ideas with his hands let alone that with him handling sea-life. Wiping his hands like clearing a slate from dust he would read off his hand gestures, and pass markers on them to bring him back to text. Flowing fingers together, through each other, and between each other, extending his arms at arm's length he was seen once as mapping when picking food to eat from the market shelves. Through to a different stop or same stop as his thumb would end. Marine had excellent marksmanship for aiming for a specific position of perplex for a protocol.

Manson Blue, a strong Sashan who was excellent with people. He knew his environment and who was living around his closest proximity, the proximity barrier of the food shelves to the polished floor of the ball court. His heart had haemoglobin but was like a white towel of merci. The people too around him loved him too, simply because of a handshake and a smile. His childhood friend, Barsy Marine called his best friend Blue because he was honest. When no handshakes meant no handshakes today, he'll cool off tomorrow let him be. If he's there, he will stand with you, let him stand and he'll be peachy once again.

Blue and Marine had known each other since they had met at the cliff's foot to pay tribute to their lost ones. Now twenty-years from the time they witnessed the burial of their loved ones they both praised each other more to be stronger. Blue had lost his mother, and Marine had lost his sister to an infection that had spread over Sasha during their birth.

It was a violent breed of bacterium that was transmitted through the fish from changing the landscape of East Sasha. Metallic ions from welding contaminated the waters and spread to become an infection cultured at sea. Families of fishermen were noticed first to have symptoms leading to death, killing off most of the suburban population of Sasha. Presenting symptoms included fever, malaise, shortness of breath and dehydration, that without immediate attention the person died with septicemia. Much later a vaccine was administered by needle that harmlessly piercing the infected with the specific-antibiotic allowed remedy within thirty-six hours. Pinching the skin prior to administration of the cure allowed the young phobic to become rational. Fortunately for Blue and Marine they survived, but only to share the grief to

Colours of Enlightenment & A Potion

watch their father's suffer. Blue and Marine were made well aware that they as their fathers' were made to die together.

After leaving Prof. Dev Esjah and the workforce the friends thought to catch up on some physical exercise. They left the testing center before dusk and walked to the gymnasium. Walking past the gymnasium halls they could hear Lindsey Butcher work the women of Sasha in gun firing. The women had guns to say the least, so Lindsey Butcher's passion was fire arms and combat fighting. Lindsey Butcher and the girls heard the guy's walk into the gym as nothing was more distinct than Marine's accent and Blue's laugh. That to say, wherever they were people heard them.

"So what's your name?" said Blue to the air.

"Jessica," replied back Marine.

"How do you spell that? Never mind how old are you?"

"Mmm... shouldn't ask me that. But I don't want to be boring so 24."

"Ha you too funny, I'm 12, so are you single?"

"No. Oh no, no one's perfect," they both replied, and began singing, "I like this, I like that, you like what? I like this, you like that, you like what? That'll look nice, that'll look nice, and that'll look nice, on you. But as it's a no, I'll have to go. Go, Go, Go!"

As for Lindsey Butcher, she had lost her father to the infection that had brought the three of them together. Her behaviour fell in a comparison to passing off her hellish figure, thus her mind was set to survive at any means. Lindsey Butcher was well much like her father, fair and rugged, with a soft complexion that would make any girl envy her. Nevertheless if Eve came with ignorance she would let that pass, however if Eve was purposeful then into the wall she'd go.

"Okay Barsy," said Marine, as he threw down his bag and began changing into his sweats. "Who are you going to take out tonight Manson?" Marine asked Blue.

"Most likely Gloria, to the Sea Diner," replied Blue.

"Most likely?" quizzed Marine.

"Well there are others, but tomorrow is a work day, and I am not that cut out to make any type of celebration so soon. What about you? Want to join us? Three's company, and besides what's her name will be there," Blue asked.

"Aryan, her name is Aryan," Marine replied.

"So she has a name, didn't realize she had a name, and mighty what a name someone has given her, well she does fill out her name, I give you that Barsy," said Blue whilst they both headed out of the locker room, "so what about Aryan?"

"I'll think about that later. Now I have to work and study. That is the best form of means to travel to the Rock to see the planet's other-side."

"Now that is a thought, the other-side of this planet. Do you think if there is life there, they will be as us? No, no Gloria first, and then from the other-side," said Blue.

"Hey guys," said Lindsey as she pulled up her socks behind the men, "what you two talking about?"

"Work," quickly replied Blue.

"Food," replied Marine with a puzzled look at Blue on why he said work. "What about you Lindsey, have you made plans tonight?"

Colours of Enlightenment & A Potion

"Going to the Sea Diner with a few girlfriends in my class, nothing special,"

"Oh Blue, will be there? I thought you said you were working?" asked Lindsey to Blue.

"Working, eating, all the same really, you know us, always mixing things up," replied Blue, "So anyone that we know from the class?" returned Blue.

"I am not sure, why?" asked Lindsey.

"Oh don't take any notice of him; he is still trying to resolve what would come first, the voyage to the other-side of this planet or him," sarcastically saved Marine anymore questions on Blue by Lindsey, "I will be there tonight too, meeting a friend," Marine said.

"Well that's good. So what's her name Barsy?" asked Lindsey.

"Aryan. Tonight her name is Aryan, Lindsey," replied Blue returning the favour.

There was fury on Lindsey's face that was unbearable for Marine to see; he shivered for a second and began working on his work-out.

Expressing her jealousy at no cost Lindsey Butcher leaned up against a wall to wait to be noticed by Marine. Instead Blue began asking Lindsey all questions involving anyone but Marine, and Lindsey eventually swung her hair away from the men and walked back to the girls next-door.

Sasha was much different to other civilizations. Long ago they had brought about their doom which changed generations. Both genders on Sasha were considered equal in thought and opinion. Much time had passed since they could remember what life was like before their first catch, so that being said they cared not about yesterday but for tomorrow.

Chapter 6
Joule's Lair

Brushed as a scaly acrylic paint of burgundy and purple on each scale, Joule stood 18 feet tall, and 54 feet wide with wings' stretched out. His skin was grafted as a squids but with a hard exoskeleton. Meaning to say Joule could camouflage to his surroundings, both in texture and shade. He had a serpent's tongue coloured deep purple, and around the inside of his mouth keratinized mucosal epithelium. This layer of skin was different to the rest of his scaly structure; the inside of the corners of his large jaw was protected with para-keratinized epithelium needed to protect the eyes from his ignition ducts.

Joule had deep black eyes, and a horse's forelock that was stiffened with copper which held Joule's mane back to the arc of his spine. There were a couple of holes in the collagen and elastin protein sheets that stretched between his right wing appendages. Joule mostly had them for affect as the shine from his dark black eyes performed miracles. Joule was a being of one's own self.

Joule lived in the castle created by Master. There was an open nave with a transept, a double transept, and the tall sculpture held up by flying buttresses. There was a narthex that had a spire ceiling which lit the opening. And Joule would at times sit in the nave and watch Master move rose arched windows with no glass, from one end of their castle to the next.

Colours of Enlightenment & A Potion

The castle had many entrances, with them all being bathed in the crust of rock their castle sat on. The entrances could be seen, but could not be seen into. The castle from a bird's view could be seen as orange-red that contrasted the blue rock around the crater. The lava surprisingly did not shine any other part of their home. Thus from the reflection off the lava their castle was lit to be seen from the outside, where the outside of the castle was nothing but dark blue stone.

Within the blue rock entrances were seen. A few entrances had shafts; a few had columns, and some housed pendentives or squinches, which brought life to their rock in space. Sixty-four in total were the number of sculptures that indicated the start of an entrance into the castle. Some had promising positive destinations whereas some to dark dwelling dungeons. The reason for the precise number of 64 held count for ghouls and goblins as statues that resembled peoples' wrongdoings. There was nothing seen around these tympanons but irregular rock, and stone, Master and Joule.

Master wore blue cloaks mostly; dark blue that sometimes appeared as gray or black, and the only time Joule could tell the difference was when a flame came for deliverance. The timeline that Master lived by reflected that of all the galaxies he had created to hold time. Regardless of that he amused himself to only hear time when time was right, or to hear what time he was in. Fair enough that Joule and Master lived for eternity, but time itself filled the circle. And in that circle Master wore the same threads.

He was a large man that must have fed himself on mostly potatoes. He had a beard, a white beard, which probably once was black. He carried with him a tiny dagger, a bangle, a comb, all covered by a robe with a large hood. When Master slept he would lower his hood, comb his hair back from both his brow and beard, raise his hood to hide from the starlight, and be able to sleep vertically afloat.

Master had created spells out of his own will but through his passion he was able to nurture them. Through words written from all languages across all galaxies he was to regard knowledge as his thirst. Past histories of planets' hope fueled Master to look out to space and sleep as he did. When mornings' would arise, Master would search for unanswered, existing, new born prays through his momentum of pray. By mapping his search to answer prays at times released energy of light to space. A pray that could be seen as answered from great altitude as a newly born star in black space.

Smiles under beards, with scales, and rocks on fire, building fortress walls around castle walls, complementing stone temples, and scripture sought on companionship, all being churned to live together to bring around an existence of red matter. The roar into whatever Joule chose him to be, he chose a dragon. Master was overjoyed to see the being in his supreme glory choose to sit moreover the option of flying, eating or building faith to any of Master's kingdoms. They enjoyed each other's company regarding that neither needed each other evermore. And furthermore in their warm chambers they watched the universe turn to the wave of Bani.

The Utensils

Chapter 7
Firing Rocks

In the world of Bani, within the land of Goman, Tarun anxiously waited with Faran within the castle walls of the king's kingdom to speak to the king.

"King! King! My Lord, I am honoured to meet you, I wish to show you my findings," spoke Tarun, as he slowly approached the king of Goman.

King Lex, as Alexander by his princess, was in the stables feeding the horses with Faran's company. Faran had thought of feeding the horses with what he liked most, and that was jellybean candies, the king had heard, and insisted to join Faran. Whilst feeding the horses, Tarun who now was twenty-two could not contain himself further without making the king aware of his arrival. King Lex had noticed his presence which was hard not to notice as Tarun itched closer and closer to the king.

The king was regarded as most important as he held the writings of ancient script. The whole of Goman followed these writings of Sant Basha dialect, which was spoken from the king on the beginning of each new year. The original script was shown to Gomen at this time, but all copies were regarded as the same. The script was named Granth, and held writings of ten teachers that first grew Goman.

Goman kings read the Granth, who was regarded as a real teacher, a teacher they named Guru. The first of the ten gurus, Guru Nanak Dev Ji, paved a message that a messenger would arrive presenting all attributes to Khand, as this Khand was entrusted upon by the heavens. An official order made sacred within the castle that revelation can be taken by force. The order was carried through five generations before He was stolen.

The tenth guru, Guru Gobind Singh retrieved the Granth after that left by the fifth guru, Guru Arjan Dev, and included the ninth guru's work, along with his hymns and poetry to complete the Scripture as Adi Granth, who was regarded as present and future, (the five initial gurus), whom should be followed, and the message of Khand repeated reminding Gomen to live in peace. Plus trust in repetition of the Granth for salvation.

A last message received with the writings was for the faith from Sasha Khand. No guru was presented after Guru Gobind Singh, but instead kings to uphold the Guru Granth Sahibji as the true ruler of the land.

What was to be known across one man's vision that others began to follow? Was it the desperation of the necessity to be wanted, needed? Instead faith was spread to believe into something else, somewhere else, someone else, to carry on living in anticipation. Unlike the vision was spoken to build more listeners, let alone to be military, the listeners were delivered the word with accuracy. A return from the Khand to Guru Nanak Dev Ji to built an army was the reason for their existence at the end of the second millennium A.D.

Colours of Enlightenment & A Potion

"King, this is my brother Tarun," said Faran.

"Show me Tarun of your findings later," replied King Lex, "I will send for you and your brother later tonight, and you shall both eat with me. How does that sound?"

They blinked and King Lex left their side and opened the gate of stall 3.

"Splendid, a male horse," he said.

He reached for the neck and walked the steed out of the stable. The men fell in light conversation as the king himself prepared the saddle. Fastening the straps around the animal he buckled them tight. Then jumping as fast as the horse could gallop, King Lex mounted the stud and paced towards his castle.

"Wow," with a long pause Tarun stood, "didn't know he could do that."

"So will your 'findings' be as great?" teased Faran, and began laughing.

"The show is on the road. The show is on the road," sang Tarun as he looked at the horse that Faran and King Lex were feeding.

The blacksmith saw the king leave and walked over to the brothers to enquire on what Tarun must have done.

"Young lad, that must be a pretty amazing story you have planned for the king, or that he wishes for you, and your brother to become a quest for the Rock in the sky," said the blacksmith, "mind ya…"

"Had you told him sooner for what I was speaking about?" Tarun accused his brother, "and who are you that knows the same thing too?" he asked the blacksmith.

"Marc, as in Marcos, and I only know as much as your brother has told me, and frankly I'd run away from you no time to sooner too," answered Marcos, and began walking back to his work. "Your right Faran, he is special," finished Marcos as he pointed one to the sky.

Tock. Tock. Tock, went Marcos's hammer and anvil. The horses began to laugh. The only idea Tarun was well aware of was that his idea might never work. Faran knew all too well not to mock Tarun. Startled with surprise that Faran was so close to the king came later as Faran fetched water for the horses. Tarun walked over to the open gate of stall 3 and pushed it closed.

The full expression to gather his thought as a loud bang, as to launch a rocket into the sky and onto the Rock sounded absurd to himself as well. Faran looked over at Tarun staring at his own open palms and fingers, crossing fingertips, and he was rattling them, mentally thinking in his own world. Tarun tensed his eardrums and inhaled, he smiled over at Faran then back at the wall. The rattling stopped moments after by composure with both index fingers in pulse., He remained still writing his thoughts onto the wall that he faced.

From within the stable there were ten stalls for the horses. Each stall was filled with hay, buckets of water and a horse. One end of the stable was tiled with cobblestones leading to the castle courtyard, and the other reached out into the woods. Of the horses, six were female, one was gray, two were brown and three were black. Out of the four male horses, two were black and two were brown. Regardless of the horses' coat but

Colours of Enlightenment & A Potion

more dependent on age, ten horses were tried to be kept at all times within the stables. The building was tinted with a deep brown, and most light would enter from the two entrances the stable had.

So what that meant for Faran was to find a male horse and place him to the king's count. Faran counted his stable full of food and water for the horses to drink, and counted stall 3 too to be cleaned by Tarun before he returned with a male horse. Faran released the horse from stall 6 and trotted him into the woods.

"Don't try to make yourself to comfortable here, everything the way you found it," requested Faran to the walls echoing to Tarun.

Soon after sweeping the floor of the stable Tarun decided to look outside. He walked to the front of the stable and opened the door. People were walking across the courtyard, some holding bags, some pushing trolleys of vegetables and fruit, and other people making meaningless conversations as they all avoided bumping into each other. Appearing from the crowd came a man standing slightly shorter than Tarun. He was dressed in a brown overcoat and wore a brown hat.

"Can I see what horses you have? I wish to arrange a stroll with me and me misses in a fortnight?" said the man.

"We have nine horses at the moment, six lasses and three lads. Strong steeds for the king's people however I can't allow you to see them yet as the horse keeper is away. I will leave a message, what is your name?" asked Tarun.

"Name is Crogar, and I will be back before dusk to see him then," replied the man.

"That should be fine," finished Tarun and watched the man leave.

In any situation Tarun never felt afraid of other individuals. His best form of defence was an offensive one from stance fingers and thumbs. For instance if Crogar's intentions were bad he would have followed Crogar's thoughts into the stable's timber, and mark the etiology as Crogar falling over. Tarun turned and head to collect a pitch folk and a wheelbarrow from the supply closet instead.

He began clearing the empty stall. He looked around at the horses as he cleared horse dung and molten hay from the stall's floor. The male horses began gnarling as they watched Tarun sweat over what would have taken Faran minutes to do. The day began to get warmer. Tarun had cleared the stall by noon and prepared to have himself a ciasta. Lying down after all fresh hay had been stocked, and gathering fresh hay himself on a hot day he fell asleep.

Chapter 8
The First Attempt

Inside the mind contained by Dev Esjah a thought of conducting an orchestra within his office walls was playing. Prof. Esjah was in his office in the university of Sasha under a light that reflected beech red hue off his table. Alone in the room he moved the light that illuminated the space and material around him. His hands were tightened around an invisible area of spherical size. Prof. Esjah stretched out an imaginary answer to float ahead of him; he stood with his arms and palms out building a foundation for this answer. He remained in thought staring at the perplexes of space between him, the possible answer, and the walls of his office; he was mapping his research of wisdom through years of knowledge. Using vast movements of interruptions and pauses, a continuous form of speech motored between his mind and sensed by his muscles of his fingers and thumbs, Prof. Esjah prepared the answer to reach standstill.

"Fire in three, two, one!" said Marine.

There went an object with mass of five-hundred kilograms into the air, and there it hovered with that weight within a few seconds for a few seconds, before returning back to the ground gently. This was what was expected from the ground crew following the ambition from Prof. Esjah's senior at the university.

Sasha Khand, the name of the university, which was founded on West Sasha. Sasha Khand was developed within the city's infrastructure that made all of West Sasha, and all the strongest people of Sasha operated around the strongest students of Sasha. The launch site was facilitated from the university but tested on the opposite end of the island.

The Rock's width and length covered the palm of an open hand when standing on Sasha. Reaching the Rock's surface had become as easy as reaching their arm's out. Sashans' had planet observation devices on the Rock to monitor the shortening of years Bani was showing.

Through the lenses on the Rock, Sasha had seen Goman's existence, and had been watching the turn of Bani for several years now. Slowly accumulating how Goman spun so different from Sasha. The situation was far from meeting the Rock, but to also explode off it and land on Goman. Prof. Esjah and his team had been working on how to lift off their planet without destroying any part of their land. They had come with successful plans on making this task operational, and tests made Sasha Khand more confident that space travel by them could be possible. Further from that, they needed to land a person on Goman. Landing him safely was a one shot opportunity. Shooting mechanics as cameras and thermo-scopes came from Lindsey laughing with Prof. Esjah on how to survive the landing on Goman.

"Telescopes, and magnifications, and climate control computers could all be set up in the area used for the gym," laughed Lindsey to Prof. Esjah, which in turn forced Dev into welcoming her into the project. She saw images far and wide of their planet and slowly her heart stopped when she witnessed Bani turn away

Colours of Enlightenment & A Potion

from Sasha. Needing more room was a sure definite, "I'll clear some space so you can get set up."

"The stone in the sky is actually a piece of rock from our planet," informed Prof. Esjah, "It has been floating around us since Bani's been floating around in space. Surprising that there's more attraction for that rock elsewhere than the gravitational pull to our planet. Amazing how the energy in space is keeping us separated."

Alarmed by Prof. Esjah's perception of astrophysics, Lindsey looked around the gymnasium and saw how it would be like with no life. She blinked after several seconds and dreamt for hope to be as beautiful as their final run. Seeing Goman again in all natural beauty she began to cry.

Prof. Esjah advised her on the workers already on operation for sending a Sashan to Goman, and listed Lindsey to work within that crew. The distance to travel would be too great for a lady officer to withstand, physically as well as mentally. The thought of never returning home and living within a foreign environment was not a safe decision for Lindsey Butcher to make.

Lindsey Butcher's role in the excavation was to find an honest, fair working, sane individual that had nothing to lose, a discreet volunteer to undergo such a requirement. The individual was to be a disciple of Sasha Khand and enter Goman, and impose to see the highest order to notify them about the annulment of the planet. Plus the individual would have to remain on the Goman side of the planet, possibly to live alone if no one was to be found. How would Lindsey demonstrate to a strong candidate that he should choose to be fried alone? The matter was shocking to the coach. Lindsey

Butcher better thought to find, apply love, and forget the candidate successfully completing his acceptance into the program. The conditions for Lindsey being the faculty of the university, physiological, psychological and physical decisions in the matter of social behaviour of the program was best suited to her.

Prof. Dev Esjah informed her on who else would be in on the program, Manson Blue and Barsy Marine. During this time the two engineers had been fixing electronics and welding most walls to the launch area. The launch area was constructed in East Sasha. Lindsey needed to be away from any part of this operation to find the right person. For Lindsey Butcher and Prof. Esjah, a suitable candidate would be one with an honest heart whom could be informed without force or encouragement to volunteer. Anyone close to the university may accept the challenge for glory but most likely would repel when asked to die as an alien. Notwithstanding the ideal candidate should be that of Sasha Khand, as this student could best enlighten the people of Goman.

Living on the land they called Goman would be challenging. The camera on the Rock could not show civilizations of the foreign land; nevertheless, Sasha felt the duty to investigate and provide assistance if any, to signal back by using the Rock as a satellite, and communicate affectively if a candidate crossed through. Unscrupulously the bringer of bad news may even be murdered on the foreign land. For further the thought, allowing a race to die without acknowledgement of their brother or sister would be as unbearable as turning a blind eye to Goman.

Colours of Enlightenment & A Potion

A suitable candidate should survive a thrust from Sasha into space and survive a forced landing onto the Rock. All timed and prepared to leave the Rock, to land on Goman, to survive alone forever if no one was found. Radio communication would survive for several years, but theory would lead to silently muting insane responses by both parties. A strong male candidate should be found that could handle himself in a different environmental nature. Preferably someone presented with a life to rot and degrade; preferably someone needing a chance to escape their reality.

Chapter 9
The Possibility

4,501 million universal years ago in a time called Hadean, Earth had appeared. The earliest animals to inhabit that Earth came from the deep sea. The animals were recognizable on land 545 million years ago, which grew to the fascination of the Jurassic Era around 209 million years ago, and then after being struck by a meteoroid Earth had come into the Cenozoic Era. Plants began to grow again around 146 million years ago, leaving animals to grow after them. And not until 11 million years ago did human species recognize the volcanoes from Hadean. Unlike Bani, Earth was made on one time line with the only thing the days having in common was a sun.

From the woods Faran had returned with a horse, a strong wild male one, and walked him into the empty stall where Tarun was fast asleep. Without waking his brother and keeping a strong sense of surprise for him, Faran decided to leave the wild horse with Tarun. Faran patted the horse he was on and walked him to stall 6. They watched the reaction of the new stud as he gazed across the stables at the females. The new horse nodded to his keeper and the horse Faran was riding, then he glanced at Tarun in his stable, he gave a loud grunt enough to startle and wake Tarun from his afternoon break. Tarun looked at the horse with his eyes half shut and fell back asleep.

Colours of Enlightenment & A Potion

"Had there been any customers?" asked Faran from behind the stall gate.

Tarun slowly opened his eyes and looked back at the horse. He stood and stretched making the horse know of his presence. Stepping over the horse's face Tarun looked well at the horse. Noticing the horse was indeed male by the glare in his eye, Tarun exited the stall allowing him to rest.

"One geezer. Said he'd be back later for two horses, wants to take his girl out on a ride. Said his name was Crogar. And that he'll be back before night," replied Tarun.

The man that had come to see the horse keeper for the horses returned as said before the stars could be seen shining in the sky. Faran bound Crogar with two horses, for two days, for a fortnight's time, with each horse of opposite gender, and both horses having brown coats.

Night had crossed into evening and the horses left grazing outside the stable were brought in and given fresh water. After closing the doors to the stable Faran walked home to wash and change.

Very soon after Tarun was seen bouncing outside his cabin full of excitement to dine with the king, that Faran became filled with overwhelming curiosity and increased his stride.

From the main castle arch to the king's courtroom, travelled a distance of twenty-minutes. The path walked from cobblestone floors of yellow-gold surface to darker gold-brown walls of the castle. They walked on stairs that climbed to a thick wooden set of doors. The ground changed from a cobble texture to a smooth stone finish within the castle. There were several lobbies that all had stairwells ascending and descending through towers that stretched tall within the castle. The king's courtroom held the widest stairwell with banisters that were made to be more authentic than purposeful. The stairwell to the courtroom was well structured that if the castle was torn down, the stairwell embedded into the mountain rock would have been preserved.

Hymns were heard coming from the open king's courtroom. The priests, knights, and the king's alliances followed their time to reciting guidance from their Guru. All accompanies realized the truth from the Granth, that the best form of survival would be by His side. To be in view but not seeing, to hear when there's no sound to listen, and to pay caution to thy words when around those with the Granth. The words recited off the walls to pay final pray to 'Gur' and 'Ant', two words Gomen regarded as safe to finish a sentence, meaning Eternal Guru. The words together said without eye contact prepared what was the way to be with 'Akalpurukh' altogether. Akalpurukh, meaning 'think harder', Guru Arjan Dev with Spirit of cause and effect, Akalpurukh, The Creator, He who has prepared the hymns to finish before work occurred. The king wiped clear the page of scripture he was reciting from and closed 1430 pages.

"He said he was reciting the prayer of the 100 stanzas Gita. He read it to me as if he had learned to do so from a Pandit. Now the intellect of our son is very great. Who knows what he will be when he is older?"
Adhyai 7:40

Colours of Enlightenment & A Potion

The door of the courtroom closed and torches became alight with two stones that delivered a spark to light the room. Candles sitting on a wooden chandelier were lit and raised to the ceiling of the courtroom. The light that shined from the torches and the candles shone light over King Lex and Tarun.

From the opposite end of a square polished table where King Lex stood, Tarun pulled two stones from his shekel: one stone of limestone and one stone he had found from a lake bed. He placed them on the table facing the king. King Lex had noticed him and stood against the table with one finger. The people all around noticed King Lex looking at a new arrival and paused in speech. Tarun hit the two stones together and rubbed them for several seconds. The courtroom people watched. He gathered the solid particles and funneled them into a 10 milliliter canister. He filled 6ml with water and gently covered it with another small stone. Tarun stepped away from the canister that began to fizzle on the table. He covered his eyes with open fingers. Steady and pop the stone went to shoot from the canister with great pressure to bounce off the wood and wax chandelier.

Some solution had reached the king's eye, however this wasn't any synthetic solution. King Lex faked to wipe a tear from his eye and applauded Tarun. Everyone stood there staring at each other. Tarun stood there in shock.

"That's fantastic! What do you attend to do with this Tarun?" asked King Lex.

"Thought we could have a larger one, and somehow g-et to the Rock, King," stuttered Tarun.

"Thought about making more glass from what you have in your hand, but never thought about seeing what compound you have in your other," returned the king.

The king gestured with his hand for the stones. Tarun walked around the table and handed the stones to the king. The king placed the limestone down and examined the other stone.

"It's a little cold and moist, and there's something covering it," continued King Lex.

Tarun had never thought of the rock he had found to be thrown at the clay vase holding mother's flowers in and exploding. A rodent had ran into the kitchen and behind the vase one summer's day, and through surprise Tarun tried to scare the rodent out, but instead shot the vase to a million pieces. He was to have gathered this rock with all the others, and to have saved them until asking the king of their differences. Instead the rodent survived and Tarun was to walk to fetch a pail of water, plus collect another stone. Several seasons had passed before Tarun could control that reaction, furthermore the king seemed pleased.

"I found the rock in the foot bed of Lake Sunara," said Tarun. "You had already heard of this sire?"

King Lex rubbed the surface of the stone and smelled his finger that was covered with shiny black goo. He licked the material, "tasty," said the king, "tastes like salt."

He looked thinking about the limestone, and decided that the salt became attracted to the carbonate in the limestone, and funneled in the canister was a salt based carbonate. That under small volumes of water

Colours of Enlightenment & A Potion

would produce a mass of gas great enough to shatter windows.

"I will call on my helpers to aid you in experimenting with other ideas you may have Tarun. And possibly we could come up with something more useful to Goman than throwing things in the air."

"I will be more than grateful, King."

Tarun started gathering his things back into his shekel with a smile. He knew that the king would be surprised with what he had found. Nothing in Goman represented strength greater than the explosion in the canister, nothing but that for Marcos's hammer and anvil. And now some small pieces of rock kept in a sealed environment, and allowed to dissolve with water molecules, caused a long lasting echo in the king's courtroom. Moreover the reaction raised King Lex's pleasure to look further into this new finding.

The two brothers finished their meal with the king and his house guests. They listened to the king's men as they entertained the king and queen. Once dining had ended with water, Faran and Tarun walked with King Lex to the new galley quarters within the castle walls.

"Request a note to their folks that they will be living closer to us," King Lex said to a kinsman. "And invite them to the fortress walls if they like."

King Lex looked around at the men and instructed them to work within the stables during the day. He also instructed Tarun to work with the castle's chemists in the alchemy lab during some afternoons and by the king's mathematicians during some evenings.

As pleased as animals finding themselves to safety the men felt as one with the king's kinship. Faran was pleased to see the king overwhelmed with Tarun's idea. And as for Tarun, he could not have been more pleased to see the same appreciation of importance from the king for his experiment, the same appreciation that the rodent felt whilst surviving the kitchen explosion. Tarun felt a sigh of relief that the demonstration went well. King Lex who felt a sigh of relief that there was still hope left for their existence.

Chapter 10
The Track

The night was busy across East Sasha Bay. There was much light blinking off the ground around the busy working force of Sasha Khand. The light of the night itself was seen as royal blue across the whole face of the sky. The Sashans working could be seen from afar by the light that reflected off their helmets from their spotlights.

"Move that block in there," said Marine.

"Move that one too, and move the other one alongside it," encouraged Blue.

The two guys worked hard and moved the others to build the dream.

"Clamp, turn, turn, turn, tuuuurn!" shouted a recruit.

"Next one!" voiced Marine.

"My turn! My turn!" shouted another recruit.

For one acre down the men dug a channel to hold an ore of iron across to keep the water out. They mounted the iron and concrete to the edges of where the channel bay left Sasha. They were building a launch pad for a one-man hub disc to fire from East Sasha Bay and onto the Rock. Apart from seeing the distances the experiments could fire, Prof. Esjah knew that only one force could safely land the manmade vehicle on the Rock. Leaving the atmosphere would cool the hub upon landing, and the volunteer would fire off the Rock to Goman.

"Slowly. Slowly now, we don't want to break it," said Blue.

"Break what? Our neck? It's a steel alloy bar, Blue. I don't think it'll damage easily," mocked Marine alongside.

"Come on move it! Move it! Push!" Blue helped the men stand still on the ground as an iron bar of one foot thickness slammed into its place.

"O.Kay, everyone out! Tappers across!" Marine said.

The men started rattling the firing hub socket and began clearing the gas pockets. Ratta-tatat. Ratta-tatat. The beat started echoing towards the night sky as the men grabbed their tools away from the iron canister. A seal folded across the canister as the last man stepped out and onto the sand of Sasha's shore. There was a crane hosting a narrow metal disc massed over the opening of the firing socket.

"Start the air!" signalled Marine.

Everyone stepped back and a huge gust of air rocked the crane holding the hub. The air reduced and Marine waved the people holding the pulley to bring the hub closer to the socket. Other workmen got involved and held the metal casing of the hub and brought it into place. The hub began hovering enough to hold the door line and was clamped into place.

"Reduce the power!" said Blue.

The hub slid into the firing den and all that was left to do was fire the can into space. Blue looked over at the analyst. The analyst gave the thumbs up to Blue.

"Close everything down!" said Blue to the crew.

The whirring, screeching, grinding sounds of engines and motors began to fade and disappear. Some

Colours of Enlightenment & A Potion

lights began to switch off leaving only the emergency lights around the hub on. The workers stood in silence appreciating the night. This was the only part of the day they have happened to enjoy in weeks. And the workers stood in silence to absorb the engines stop to silence around them. All sound faded until only the waves of East Sasha Bay could be heard.

"Now I hope the maverick is ready for this," said Blue to a recruit.

"I trust Prof Esjah's judgment," said the recruit, "everything seems to be fine."

"The traveler should land with no problem," stated Blue.

"Just make sure to remind him to sit in the first half of the hub," said Marine.

"I'll remember to notify him of the instruction manual," said the recruit between Marine and Blue.

"Hope he remembers us when he's gone," Blue gave Marine a puzzled gesture and looked over at the recruit that said that.

The recruit stepped behind Blue and gathered his coat and hat. Stabling himself, his collar, he looked over the table and at all the workers. He saluted them with a gentle nod and moved towards the door of the main office.

"No reason to be of any concern," asked Marine walking over to the recruit.

"No concern, works with me. Nothing to worry about Barsy," said the recruit and patted Marine on the shoulder.

He reached for the door to walk himself through and Marine stopped him.

"What's your name private?" Marine asked.

"Malek Esjah, Jr.," replied Malek.

Marine carried on looking at him and said: "Esjah, Jr.?"

"Look nothing like my old man, look nothing like my old lady, to be honest I look more like you," Malek said bracing to look at Marine.

Marine walked with him into the building for a few paces, and then holding him square on the shoulder he pushed him into the office of Prof. Esjah. Marine quickly caught Prof. Esjah's attention with Esjah, Jr. stumbling in to straighten himself out. Marine looked at Malek tightening his collar, a few cold seconds passed.

"Are you sending him there?" asked Marine.

"I'm here to help you with the other," interrupted Malek.

Prof. Esjah laughed and finished his sentence: "He is to help you with the other."

Startled at the timing of both responses Barsy Marine paused: "Have we found someone?"

The Esjah's looked at each other then looked at Marine and blinked twice.

Marine slowly took off his hat and wiped his face. He cleared his tear sockets and strangely plucked a few hairs out of his nose. He then wiped his mouth with the back of his hand, slapped them loudly together, and rubbed them with pressure to remove any possible reason for existence of bacteria on his hands. He then smiled and placed back on his hat.

Chapter 11
The Insurance

Goman's tavern was called, The Potato Inn. Landlady Caffe opened her tavern roughly before noon to let her staff in. She would leave the doors closed till more people began walking in front of her tavern. Her usual customers were pavers and cloth maids. Opening the doors, the people would enter and sit on their own accord as one dish began to be served across the tavern floor. Mash potato, gravy and meat. Either part of a poultry or side of a hog was ordered. Drinks were filled through draft and into large glasses that could hold four grown fingers in their handles.

Noise began bellowing from the tavern and could be heard across the courtyard of the castle to Marcos. For Marcos he could no longer hear the constant clatter of sandals across the courtyard. Besides his hammer making most the noise around him there was very little chance that he could hear anything, let alone a man being thrown out the tavern. Surprising that Marcos even saw the body fly out of The Potato Inn, but he had happened to catch a glimpse of light fracturing as it fell across his sight during daylight. The blacksmith never imagined anyone starting trouble in Goman or anybody hitting the courtyard. Marcos stopped halfway through a stroke on realization to what just had happened and looked towards The Potato Inn.

Four men had grabbed the victim and thrown him out of The Potato Inn. They looked at each other and then looked at Marcos; the courtyard began to look at the victim. A well-built man of stronghold lasting a lion's weight stood up. They looked at him and his unusual disfigurement. One quarter of his dental arch brought crowding to his teeth in the maxilla, and his lower jaw skewed to the right of his facial symmetry. He brushed his clothes and smiled with his lips closed. He smiled looking at the four men; he looked to catch a horizon and grew his smile further.

This man was smiling about something personal, and no one from the four men that threw him out knew why. Grabbing his belongings he pushed his hand into his bag and pulled out his radio communication device. This piece of equipment that the man had was broken in three places. Firstly the shell was broken, some wires had come loose, and the microphone film had torn. He glared to the black line of the horizon and gathered his thoughts. The man prayed for the four men that had thrown him head first outside.

The man placed his first two fingers beside his thumb on his right hand and scrolled his fingers to stance. The other people became alarmed and stepped away from the man. Then the man patted his heart and said: "Sikhism, Sikhism, Seek on Him, Seek on Him, Shish."

They all looked at each other and then the man. The man was watching Caffe. Caffe was sounding Om (the hymn of peace) in her head whilst she marked the strange man. She presented ॐ (Om) to have nerve to see him without showing fear. Caffe braced her index and next fingers with her thumbs and felt her heartbeat. Marcos stepped up running. Just as Marcos approached the stranger she released her awareness and cried:

Colours of Enlightenment & A Potion

"He ordered something different!"

"What do you mean he ordered something different?" Marcos stopped in his own tracks whilst her words caught up to their meaning.

Not remarkable as this man looked nothing like them. Marcos thought for a second. Pushing into his thought he grabbed the man and showed him across the street towards his shop, The Blacksmith's Wagon. Marcos urged something towards Caffe pointing at The Potato Inn. She moved her heels towards the inn and Marcos guided the strange man into his workplace. Marcos pointed up at the sky with his right hand and all Gomen standing in shock looked up, and then began their business again.

Walking over to a flagpole Marcos unfolded the flag. The bright colours of red and gold reflected the light and the flag was left blowing in the wind.

"Sit down," Marcos insisted as he entered the strange man into The Blacksmith's Wagon.

The stranger stood longer so Marcos looked over at a wooden bench he had for all his customers. The man sat down.

Marcos took a few of steps back, "So you look like you should meet someone else. Seems like you'll have to sit here until the boys get back from the fields."

"Bani," the stranger said.

Marking his territory by stretching he moved over to a water basin and drew himself some water.

"Pani. I get it. Brilliant you speak the same as we do. Just sit, and help yourself to as much pani as you like. You call it bani, we call it pani, good, good. Look at the size of you. I'll be back with, well..." concluded Marcos.

> *"If one is to wear the sacred thread and then later commit sin by killing in pursuit of wealth. In their final days they also do not eradicate their enmity and continue to slander and lie,"*
> *Adhyai 9:17*

Many may not be able to trust a stranger, neither would they if the stranger was a slave. Marcos could see no problem in realizing that this stranger was searching for them, and left by the side exit to see if anyone had informed the king. As soon as Marcos left the stranger's side he heard two pairs of clatters echoing down the castle walls. Marcos stepped back into his shop and suggested the man to stay. He stepped back outside.

Tarun had heard all the noise that came from the tavern, and now had heard Macy with King Lex riding down the castle courtyard. Macy was the king's favourite female horse. She had a cream-white coat that shined fluorescent pearl with sunlight, a gorgeous thick mane, a tight body, and jet-black eyes that seemed to shine stars from deep within her sight. She came to a stand just as a bird would on moving land and stretched. Macy looked at the stables where she was expecting to find Faran, but instead she saw Marcos hailing for the king to come inside his workplace.

The stranger saw Tarun leaving the stable behind the horse's legs and saluting the man on the horse. The stranger had wondered if the beast had scent his presence. Hearing the horseshoes gently tap the stone floor the stranger believed that the beast was

Colours of Enlightenment & A Potion

aware of his presence. The stranger drew back at the curtain to The Blacksmith's Wagon and stepped outside. Macy took a step back. Marking the king on the beast he decided to bow in respect to what he could see. The prestigious presence of this man's clothing compared to that of Marcos' demonstrated to the stranger that the man on the horse was of importance.

King Lex dismounted off Macy and stepped up to the stranger. The king walked him back inside Marcos's workplace away from the observing Goman crowd.

"You can come too Tarun, maybe you will be more help than the rest of us. Does he speak?" asked King Lex to Marcos.

"He said bani, and ..." Marcos replied.

"Bani, huh?" interrupted the king, and looked at the stranger, "so Bani is what they call you now,"

"No sire, he went to get some pani," replied Marcos and pointed at the water bowl.

"Right, amazing," King Lex walked closer to the stranger, "Alexander," King Lex said.

The stranger replied: "Jai Sainapat."

The king took a step back. "So you're not Pani, you're Jai Sainapat. He's Marcos, and you're Tarun, and I'm Alexander. You got that Tarun?" said the king towards Tarun to catch what he was thinking.

Tarun was watching the stranger, who was watching the king. The stranger now turned to watch Tarun after observing what the king was thinking. Marcos began to look at Tarun too.

"Got news for you, you must be told before time speeds up," Sainapat said to them naturally.

They stood staring at him.

Sainapat collected a piece of coal, and was to throw it at the furnace but saw that the door was closed. "Perfect," he said to himself. He walked over to open the door to the furnace and walked back. Sainapat glanced at the other men. He looked at the piece of coal and looked at the men's hearts; he turned the coal crumb over and stomped the ground. He stared at the fire in the furnace; he pitched on his hind leg to stand firm for a moment's time, and he threw the coal into the furnace like pitching a baseball.

The coal flew straight into the heat of black, gold and red. Sainapat started watching the floor. King Lex, Tarun and Marcos all stared at the floor for a moment's time. Sainapat was slightly relieved that the men understood his message. Then sense hit them harder, and they began watching the king. Sainapat held back his modesty and his stomach began rumbling. The rumbling shrieked through his body for King Lex and the men to hear.

"I'll get a horse if you like sire?" Tarun said.

"Wait a second," hushed the king.

King Lex suggested Jai Sainapat to sit. He asked for his bag and handed it to Marcos.

"A stone, this, this heavy thing, a scroll, a bowl," Marcos began shaking a metal canister and planted it on the table. "He has a weapon, this knife." This he saw whilst lifting out another can of something. Marcos began shaking this can too, and to his right judgment Sainapat's stomach rumbled more.

Masala dosa filled with aloo and sauce. Sweet succulent amli with cuddy, warm and poured over the wrapped dosa. Dho chaatni ki thali, es ki baath roti ka

Colours of Enlightenment & A Potion

hot puri. Chaatni ki thali mai athana, some pickle mixed, or that mixed with mango, na thali ki pass balti.
A full dish of khand as creamy chocolate cake. Garam na tanda dhono pilaris, chaiya tum ko kub chaiya. Lassi with buraf, lal and peela mercha, dhono murkki na guy, oos ki baath tandasa, tandasa pani.

King Lex walked over to Sainapat and placed his hand on his shoulder. He grabbed the back with his other hand and began placing the things in the bag starting with the heavy items. He tied the bag and handed it back to the stranger. Om began to play into Sainapat's ears from King Lex. King Lex stopped and stretched out his hand:

"Ommm...," said King Lex whilst pointing to his head, "Alexander," he continued and waited for a response from Sainapat.

Mmmmm..., thought Sainapat and blinked then said: "Jai Sainapat."

"Yes Tarun, fetch a horse, make him a strong one," King Lex told Tarun.

"Tarun," Tarun replied to the air above him.

"Mm," replied Sainapat again and smiled.

Tarun left The Blacksmith Wagon and cut out into the courtyard whilst the others sat watching each other. Tarun glanced over at the tavern's doors where Gomen were starring towards him as something unusual was happening. The four men that had thrown the stranger out were still keeping guard but now at a greater attention. Tarun opened the door to the stable.

"So what do they feed you?" King Lex said looking at Sainapat's brawn.

This man was roughly the same age as the king, but his size and share difference in posture and width, King Lex knew he wasn't from any place in Goman. Nevertheless the king was more relieved than scared that something quite different could look so much alike. A master of fine arts the king placed his existence to two ideas, that he was born to look like that or that where he was from they lived to grow like that. King Lex didn't want to agitate the stranger further until he had seen him on fairer ground. Fairer to the stranger that is, the king smiled at him. Sainapat smiled back.

Chapter 12
Ground to Grow

Wielding began to glow the ground close to one of Sasha's cities from late enough on one entry closer to the descent into their sun. Wielding took part all the energy delivered from the turn watermill that span due to the waterfall that fell in East Sasha. This mill developed energy and amplified the current through Sasha. The current was made by the energy of the falling water, and the cogs turning the waterwheel collected voltage within a battery, the battery remained charged as long as the water kept falling.

Sasha had two cities, one in the east corner and one in the west. The current harnessed from the waterfall was in East Sasha. Poles were wielded between the university in the west and the hydroelectric power station in the east. The current was sent back to the power station from the city in the west to the east as an alternating current. No cables were needed for this source of energy that powered all of Sasha.

These power points were anchored close to each other and a strong current was sent charging from the anode to the cathode at both ends of their field. The grid that held the university powered another anode to deliver the current back to a cathode on the power station side. Along with power posts that were wielded into the ground so were iron rails that shared the same distance.

Wielding at this point was occurring in East Sasha. Shimmering bolts were screwed tight and secured to the ground. The university engineers carried on fighting to build a deeper channel in East Sasha. This new depth to plough the east channel of Sasha was to adopt a space hub. Locking caissons into place the Sashan engineers had built a disc-opened socket into the ground between mainland and a small stretched out mount of an island occupied by stone and sand.

"So Jai, you still for this?" asked Lindsey.

"No time like the present," replied Sainapat.

Beneath the concrete laid air spaces that lead piping to an air compression chamber. The idea was to fire Sainapat into space hoping he would land on Goman, and deliver news of their existence to any civilizations there. The idea to blast him into space was to drop a precise quantity of sodium carbonate into the water chamber to acquire a reaction through the pipes and into the air pockets to fly the hub into space.

"Hope I don't fly too far out," said Sainapat.

"Me too," pronounced Marine, "we need you, and what we have examined from past experiments you will be most welcome there," carried on Marine.

"Do you think they'll be people there? People that will be able to understand us?" asked Sainapat.

"We believe they'll be a type of civilized culture, but them for understanding you is past my judgment. Just remember to keep radio contact once there," Marine told Sainapat, "there should be no problem, Saina'. You weigh half of what we have already fired into space, that you coming down will be a sure thing," said Marine to comfort Sainapat.

Colours of Enlightenment & A Potion

"That's good to know that I am not the first subject," smiled Sainapat.

"Well that's not ..." carried on Blue whilst being knocked by Marine.

"I'm sure we'll work on something to bring you back," smiled Lindsey.

Sainapat knew all too well that he would not be returning to Sasha. Nevertheless he mocked alongside the crusade to save civilizations organized by Prof. Esjah. Truth was that Sainapat was excited. He worked close with the engineering crew and studied that the most challenging task would be adapting to a foreign land environment.

The engineers and Sainapat had fixed cameras onto the Rock without the need for man to enter space. From the images received from years of examining the spin of Bani another land was seen, but no evidence of intelligent life could be noticed. Time had come for goodwill and for Sasha. They needed to send something to Goman so they too could be aware of the other's existence. That something was actually a someone, and that someone was Sainapat.

Many thousand bolts, 129,000 nuts, 340,000 kilograms of gravel and sand, through 100,000 scoops of buckets swung over the shoulder and deposited onto the far side of the island off the mainland. 14,987 slabs of concrete shaped as curves and, 50,498 slabs of straight concrete to line the command centre, and the gas pipelines were listed for mining, shaping and cleaning before ignition could occur.

Commencement began when the first command post was open on the cliff's peak. The Sashan people called this point Mine Yellow. There were to be three more mines to be constructed within the cliff of Sasha.

The initial program was for the clearance of trees once Sasha planned for their exile. Barbwire was stretched around the mine sites. No more mosses on trees, but vines instead began climbing their barks, weakening them by absorbing the water, and making chopping easier for the lumberjacks in the coming years.

Sainapat would be in Goman by the time roads were paved for the people of Sasha to climb and enter into these mines.

"I hope you all stay safe whilst we carry on this task," said Sainapat, "otherwise what would be the point of surviving a nuclear burst if you can't even take a walk in the park."

"Wouldn't quite call it a walk in the park," said Blue.

"Walk, crawl, whatever," agitated Sainapat further on Manson Blue.

"The walk is actually a climb, the crawl is actually a pull, and your' whatever is actually this," Blue said whilst pointing to his left bicep. They both began smiling and admiring Blue's bicep. Blue started stroking his bicep tenderly.

Four hundred thousand, three hundred and seventy-nine seconds, still had to go by before Sainapat could be away from Blue, and allow Blue to concentrate on the bigger task. Sainapat and Blue had become stronger friends since Marine realized Lindsey's feelings for him. Barsy Marine and Lindsey Butcher spent hours together, and Manson Blue was left to throw hoops alone at the gym. The only time that

Colours of Enlightenment & A Potion

Marine and Blue got together was when they sat with Prof. Esjah to discuss the future of Sasha. And Sainapat being roughly the same age as Blue and with the same look to life, which was nothing but friendship, they began spending more time together. Eighteen more hours in Bani's axis rotation till Sainapat's launch and there was a knock on his door.

"Place some sweats on and come shoot some hoops," asked Blue whilst walking into Sainapat's quarters.

The men were in East Sasha with most of the operations finalized. Other tasks were being checked over thoroughly by the ground crew leading to no work for the men to do. Blue thought to keep Sainapat active with some basketball.

"I remember when we placed this board down," said Blue to Sainapat as they entered the basketball arena, "Marine would always be getting in the way of our fathers, and I wasn't supposed to touch anything. Then I remember climbing on to the polisher, and asking Barsy to plug her into that socket there," Blue pointed at a power socket, "and wooosh I went flying into that wall there," Blue pointed at the wall on the opposite site of the socket, "that was fun."

"I remember playing ball with my brother before the infection hit him. Still as lousy at it as ever," carried on Sainapat, "not really my desire."

"Well try this then, you know what they say, those that can't play, teach. Well there is your fixed point," Blue nodded towards the basketball rim, "and here is the ball." Blue handed Sainapat the ball, and walked under the basket.

Sainapat was standing so the basket was at his two o'clock position.

"Now watch your ten and shoot for the hoop," finished Blue.

"What? You want me to look this way, and shoot to the right?" asked Sainapat.

"Ya. Take a couple of warm-ups, the art of targeting the bull's eye without actually looking towards it. Try," suggested Blue.

Jai Sainapat threw the ball towards the rim whilst keeping his focus at a second point. The ball missed the hoop, and Manson threw the ball back to Sainapat. He took another throw. This one was closer but still no net. Manson dribbled the ball towards him.

Blue looked at Sainapat standing to his left and threw the ball. Swish went the net.

"Now that is what they call vectors, my good friend. Nothing for you to worry your pretty nails over," Blue said patronizingly.

"My turn, I see what you mean, let me try that a few more times," said Sainapat jogging towards the ball. He jogged back to Manson, looked at him, took a deep breath, and on exhale released the ball towards the basket. Manson began looking at the net and Sainapat kept his vision on Manson for a second longer. Swish went the net.

"Seems like all your nuts and bolts are tightened," implied Blue whilst watching the net swing to a still. "Don't hesitate to call. I will understand if you don't."

"You at best means keep the Esjah family thinking. And keep 'whatever' tight," requested Sainapat to Blue.

Colours of Enlightenment & A Potion

"What makes you do it?" directly said Blue.

Sainapat took a moment to answer: "I'm a hard breed. That to mean, I'm the opposite of laughing, nothing. Oh I'm sad; I've been thinking about that, oh, I'm sad, ha ha. I realized that life only goes up, what we decide is how fast? There's a time for laughter and there's a time for thought and that is black, and there's a time for sorrow that we pray never arrives too soon."

"I like the sound of that dogma."

"Nevertheless not all questions need to be answered. Personally if I knew the answer to a question but had no time to reply then you'd need to remind me if it was important later and I may help you on answering whatever," continued Sainapat. "Always pleased to please, I guess," finished Sainapat on that thought.

"Ah, to bring nothing but joy of course," returned Blue, "you and I are much alike."

Both men fought for the ball and taught each other some more motivation to live from. The echo from the ball dribbling had made its way to Malek and Marine. The arena door opened and the one-on-one became a four way.

"Someone in the background walking to the exit, some cameras, some more exits, the man walking up the stairs, through the switch to you, shine off the board, sign on the right, the mic' of the commentator, the shirt of the ref, someone back in the background, back to me, the shirt of the ref, the play," encouraged Sainapat out aloud.

"A-the tackle," Marine said and bumped Sainapat off stance winning the ball.

Sandeep Patel

One hour became a hundred-thousand steps, and a hundred-thousand and seven kilowatts of potential energy that hour. Nine-hundred thousand and one joules of kinetic energy pumped through their biological gradients, in and out their mouths, until the last available amount of energy was used by them to reward their appetite before launch.

The Boil

Chapter 13
The Boil

A voice of one calling in the mist of space:
"Toil and trouble, and all things cast in threes. The night is young and there is plenty to play with three. Three of us and more of you, beg us pardon as we wish to play with you. Truth with us so you can never be alone, leave that hag and come home. Look how nice we look with our lace stitched with darkened wool. Carry to seduce you Master though the night is still blue," came one voice from three souls across the galaxies. "Honey, marinate the warmth."

"Slow now and in forevermore," came Master's voice through the galaxy.

He moved his hands to sign out the helix of his best scripture and made it float in space across his outdoor deck. The light from the helix moved space lightening his castle.

One, One, One, Two, Three, four, five, six, seven,
Six, seven, six, seven.
One, two, three, four, five, six, seven, eight, nine,
Nine, ten, nine ten.
Three, four, five, six, seven,
Eight, nine, ten, eight, nine, ten.

Sandeep Patel

I love to serve you with poultry,
And some baked beans,
Marinate with honey ginger,
Till all flavour has sunk in.
Add some lettuce and some sweet corn,
To a large bowl,
Dress with some cherry tomatoes,
And some cilantro,
Potato salad don't you dry.

Oh Potato Salad,
Don't you miss me?
I love to serve you with poultry,
And some baked beans.

I add some cinnamon to the right,
And strengthen the heartbeat.
Sprinkle a little black pepper, sneeze.
There it is again, a potato salad,
A potato salad I see.
A chocolate bar for desert filled with sugar,
Or some peach slices for desert with juice sugars.
Potato salad don't you dry.

Oh Potato Salad,
Don't you miss me?
I love to serve you with poultry,
And some baked beans.

Colours of Enlightenment & A Potion

Something, Something, la, la, la, la.
Something, Something, Something.

How come it's okay to sing to the self,
But to talk to the self is not?

Master continued singing to himself as he filled his imaginary cauldron. Warmer and warmer his realm became as he carried on singing. Hotter his surrounding scourged as he pleased himself with the sound of his own voice. The release of hymns and exotic music overwhelmed his heart and he could no longer contain himself to sustain his emotion. Music started pouring out with the lava and Master began to dance. He stopped on a note that caused some of the ground beneath him to break far out into space.

The Rest

Chapter 14
The Biomes

Across the planet from left to right on either side or west to east on a horizontal axis the atmosphere folded together as the planet turned. Just as an Armageddon-ater, another Armageddon-ater, spark fuse Armageddon-ater, this grind of salt was not as smooth as Avagadro's number. The planet was a levelled rock; split atoms from the core crystallized a growth of stone lateral to the circumferential hit between two highly charged gases, leaving the planet to look like a giant schist stone.

The nature for this stone had come from afar. As the atoms split to form stone through one reaction another produced heat to break moments of silence in space. They collided to create a black hole for a moment's time, which in turn inhaled distant gases to accumulate and react with them.

The spin of Bani rotated through a perpendicular hold from their sun's gravity. (Imagine untying a ball of string from two ends, however the ball is not a ball but instead a huge plank of wood made of rock, with own naturally changing moon with a distant piece of rock orbiting). Bani fashioned to turn north to south towards an axis away from the sun, with Bani's satellites on the contrary. The planet moved from one point of an arc to the other as a pendulum across space from their sun. Nothing was to change for Bani beside the planet growing and pulling closer to the nearest star.

Sandeep Patel

There was a small chance to believe that the civilizations that grew there had not studied their planet closer. There existed a concrete consideration for allopatric speciation from the lands parted by water. Bani span and created heat from the ionized reaction initially growing exponentially, and now the size of our Neptune, the weight changed the rate. Only a million miles from their closest sun kingdoms appeared.

Oceans separated the lands of Goman and Sasha from seeing each other, let alone the land that slipped slightly more off as a tangent than Washington Irving's head. This planet's arc across one face of the sun generated enough heat to grow all food web consumers on both sides of the planet.

River systems flowed from condensing clouds that built mountain lakes, which poured water through and out of the mountain to flow to the oceans Bani had. Here the water would either be evaporated or flow to Bani's other face. Another wonderful thing about the rock of Bani was that Bani had its own irrigation system. In the waters, the earth, and either side of Bani within the ocean there was a void to the other side.

From the eastside of their sunlight to the west on the side that sat Sasha, the condensed clouds gathered and would become further dense. The water vapor would sublime and begin to further still freeze the Alps of Sasha. To the drop of the cliff the rest of Sasha stretched finely to the central point of that face, and further still east of the land.

Waterfalls from taiga-land above the cliff's brow flourished the foot of Sasha. But as the fate of Sasha was not by far the fate of Goman, the Sashan water touched more sand than clay. Bounding by a

Colours of Enlightenment & A Potion

disproportion of soil, Sasha fell onto a savanna stroke desert and that was where man lived.

The lakes from taiga altitude brought seafood to the people of Sasha. Cod, Bass, Tilapia from lakes like Malawi; Salmon, many fish, and algae sanitations bloomed plant life and crop for most years for Sasha.

Chlorophytes being green algae, evolved from water based plants to more phototropic plant divisions on land. Bryophytes evolved from chlorophytes, and brought about seedless vascular plants with a water system passing through the xylem vessel, and sugars flowing through the phloem vessel of the plants.

Ferns were scattered at the foot of the cliff, mixed with the algae and high risk of dehydration, the only other plant life was at the cliff's ledge. Gynmnosperm plants that produced a seed with or without pollen produced pine trees, cedars and redwoods, and these covered everything above the snow on the top west side of the cliff.

Goman's mountain island roared with tropical forests that led to temperate deciduous forests, to a mediterranean chaparral environment with freshwater lakes. Water from the clouds ran down the mountain to the lakes into the rivers then into the seas that sank to the ocean where richer tasting sea-life mated.

The sea-life sub-sequentially released the growth of algae, which was substantially replaced by angiosperm plants, which produced flowers, and Goman was dominated by farmland within gymnosperm plants. Mendocino trees grew as tall as two football pitches to the way to the castle from the seashore. Thousands scattered the land and waterfalls were seen bathing them in between.

Goman's climate was by far generous than that of Sasha. But as life was not called for Sasha, and Goman knowing nothing of Sasha, plus no life to bloom on this planet whatsoever, all seeds would eventually grow closer to their sun's center. Nonetheless life populated the planet, and the oceans were homed by various live organisms from as small as an amoeba to as large as omnivores blue whales.

Chapter 15
The Stones

From what formed Sasha, Goman formed much differently. Sasha was initially presented through some seismic activity large enough to break and raise the ocean floor to the sky. The final polish of Sasha was due to weather eroding the land from the hurricane winds over the void in the ocean.

The rock of Bani was mostly made from iron, and either the ground shook spewing out more iron in the form of basalt to coat the ocean bed, or there was no more volcanic activity after placing Goman on Bani. As an alternative a castle was carved into the peak of what brought life to Goman.

Sasha embedded living on much quartz, whereas Goman piled with conglomerate stone and mud. Besides the cliff of Sasha there was no sedimentation of rock above the desert sand. Granite of old igneous rock covered the planet cracking into transmissions between rocks of quartz or magma in and on Bani.

The soil was composed of feldspar, sandstone, limestone and granite. High amounts of iron, silicon, sodium and calcium covered the islands of Bani. Small traces of gold, platinum, palladium and silver could also be mined from either side.

Thus more basalt was seen on the side of Goman. This gave minerals within the volcanic debris as magnesium, feldspar and quartz on sedimentation.

As the magma had cooled on the eruption of Goman, silicate a useful material to provide strength formed. Quartz crystallized last bringing seashores to Bani.

The earth was warm for Goman with green luscious valleys and strong trees that banked on their earth. The rings of memories for the entire universe were harnessed within the landscape of these trees.

Moreover for Sasha, they had an abundance of iron ore and various other types of metals. Living within the cliff would become the safest place to be once the fate of Bani reached oblivion.

The Rock that orbited Bani was consolidated with iron. She was formed when Bani first split as schist. The growth bellowed out enough to crack some of the main stone to a far orbit around Bani, whilst catching a rate of gravitational pull to the closest star. Nights were no more different than days but the seasons shrunk the years.

The moon was filled with basaltic lava flooded by volcanoes dying from no atmosphere, and covered large parts of the surface seen from Bani. These lunar surfaces were seen as dark spots marking huge craters, and light shades were the highland areas far above them. The mantle of the moon was iron, and the surface was rock with regolith consistency of mineral silt, sand and pebbles of silicon, magnesium, calcium and metal oxides. Overall the moon turned the tides of Bani, and the daughter cell orbiting Bani controlled it, so naturally Bani turned slowly with its own pace closer to the infernos of the sun.

Chapter 16
The Kingdoms

On the rock called Bani; one side formed as a huge block with a dry opening and the other as a glorious island, both had their abundance of wildlife. Far from the kingdoms of *monera* and *protista*, that *kingdom animalia* occurred. And the only method for *kingdom animalia* to occur as a multicellular organism stronghold would be to discuss life under the natural observation radar.

Chlorine presented itself in nature as a hard salt or as soft seawater. This chlorine could bond pretty much to anything, especially metals that orientate themselves as crystals of salt. The chlorine became attracted to nitrogen molecules, or nitrogen began to like salt that lead to amino acids being made. Slowly swimming freely one cell organisms developed.

The microorganisms and their properties affecting the ecosystems drastically effected a change to Sasha's sand ferns and Goman's vegetable farms. Unfortunately for Bani, there was no conclusive recognition between that of man coming from the belly of a fish or the curiosity of an ape, that to be said, the kingdoms still presented themselves.

The *kingdom monera* consisted of prokaryotes. These non-nucleus bound organelles brought about consumption of energy accumulating on Bani. The prokaryotes became divided into autotrophs, such as chemoautotrophs (chemical acquiring energy seekers, like bacteria), and photoautotrophs (light acquiring energy seekers, like plants). The prokaryotes grew and developed with their surroundings that when plantlike prokaryotes changed to liking oxygen, a new kingdom grew alongside *monera* and they were the *protists*.

Kingdom protist on Bani provided most of Bani to grow from algae to trees, and *kingdom fungi* to *kingdom animalia*. Prokaryotes became studied into eukaryotes, and the theory of mitochondria and chloroplasts brought evidence to study bacterial strains.

What was most exciting about a bacterial cell besides binary fission was that some had flagella and some had more. These cells would move around, eat and grow protein of their own; some stabilize multicellular organisms for life, whilst others develop resistance to survive host defences in other organisms, voluntarily or not.

Strains of bacteria can conjugate together, mutate altogether, transform completely or transduct parts of their nuclear material to each other, chemically or with heavy dose radiation. Using pressure by the slapping hands together and rubbing them would kill most bacteria. Antiseptics, soaps, detergents and bleach would remove more prokaryotic cells, but with those producing spores autoclaving was conclusive.

Other special and wonderful characteristics attributing the bacterial cell was that they could live with or without oxygen. Respectively aerobic and anaerobic bacteria make most of the functions in man alive. That man was no different from a prokaryotic cell. Survival of the fittest evolved to a mutual habitat between eukaryotic retinal cells and prokaryotic gram-positive bacteria cells in digestion.

Colours of Enlightenment & A Potion

Fusion of gametes over and over again brought about a morula, blastula and three derm layers, of which one comprised the neural highway paving cardiovascular cells and stratified epithelium. How much of whatever laid down was according to the protein scramble when the two gametes hit and that was man clothed or not.

For eukaryotic organisms with male and female sexual functions such as sponges, i.e. *porifera,* there follows more diversity resulting in jellyfish and life with radial symmetry. A study into marine biology over biochemistry and microbiology developed more awareness to eukaryotes.

Viruses were found by chance when tobacco fields were evaded by the tobacco mosaic virus. An antiviral agent through bacterial staining removed the virus for the plants to grow. Fields of crops and land for locusts to cover was covered with pesticides to allow the ground to churn. Viruses are not accustomed to share; nevertheless there are some that lived dormant in eukaryotic organisms. The ecosystem of Bani believes itself that viruses should not belong to eukaryotes or prokaryotes yet they still existed.

Evolution within the kingdoms, that natural selection within the genus divided the *kingdom animalia* further. Profound timing made *molluscas,* snails and slugs on earth, and octopuses and squids in the waters. The earth turned by the *annelida* organisms, as earthworms; spiders, ants, creepy crawlies with a chitin protein making a hard exoskeleton were *annelida* too. These animals were especially important as they fought infections and spread of germs within earth; the *annelida* also had to remain attractive to attract the second consumer. And *chordata* animals some invertebrates and some vertebrates prowled Bani; the waters had fish and amphibians to reptiles and the land had reptiles to most mammals, where the sky's were swarming with birds.

Sasha hosted two sets of wildlife; one was as an Australian outset and the other a Northern Russian on Earth. There were dogs to wolves, rattlesnakes to kangaroos, kwela bears to mountain goats, and white leopards, birds of prey as ospreys, hawks, and turkey vultures.

Goman was seen in the eyes of monkeys, amazonian wildlife, parrots, snakes, crocodiles, and alligators, other beasts to cows, poultry, pigs, donkeys, roosters and ducks. Deep within the jungles of Goman where waterholes bathed so did some animals, as elephants, bears, mighty horses, birds of prey, other passerines, to lions and tigers.

All organisms in the kingdoms had a specific order in which to survive. Man had developed this into breathing and exercising. The eukaryotic cell derived building blocks to accumulate oxygen and vegetation to survive.

Alveolar cells exchanged carbon dioxide for oxygen for most creatures on Bani. In man the oxygen was taken to the heart, and pumped within the blood to the organs and respiring tissues within their anatomy. The blood flowed through bones nourishing them with calcium and by cranial nerves nourishing them to fire continuously.

Shots of neurotransmitters from the nerves' triggered the creature's muscles to move, and some ions were exchanged between the tissue layers for life

Colours of Enlightenment & A Potion

to act. (To actually observe this would be as amazing as watching water droplets sink into water). The muscles moved the man who in turn managed his work in order to keep his cells in homeostasis.

    Loaves and sodium absorbed for nourishment kept the kingdom cells firing everyday; this included passing bowel movements for more grain, oats and barley. Back around went the cycle to the prokaryotic cells; fungi that made yeast by fermenting carbohydrates above their capacity of needing oxygen, and the yeast turned the starch from the grains in the flour into loaves of bread once more.

Chapter 17
The Atmosphere

Sources of energy for Bani came externally from the sun and internally from the electromagnetic waves between the poles of the planet. The magnetic field filled a capacity for Bani to hold an atmosphere. Nitrogen, carbon dioxide, oxygen and other mixed gases occupied Bani's hemispheres. The current of the gases were moved by the pressures of humidity and frost in the wind. With the wind moving the life of the planet, the planet aimed to draw from the proximally directed twist of the closest star.

The atmosphere to sustain life for the plant and animal cell was to have a balance pressure with its surroundings; this was fixed around ten thousand Pascal. On the moon the atmosphere was largely unsustainable being close to the vacuum of space. From what was present for Bani, the atmosphere developed meadows and fields where animals would graze.

Air flowed by a high-pressure system that brought warm air from the oceans and cold air from the sky's. There were two seasons that both Goman and Sasha experienced. One was a hot, dry and humid one, whereas the other was mostly as rain and moisture for the land. On comparison to Goman, the clouds over Sasha would disappear by the time the desert faced them. For Goman the clouds remained consistent

Colours of Enlightenment & A Potion

throughout the island. The mountains of Goman were not as affected by the weather. A low pressure system at the foot of Sasha's cliff would draw warm air onto the cliff slowly mechanically wearing the stone down.

Mostly the pressure systems brought an El Nino affect on the seashores of both lands. These effects allowed the people to bathe freely in warm waters. No tornadoes threatened the land on either side of Bani, but hurricanes out in the oceans occurred frequently. The ocean water was as salty as the seawater however the lake and river water was pure to drink.

The people of Goman were not to suffer devastation from natural disasters, but to admire the winds that humidified their meadows. Cold fronts were felt at the times when the Rock disappeared behind Bani. These times through millions of years formed snowcaps on Mount Dev Ji of Goman and on the Alps of Sasha.

Through the turn of Bani and the water irrigation system within the planet, the magnetic turn of ions, through the buildup of space gases, and along with hydro-energy from carbon, nitrogen, sulfur and water cycles the inhabitants of Bani lived. They would adapt from creature to creature till the realization of their planet's warming, where they would rule in order to accomplish the survival of that translation. Lastly they would work to preserve their land with all their might and possibly overcome an inevitable end.

The Specimen

Chapter 18
Jai Sainapat

An hour had passed after Sainapat gained consciousness when the ice began melting off the hub. A one-man hub shaped as a disc wide enough to fit Sainapat fired to the Rock from the planet and had cooled upon landing. Like a biscuit sliding on ice to the back of the net the hub cooled over and parachuted gently onto the Rock.

He looked out of a tiny square that held two sheets of glass kept apart by vacuum. He wiped the window to take a look out into space. Sainapat saw for sure that there was another land on the planet and that land was colourful. Marking a lever and pushing hard onto a panel with his full palm, he was cast upright and upside-down. Firing started immediately for the second time off the hub. With a thrust that pulled most blood to his head he gripped onto the safety bars and soared away from the Rock to Bani. Bani's gravitational pull turned just as the gas stopped firing to the burners of the hub. Sainapat felt the pull of the planet.

Sainapat drifted back into sleep and many moments later he began to become warmer than usual. Waking by gold bright light though his eyelids he thought best to leave them closed. Sainapat covered the light with his right hand and attempted to open his eyes. The light fell in brightened as he passed white rock above the clouds allowing him to see the green mountains of Goman.

Sandeep Patel

The landing couldn't have been better predicted for Sasha Khand even if Sainapat did not land on Goman. With predictability over crashing into the mountain's face or cracking through the rock below the surface of the sea, the best outcome would be to safely parachute to a valley between Goman's mountains. One valley in particular allowed a lake to bathe where he was to land. The hub was designed to open when he entered back into the atmosphere of Bani, he was then to parachute over the ocean and to that location.

Trying to stay under stealth would be the prime directive for him to follow. The conscience if any should be brought to terms slowly unless Gomen haven't figured him out already.

From his descent he saw that there was civilization. A castle within a fortress stood towering everything in Goman, and the castle was lit with movement. From the cameras that were planted on the Rock no movement could be outlined for Goman. Besides that the center village of Goman was well sheltered with trees, and depths of valleys, that whatever type of heat signatures there were was impossible to know. Sainapat witnessed how large the kingdom was that he felt a little afraid.

He came across a valley that sat deep below two mountain ridges. Half the distance high above one cliff housed a cave. After landing and finding himself a safe spot to rest, Sainapat placed his hands together, and with amounts of pressure tightened all his muscles in a matter of seconds. He released contact but maintained pressure to the tips of his toes. He released further and stretched out. Sainapat began tapping his first fingers together and looked across the horizon. Sainapat then

Colours of Enlightenment & A Potion

began to climb to the cave in the mountain. The journey to start off with was not difficult, through some woods that sat raising the land, and a change of terrain over a hill into a grass valley, Sainapat made his way. Clenching his hands and heaving up the slope, panting and stretching to grasp a better momentum, Jai Sainapat made his way into the foreign land.

From half way into an altitude Sainapat looked further to see the horizon. Thrusting his bag of supplies over his shoulder he marched forward. He could imagine the shade of gray resembling a path from his photos that he had learnt from home. Forwarding on his pace the route to the top of the mountain would have taken him several days. Now plans had changed. Sailing down with his parachute he had seen his goal and this track was to take fewer days.

Through luck he had noticed the tower of the castle and needed to climb like a spider to reach there. Tiny, tiny spider climbing up the mountain, tiny, tiny spider to be caught and ate. He thought to himself as he kept his mouth open during sleep time. Sainapat then tried to ignore spiders and any other type of creepy crawly whilst he forced himself further up the mountain. He had gathered himself two truncheons that he made from strong branches of trees and these he used to stride himself further closer to the tower he had seen.

The shelter point came alive after a two-day run towards a terrain, the changing of the same land into two ideally different environments allowed hope for him. From moving across the woods, he moved over a hill and everything ahead of him changed. The ground that was covered with branches and mud turned to dry grasslands, and beasts resembling buffalos could be seen grazing by the foot of the mountain. Sainapat had reached the foot of Mount Dev Ji.

Plantation could be seen around this mountain. Farmers by the hundreds could be seen plowing, seeding, and harnessing hay, wheat, bailey and oats. Sainapat's path would involve walking pass these people without raising too much attention. The path was difficult as Sainapat seemed to be an average of four inches taller than the farmers. Sainapat needed to get much closer to the castle he had seen before arising any attention to himself. He decided to wait in the woods to walk in with stealth during the night.

Unpacking his bag of supplies with enough discrepancy not to awaken any person or any beast from their work, Sainapat quietly made himself comfortable under a foreign evening sky. A small wasp like looking insect flew close to feel him. At first he was startled but then he opened his hand, however the insect flew away.

"He plays happily with the other children and does not ever use abusive language. He always says sweet words and never fights. Every being who meets him praises him. All of the children remain attached and surround him."

Adhyai 7:42

Sainapat had five cans of food and collected his knife to open one of them. He emptied a smooth texturing smell of spaghetti bolognese out into a small bowl. Slowly he split a pair of chopsticks and ate his

Colours of Enlightenment & A Potion

food allowing the flavour to savour his taste buds. He imagined watching people eat when he ate, looking to the left and right, diagonally munching on his food like it was his last supper. He pulled up to look at his food and consumed another bite. During his meal he safe guarded his axis' by horizon godpseed and continued mastication of his dinner.

The sun began to set. Sainapat discreetly watched the farmers slowly fill their carts and wagons. He watched the farmers start heading closer to a stoned valley. Others diverted to the right and began a path around the mountain behind some trees and rocks. He decided the shortest entrance to the castle tower would be by the route the farmers were taking. Sainapat waited with his spaghetti to watch all the farmers disappear and the land darken.

To the north of him all the light vanished, not even the mountain could be seen. The sight of pure beauty he then witnessed when lights began shining the blackened mountain. The walls to the castle became more evident and reflected a picture of a golden city floating in the sky. He watched with amazement hoping that the sight would not disappear. He loved how something so simple could bring so much beauty that he stood trying not to blink.

He finished his spaghetti bolognese and walked to a stream that he had passed to clean his bowl. Strapping his bag closed and tightening his beanie he looked up at the glowing castle again. Quietly he paced out of the woods towards the farms and quieter still towards where the farmers had disappeared.

Sainapat found himself within small alleyways winding within and between each other. The area was still quite crowded and he ducked under his beanie. The streets were lit dimly with torches. Food could be smelt from every street at the foothold of the mountain. People were frying batter with various blends of spices either as potato, onion or peppers. These foods were shaped as spheres, squares and triangles, and were being sold to all the farmers and the village people. There was a strong scent of boiled corn which made Sainapat's mouth water. Some other people were making kite string, whilst more were making crafts in wood. Jai Sainapat carried on walking through the crowd up the mountain and towards the castle gates.

Chapter 19
West Sasha

She walked into the library to see if he was there from the last time she had seen those broad shoulders. The last time this person caught Lindsey Butcher's eye was when he helped a student pick his books up from the library floor. The reason for the student's books to fall was because this person that Lindsey had seen walked past the individual, and through fright the student knocked into a table dropping all his books to the floor. The person walked over to the student and helped him load his books onto the table.

Looking at the man's honour, she knew that he would be right for the assignment. That was if he chose to volunteer. The man was in the library sitting on the same table as before but on another seat, and still facing between the window and the wall. She didn't want to disturb him, plus she wished to learn more about him before approaching him. She decided to wait till he left to watch what he would do.

The 19th hour, 20 minutes had hit by and the man began to pack his bags. Mostly what went into the bag were comics as far as Butcher could see. This man slowly got his things together and left the library. He walked clockwise around a fountain into Oakland Bay Street. Lindsey Butcher stayed a few paces behind and gently followed him. The man stopped to buy fruits and vegetables; two green bell capsicums and three potatoes.

"I see him. We found him," radioed Butcher to Prof. Esjah's team at Sasha Khand.

"Let's wait a week to see what he does before bringing him in," replied Prof. Esjah.

A week quickly passed, and this time Butcher visited the library with Malek Esjah in attention to collect the man. They both sat close enough with book bags and pencils that they could hide away as well as hear the man. They heard his chair lift, and he began to walk to the opposite end of where he was. The man picked up another comic book and began walking back. Malek stood to start walking towards the man to gain attention by bumping into him.

"Sorry," said Malek.

"Sorry," said Sainapat

"Excuse me, where did you get that book from?" continued Malek.

"Shelf 490.697," replied the man.

"My name is Malek Esjah," said Malek.

"Jai, Jai Sainapat," replied the man,

"Well, I'm too interested in the poets from the time of divided Sasha and how the old kind helped to bridge the gap," Malek Esjah took a step back; he looked at the man and said: "There's still one more bridge to build. Please, can we sit?"

Sainapat looked at him with a puzzled look. Malek slowly sat on a chair. He applied pressure to his feet and tapped his toes to the floor. Sainapat relaxed his stance and sat opposite him. Lindsey Butcher pulled back a chair and joined them. Sainapat looked over to see and Malek began informing Sainapat about Bani's history alongside pictures of the other land. Sainapat relaxed from the tension in Malek's voice as Lindsey

Colours of Enlightenment & A Potion

blinked by his side. Malek increased his pitch as Sainapat began to listen. After Malek came to a stop, blinked and looked for an affirmative response from the stranger. Sainapat sat back, stretched, and rolled his hands with tension over his head. Sainapat looked up at the ceiling and began breathing through his nostrils

"When would you like to see me again?" Sainapat asked without looking away.

"We would like to learn a lot more about you, and train you for the assignment before we let you go, so you will have to live with us until then, I hope you understand?" Malek replied.

Sainapat exhaled into the air above him. From where he had come from he had only seen light gray, gray, and dark gray shadows of Sashan sand. He managed to have worked with contractors and municipal engineers building West Sasha, but never had dreamt on building away from Sasha itself. Bowing down to his palms he mapped his following years for himself, the proposal seemed farfetched, but the decision was simple. Staring into his world with the space around him he wiped his hands clean and sat back looking at Malek.

As Sainapat was elder in mind than body he had been working and living with the orphan village of Sasha Khand. His mother had died from the same infection as his father. His father had caught the infection earlier than his mother, and after Sainapat was conceived his father had died. The infection did not rise to infect a new born, but after birth he lost his mother.

Jai Sainapat was adopted by the university and began studying in the school until he wished to work. He filed to live independently like many that started at

Sasha Khand, and was given living quarters whilst he worked for the city's infrastructure as well. Sainapat had grown close to the university, and felt obliged to honour them as they helped him survive the cold days. At home that night the darkness of his life began to become enlightened.

Compared to East Sasha where Sainapat had never visited, West Sasha was lined block after block of a forty mile ecliptic radius. The university centre stood at the center, and scattering from there to the cliff, to the water, and from west to east residential homes, small food stalls, clothe stores, barbers and pharmacists mostly. There was an opening that held an artificial park, there was an area of sanitation that adopted culturing animals, and there were nurseries. The importance of the assignment made Sainapat realize that there was no truth than that which was placed before him.

After one turn of Bani, Sainapat was living within Sasha Khand after the last meeting with Lindsey and Malek. Manson Blue was the first man in-line to accustom him to his new life at the university. Blue remained close with Sainapat to evaluate and harness Sainapat's courage throughout the short period that they would have together. A transition of life prepared itself for Sasha Khand ruling fear out. As to allow fear into a life would be to make a weak heart wonder.

"So now this is where you will sleep," said Manson Blue, "if you need anything, food, reading material, a blanket, don't be afraid to get it for yourself. I have shown you where everything is, now. Would you like anything else?" asked Manson.

"Nothing," replied Sainapat.

Colours of Enlightenment & A Potion

"Now rise before dawn, and meet us in the training room," said Manson.

Sainapat nodded, closed the door behind Manson and looked around his new living space. The apartment had a large glass window facing the streets of Sasha and the ocean. Sainapat drew the curtains, took off his shoes, and looked into the mirror. He washed his face, hands to refresh the daylight off his flesh. Moments later he laid down on a king bed and stared at the ceiling. The windows started making a tapping sound, then came a little rattling, a little more rattling and then the night began to thunder.

Chapter 20
The New Ground

Engines began roaring, Blue tightened his helmet, and bark after bark started to fall with branches that came crashing down from the sky alongside them. Scramble went the talkies. The lumber was forced onto crates and heaved down the slope of the cliff.

"Wake the forest!" shouted Manson Blue. "Watch your horizons men!" he carried on.

An acre at four sites had to be dug and there was no point in wasting time. The quickest way down the cliff for the men was by rope. Tens of thousands of men had marched up the cliff from most shallow point, and climbed further still with their axes to where Sasha Khand had examined. The engines stopped roaring. Scramble went the radio-talkies again and then silence fell on the chambers of the forest. Nothing was heard for ten minutes, total silence as everyone caught breath. Moments passed between the silences of the radio and the men heaving before someone spoke.

"What do you think is taking so long?" asked Marine to one of the candidates for the operation, "we have spent years building our way through this mess," he carried on.

Marine looked at another tree, pulled back his axe over his shoulder and was about to take another swing before his radio rattled again.

Colours of Enlightenment & A Potion

"We have markers, we have all parameters sealed and marked, over," said Malek.

Marine put down his axe and grabbed his talkie: "What took you so long? Over,"

"Put down your axe and push the last crates too us," returned Malek, "you can start moving the drillers in, over and out."

"You heard that men, pick up those arms and move that iron!" Marine encouraged.

The engines began roaring once again. Marine let go of the button on his talkie.

"Get to the ropes!" Barsy Marine encouraged further.

The men around the camp walked into the woods. Tension began holding in some trees that were kept alive and apart from the vines.

"Pull!" they all began to chant in one-second intervals.

They raised an iron bar with teeth at one end that glided slowly onto a holster. The holster started spinning and the men let go of the ropes. The earth beneath them started to shake; the men picked up shovels and began to shovel more earth out. Ropes woven by the families began to scale the mining sites to mark their new home. The drill turned with the nights as during the days the equipment needed to be cooled.

Three years had passed since anything concrete was planted, but once it was the operation at all four sites went well. The arc rotation of the planet reached the end of the hemi-elliptic phase. Through pushing dirt and gravel, basalt with granite, and traces of iron, the men had worked harder than those that built the cities of Sasha.

Sandeep Patel

The land on top of the cliff melted down significantly for the areas located on the map to be seen by Joule. There was plenty of vegetation around these areas, plenty of vegetation to keep the armies of men working day and night to feed themselves.

"Mark down, and stay up!" crackled Blue's microphone, "clear out the spread and start laying the road," cried Blue in the heat of one summer's day.

The men moved across each other with brooms and back fold several times that afternoon before the buckets of sand, stones, gravel, concrete and tar could be applied to spread. The men had crates full of stone from the foot of the land they once occupied, plus sand from the seashore, and gravel with concrete mixture from the earth, with plenty of water from the stream that flowed across the cliff's peak. Crates full of tar made by distilling the chopped trees was to be applied last in the road making. After the tar had settled the chambers of the mines were to be filled.

"Shall we give the men a break?" asked Blue's second commander.

Blue turned around to the man and said: "Need some water right about now."

He began walking away from the commander to a barrel on a wagon that hosed water. Bending his knees and stretching far back with his left hand holding a lever he pulled hard at it, and water he drank by the liter full in ten seconds. He closed the lever and pulled himself up. Blue took a deep breath and wiped his mouth. Then he placed a longer exhale and took a deeper breath to feel the water saturate his blood vessels. He drank another gulp and wiped his mouth again. Blue walked back to the commander.

Colours of Enlightenment & A Potion

The commander started running towards the water. He pulled back the lever to drink water merrily. He too placed a large sigh when finishing, and one by one the men walked to drink themselves cool water on the hot day. Blue was watching the line of men gather after quenching their thirst and slowly stepped to the road's starting points.

"Pull yourselves together men. I want a hundred of you on this side, and hundred of you on this side, and the rest of you line up accordingly behind them."

The men delivered the note that they heard from Blue and lined up accordingly. A hundred yards stretched from Blue's feet to the last man.

"Now everyone spread out arm's length," Blue said. Without hesitation three hundred yards stretched from Blue's feet to the last man. "Okay, need every person to stay at arm's length from each other for once," patronized Blue on the microphone. "Make sure you're in alignment with the person beside you and be aware of the person behind you. The second person in line be aware of the third. Work in rotation and men on the right pass to the left. And men on the left hence pass to the right. Last man joins the closest man to me. Grab a broom from the wagon to pass forward."

Each last man grabbed a broom and handed it forward until all hands were filled.

"Start moving," said Blue.

All men within Blue's horizon placed sweeps to the built road. Blue stepped up to pick up a broom and smiled at the commander. The commander smiled at him and took his broom and began clearing the road.

Marine's radio started to crackle.

"Where are you?" cried Malek.

"Reaching the point of Mine Blue," replied Marine, "how's it going at your end?"

"Met Lindsey on the Yellow, and can see Manson with his team working down the gradient. Can't hear what you're saying. Finished the path from Mine Green to Yellow," forwarded Malek, "we will wait for you between Yellow and Ground, over."

"Should be four days at the most, over," returned Marine.

"Okay, over and out." finished Malek.

As well as they could see everything was falling to plan. However regardless to what Prof. Esjah's team had thought about the impact to their sun the time seemed to be approaching faster. The change in time was due to their sun expanding significantly for another star was asking for existence from theirs. The time was precisely within a three-year interval from the start of their double lunar eclipse. Everything was to be drawn from Bani including the moon and the Rock. The increase in gravitational force impounded into space from their sun would sling shot Bani straight into its core. Due to a birth of another star, Bani's star was to consume the planet sooner than the people of Sasha could expect.

Winter had approached the land of Sasha. The mines could be seen as huge holes feeding into each other on the mountain ridges above the cliff from space. The roads were tarred and settled by late autumn that paperwork seemed to have paid off. Most of the city people had moved within the mines. These mines were seen as four eyes on a white and gold/blue background spinning in harmony with space.

Colours of Enlightenment & A Potion

Joule could see these four mines. He had sat on the Rock to watch them become larger and larger, and from one mine to four. Nothing was occurring of the same magnitude on Goman. Joule couldn't make out the people that transformed Sasha but he felt that something was severally wrong. Possibly the people were digging through to Goman, or for an ant's chance choosing on their own accord to shatter the planet. Something was severally wrong. Joule spent several Rock orbits watching Sasha's movement.

Blue buzzed Mine Red: "When shall we start the next work, Barsy? Over."

"I don't know Manson, the sooner the dry off the better, over."

"There are five hundred more days to go, should we start now? Over," asked Blue.

"Yes, I'm sure you will have no problem walking in the snow, over," suggested Marine.

"You warm enough up there, I'll fetch someone for you if you like? Over," warmed Blue making people laugh in both Red and Blue mines.

"I'm fine but I'd let you know if I change my mind, over and out," replied Marine.

Barsy started picturing Lindsey in Mine Red. Some girls looked over at their commander in Mine Blue. Manson Blue looked over at some men playing cards within the mine. The men stared at each other and their cards as the snow fell over the entrances of all mines.

Chapter 21
The Path Home

The orbiting Rock was made from the semi-liquid/solid matter that made Bani. Some had cracked off and fallen distances away from the rest after settling. Most the interior of the Rock held spaces that crumbled into cubes and sheets of stone. Plenty of spaces within the Rock held water before evaporating off the moisture as she left Bani. Millions of light years from where Master had created the daughter cell of Bani that after drying out the Rock had a purpose once again.

"So as you can see the island is maturely saturated with plant life," said the botanist working on Prof. Esjah's assignment.

Her name was Victoria, and she was teaching a class to Marine, Blue, Lindsey, Malek and Sainapat on techniques for survival in Goman.

"Take you a long time to find your way from A to B, so this is what you eat," Victoria showed Sainapat a stick of sugarcane, "the more you find, the more you keep."

"No problem," interrupted Blue, "so what's all that?" Blue asked whilst pointing to the Redwoods on the screen.

This screen received images from the cameras fired from the Rock to Sasha. Some cameras had attached to the Rock without meltdown, and for several years Sasha had watched Goman. Animal life could not

Colours of Enlightenment & A Potion

be recognized from such a distance; however the fact of there being another land on the planet was shocking enough for Sasha Khand.

The botanists' had noticed the shoaling of water off the coast of Goman was at a greater rate than that off Sasha's coast. The share difference in greenery that the class could see as black and gray reasoned the atmosphere change accompanying the mysterious waters. The tide around Goman was measured into phantoms that resulted to never be able to sail to the planet's edge. The oceanic crusts had plateaus that climbed from the ocean floor to the plain resulting in raising the mountain plateaus carving Goman. The vast difference between their land and the foreign land on the other side of their planet was intriguing to watch. The seafloor had crunched drastically to keep Goman a more circle-shelved shape compared to that of Sasha, which resembled more as a cuboidal formation.

"Are there any problems with you and heights?" asked Victoria to Sainapat.

"No, how come?" replied Sainapat.

"If there is any form of smart civilization they will be placed closest to the top of this mountain." Victoria pointed at the screen with her third finger and followed it down to the lower left of the screen with her first, "now here is where you have to sail down to. If you sail to the south face of this island on their day side, we will have better signal communication."

Sainapat started blowing into his clothes by lifting his shirt over his mouth. He continued inhaling and exhaling and when they thought he was done; he coughed a large ball of mucus which he spat out under a running tap. Sainapat inhaled again, and then sneezed fast enough to at least aim it at the ground.

"Ugh," Victoria replied, "Are you done? Very well; I would hate for you to travel at night, so when you fire off the Rock wait until you're back in the atmosphere, and on Goman side before you fire out off the hub, and land towards their south," she added further.

"What's that side?" Sainapat said to Victoria.

"Well. After you land, I see that this will be your easiest ascent. You will make your way here, discreetly; you do not want to be noticed until you are closer to the top of this mountain," informed Victoria.

"That place does look really nice. I hope there is some company there for you," said Marine towards Sainapat.

Sainapat looked over at Marine, and then Lindsey started looking towards Sainapat, she then glanced at what Sainapat was watching. Sainapat had his eyes fixed on Marine's heart, and then he looked over at Lindsey's lips. He chuckled to himself as he had no intention to fall in love, and began looking for a vent in the ceiling.

In between the islands of Sasha and Goman there were mass differences in the mid-oceanic ridge that the initial magma had left. The planet had formed uniquely and the compressions of the land and extensions of Bani's magnetism had shifted the plates uniquely for either side.

"I have gathered that you will be able to breathe normally there." Victoria said. "Also we believe that all other biological systems, cardio, respiratory, renal, digestive, endocrine and epithelial, plus brain matter

Colours of Enlightenment & A Potion

will drain sufficiently from your right lymphatic duct into your right subclavian vein so you can excrete, how's your liver?" she continued whilst looking at Sainapat.

The environment for Goman was well flourished with greenery spreading much closer to the Gomen than that for the Sashans. Victoria had studied trees such as Desert Palms that surrounded them, and looking at the images from space, trees seemed to be a vital part of both lands' development. For Sasha the majority of plant life was on the cliff's brow. The plants generated energy from light to grow with their planet's atmosphere. Natural light from their sun allowed the plants to grow.

"The growth of plants is called, photosynthesis," Victoria explained to her class as she prepared detailed descriptions of the foreign land.

Chloroplasts have chlorophyll pigments that reflect the colour green or sometimes red, whilst harnessing the other levels of light energy. Victoria looked over at her diagram to explain to Sainapat, and the others that there will be no problem breathing once he was back in the planet's atmosphere. Plant leaves contain chloroplasts and every chloroplast attracts light by using grana made from thylakoid membranes of the leaf cell folding over each other. The grana attract the light to make energy-needed molecules, like adenosine triphosphate and another. In the day this reaction occurs, including hydrolysis of water to make oxygen.

During night or day, another reaction involving the use of carbon dioxide and oxygen happens. Stomata's that are pores under leaf surfaces close to prevent water loss. The energy molecules from the first stage of photosynthesis help cycle enzymes within the stroma of a leaf cell, to turn carbon dioxide and oxygen, to sugar molecules that remarkably help the plant grow. When the leaf turns another colour, consider green light wave to have been absorbed into the chloroplast, the leaf has darkened and died, but the energy has been harnessed into the tree. The leaves will then fall from the tree and be flown off by the wind for the tree to make new leaves for the spring.

"The tree may hibernate, but you will not lose your right to breathe," said Victoria.

"Could I eat off them too?" asked Sainapat.

"I recommend you take precautions in what you eat. Anything unfamiliar keep away from. And anything resembling close to a fruit we have here then closely examine before consuming," notified Victoria.

Sainapat nodded and carried on glaring at the video screen. He was marking recognizable corners to the island including a lift to the highest point. The image reflected from the screen was on a cycle of thirty-two hours, and each land shared an average season of sixteen hours daylight time. He sat watching the images whilst the team began to pack their work. He went to sit closer with Victoria as Marine, Lindsey, Blue and Malek left the lecture hall.

"Do you mind?" asked Sainapat pointing at the controls on the computer.

"Not at all. Take a seat," replied Victoria.

Sainapat began playing with the controls to mentally examine Goman and Sasha from different viewpoints. The difference in structure between the lands made the decision conclusive; He'd have to tread with caution, and will need to take a weapon or two

Colours of Enlightenment & A Potion

with him. All the cultures in Sasha mounted to that mountain in the picture. The one thing keeping them alive was watching Goman. There was nothing besides one thought in his mind. And that was to keep a good understanding, if there were cultures then bless them be of one kind.

Victoria leaned over Sainapat.

Chapter 22
Healthy and Music

Palaces were built by tribal warriors and all their workers on mountains that mined marble. The floating city of Raja Harichand, Udaipur was where Master was reading his lines. The white marble floors and walls that built Rajasthan temples' on mountain tops was where Master felt to travel. Gently built not to scratch the white marble floor, a twelve-foot green-felt wooden table rested beside Master in one of Raja Harichand's temples.

    Master walked around the table that was lit through the reflections off the walls and the skylight of the temple. The table was decorated with colour; black, red, pink, blue, brown, green, yellow and white. Each colour was painted onto spherical shapes of marble which sat on the green-felt table. Reaching the corner of the table and holding against it, Master used his left hand to lift the entire table to spin and land on the side closest for him to break the start of the game.

Julienne five slices across for a staff,
Julienne five slices across for a staff,
Julienne five slices across for a staff,
Top with a treble or a bass clef.

Colours of Enlightenment & A Potion

Layered E to F and up he rises,
Layered E to F and up he rises,
Layered E to F and up he rises,
For slices on a treble clef.

Brush frequently to apply between notes and rests,
Brush frequently to apply between notes and rests,
Brush frequently to apply between notes and rests,
Top with a treble or a bass clef.

Layered G to A and up he rises,
Layered G to A and up he rises,
Layered G to A and up he rises,
For slices on a bass clef.

Shake his voice, strings, brass, woodwinds and percussion,
Shake his voice, strings, brass, woodwind, and percussion,
Shake his voice, strings, brass, woodwind, and percussion,
Top with a treble or bass clef.

Layered with sound till cooked golden brown,
Layered with sound till cooked golden brown,
Layered with sound till cooked golden brown,
And sing with a squeeze of lemon.

Surrounding the palaces there were roads intersecting through gates that allowed the people of that world to come closer to the floating city. Around the gates that previously held governing from the rest of that world to the land further east grazed horses. There were more horses than stadia and chariots. Stern to the foot to hold huge men and their armor the horses' grazed peacefully in a kingdom built for them.

Within the white temple of Raja Harichand, Udaipur in Rajasthan, Master shot his game of snooker under the stars and began to get bored. He began to move the balls around the table and place them at other spots. Master placed one of the red balls on the white marble floor of the temple just to be out of place. Master enjoyed viewing the out of place ball for several seconds. He walked to one end of the temple and viewed his work. He then imagined it not being there for a moment, and as it was so, not knowing his own strength, as a bolt of lightning Master moved the whole vision back to his home by Joule Lair.

Chapter 23
The Settling

On Ayia Napa Ridge the people held a party to welcome Sainapat. Music started flowing between the mountain valleys and throughout the night. Not only was there music but there was also food.

Meat was cooked with the least fat possible. Burgers were flipped and not pouched which kept the tender juices within the meat. The meat was best when marinated with herbs and spices, and mixed along with tomato paste or plain yogurt overnight. The most potential damage was by accumulating enough heterocyclic amines from the meat into the blood that would lead to heart problems. Thus marinating the meat overnight solved this problem.

Village people arrived with ale well before the king arrived with the new-arrival. They began drinking, and talking within their groups on how this stranger had appeared. Seven green, and seven red bell peppers got chopped, and poked on skewers divided by tandoori-pasted chicken cubes and placed on a clay furnace.

People arrived on Ayia Napa Ridge, and the more people began eating and drinking. When people drank, people danced, joyfully. Dusk began to fall and torches began to be lit as percussion instruments were beaten, and string instruments were plucked to bring further joy to their hearts on that particular day. They joined smiles as they danced, some more elegantly than others, and eagerly all waited to see Jai Sainapat.

"I can't believe what is taking them so long? Half the town can't seem to stand straight anymore," said Caffe to one of her waitresses.

There was a stand making fresh bread. There was a stand grilling fish. There was a stand with fruits. There was a pizza stand. There were game stands, and other amusements like pie eating and making own milk chocolate snowflake stands.

Slowly galloping from the distance four shadows came to light; the king and the queen, Faran, Tarun and Sainapat. They mounted off the horses. Sainapat had no idea on how to ride a horse and was tucked in close behind Faran. People started peering over to the royalty and Sainapat, who stood tall above the others.

"Here," Marcos bumped into Sainapat and handed him a drink in a large glass.

The drink smelled bitter and a little fruity. Sainapat looked around to see that most people were holding the same glass as him, and so he slowly tasted the drink.

" "O Sri Guru Nanak Dev Ji please advise us of this as everyone wishes to hear your words and become pleased." Sri Guru Nanak Dev Ji then spoke from his lotus mouth such words to make one understand how the angels of death respect the sacred thread."
Adhyai 9:21

Colours of Enlightenment & A Potion

"So sorry for throwing you out like that, you have a name?" Caffe asked Sainapat.

"His name is Sainapat, and he doesn't speak to strangers," replied Faran.

Caffe began smiling and walked over to the queen. "Would you like to try some of my mash potato Highness? Can I show you back to my stand?"

"I would love for you to show me your stand Caffe." Insisted the queen and both women walked to The Potato Inn stand, and began watching Sainapat and Gomen.

At The Potato Inn stand there sold baked potatoes, fried potatoes, mashed potatoes some with dressing of chives and butter, some plain potatoes with rough jackets, a little salt added on chips, more spuds of spirals and crosshatched potato slices. At the stand King Lex had his arm around Sainapat and Tarun was speaking to Faran.

"Look at the size of him. I was being a fool hitting stones together when I should have been hitting the floor more," said Tarun.

"Don't say that, you have plenty of time now to hit the floor. Now hit the ground and do me thirty," replied Faran.

"Wow you sounded just like him,"

"I saw him working out earlier yesterday; he said something like that to himself. You heard him too? Well of course you did scientist. You're right you do need more brawn."

"S is for science, T is for ..."

"Tree," replied Faran, and both brothers smiled and walked over to the bruschetta stand.

The king and Sainapat started following the brothers as the queen and Caffe were eating there. There was rich soar cream with chive bruschettas, and beans with cheese bruschettas. These two types along with pita-bread, naan-bread, chapatti-bread, baguette bread, ciabatta-breads, and loaves were baked during the night. Spinach dressed with cherry tomatoes, and egg mixtures with cinnamon, cloves, garlic, ginger, or thyme to be soaked in yogurt or olive oil overnight, before being served that night. The texture was warm and dense to the taste.

"Good job having a bread stand here to soak up with," nudged Caffe towards Faran.

The girl had already joined in with drinking games with her other girls, and thought to tease Faran in front of his duty to King Lex. She whistled for someone to bring her a drink. A girlfriend carried by a man holding two glasses in each hand, and her holding another two came to see Caffe.

"Works out perfectly! I am trying to look after my figure so Highness you have this one," Caffe smiled at Queen Natasha.

"Well I need to add on some calories so I don't mind if I do," replied Queen Natasha.

She drew closer to Caffe and slowly lifted the glass out of her hand. She looked over at Alexander. King Lex stood still in his own conversation to Sainapat, and halted. As a matter of fact so did Sainapat, and Faran, with Tarun, the other man stood still, and the other girls felt slightly jealous.

"So the story of you arriving from where?" King Lex pointed at the sky.

Colours of Enlightenment & A Potion

They both looked up at the sky which could be seen by the fire that was roaring to the stars.

Sainapat pointed south and said: "Sasha."

King Lex pointed to the floor and said: "Goman."

They both joined nodding heads to each other's newfound discovery. Tarun began nodding his head too. Faran bounced on his toes. Caffe was watching Faran. Queen Natasha was watching the dance, girls touching vogue whilst dancing to soul, and men brushing into them, and the other two began making out, all to allow the queen to grab hold of the king and move him to the dance floor. Caffe stroked past Faran and walked to Sainapat, grabbing him with both arms around one of his, she moved away from Faran. Tarun walked over to get his brother more ale.

Move side to side with the sound of the beat, again!
Move side to side with the sound of the beat, singagin!
Move side to side with the sound of the beat, beginagin!

Faran watched Caffe dance with flare, and Sainapat move two steps left and right with hands down either side. Never minding what Sainapat thought of Caffe, Caffe watched always round to Faran. Sainapat watched pupils around him, and he smiled through his two steps to the left and two steps to the right. Glad Sainapat was for being around company as well as being alive, so he danced his two steps, watching the king, smelling the food, tasting the ale, and watching Faran become uneasy, so he walked over to relieve Faran from standing post with Tarun. When Faran joined Caffe there was a surge of energy like no other. A drawn energy to ripple through space pulled not only the crowd beside them but that of Sashan blood.

    Sainapat stood beside Tarun who kept stealing peaceful glimpses of him, and he too stole glimpses of Tarun. Tarun kept staring at Sainapat as he watched him glare through all the noise and movement wondering what he was thinking. Sainapat was watching the Gomen eat and some Gomen that weren't eating. Sainapat smiled at Tarun watching up at him and said, "Got to get up, face the music and dance," and pulled himself and Tarun into the rhythm of the music amongst the Gomen.

Chapter 24
The Explanation

Sitting beside Faran, Marcos asked him about Goman. Caffe was pleased that Faran spoke passionately, and nothing more than what he felt was right. Over the campfire they had laid out, beneath the castle wall on the south exit just away from the noise that would gather from the castle courtyard in the morning, and far enough not to disturb the horses, Sainapat sat beside Faran for interest in what he could learn from him.

"*Taraxacum* plants forming dandelions, and *Leguminosae* plants would produce peas, and roses would form in all colours, and that is a bouquet of flowers." Faran slowly chanted his ambition to talk about growth from lavenders to lettuce plants, and other herbs, and shrubs, Faran flowed with his desire to please Caffe.

The other guys listened in on him, and especially did Sainapat as he began to learn more about Goman. So much vast difference from what Faran was describing from that of Sasha, that Sainapat filling Faran in on the surface of the other side of the planet would become tearful. Faran looked over at Sainapat and Marcos began looking at him too. Caffe glanced towards Sainapat as well. Sainapat watched the fire, and Faran carried on whistling the name of flowers to Caffe.

"*Anthoxanthums* is another thing that reminds me of you," said Faran to Caffe.

Fact was that Sainapat had no idea what Faran was speaking about, nonetheless nor did Marcos.

"What about *poppies*?" shrugged Marcos to Faran.

"He means grasses, grass blades, I remind him of grass blades," replied Caffe.

Sainapat and Marcos looked at Faran, Faran looked at Caffe with his puzzled look.

From the distance came Tarun. He was now twenty-eight, and still with the thirst for knowledge as the next person. Plus Tarun wished to be more confident like Faran, so he joined in around the campfire.

"*Anthoxanthums*, is what we were talking about," Marcos filled Tarun in.

"Oh, blades of grass, good one," replied Tarun straight to Faran.

Caffe stopped staring at Faran and looked over at Tarun, Tarun looked at Faran. Faran now was watching Sainapat.

"How can we get him to explain his land?" Faran said to them, and handed Sainapat a *Colchicum* plant. Sainapat began to examine the purple stalk-less flower, and looked over at Faran, "eat it when you are in pain," Faran forwarded towards Sainapat.

Sainapat looked over at Faran and then the gravel at his feet. He placed the flower down. He drew a stone by the campfire closer. He gathered gravel and marked it close to the stone, and then he got up and walked over to the stone arch of the castle. Sainapat grabbed a piece of sandstone and returned to the fire.

Colours of Enlightenment & A Potion

He stood over the first stone and began to grind sand over it. Picking up the flower he placed it over the sand. Then he pulled at some grass blades by his feet, sprinkled them over the rock and sat down.

"That's nice," Marcos said.

They all carried on looking at Sainapat's creation on the ground, and didn't know what else to say so they smiled. Sainapat picked at the sand and said, 'rathi,' he picked up the flower and said, "city," and then he picked up the stone and said, 'cliff.' Pointing out the area around the stone and the sand, around the ground, he said, 'pani.'

They all looked over at the creation that Sainapat had created. An arm stretched out into the middle of the description of Sasha that he had left.

"*Anthoxanthumus,*" Caffe said, picking a few blades of grass off the stone.

Sainapat took the blade of grass with his right hand and picked up the *Colchicum* with his left. He started examining both of them, and saw that each other were as beautiful as the other.

Beauty had almost disappeared for Sainapat, and he could no longer remember the sight of his land to the glory that Faran was describing his. Looking over at the grass blades he handed them to Caffe.

From there came lilies, and from there came lotuses, and more plants became colonized by insects including bees that flourishing Goman was extremely sudden. The flames from the fire burnt hotter whilst Faran kept charming Caffe. Faran looked over at Tarun wondering what he was doing there. Watching the ground that Sainapat had created, Tarun looked up at Faran.

"What do you think all this means?" Faran looked at Tarun and said nothing. They all began looking at Tarun. And Tarun began looking at Sainapat's creation. Then Tarun began looking at Sainapat.

Sainapat looked at the stone, picked it up, and turned it around. He collected another stone, and pointed at the Rock in the sky. With a crystal of sand he placed this on the second stone, and pointed to the first stone, turning the first stone over bringing him to Goman. Sainapat was trying to explain his path from Sasha to Goman. He then motioned a pair of binoculars over his eyes. Marcos was last to laugh, realizing that Sainapat does not wear glasses.

"There was once told to Guru Gobindji, that a disciple will arrive in three forms, one as invisible, one with his word, and one as visible. And as Gobindji describes him, after he had arrived as invisible he'd become the Adi Granth, and after he had arrived as visible he'd be the Khalsa. He'd be Khalsa as the One had entrusted him with Scripture," softly said Tarun.

From the words spoken by Tarun, Sainapat had heard their acknowledgement and he pulled a small book from his pocket. He opened the book and read a line, he read the line again, and then gently aloud said; "Guru, Guru Arjan Dev Ji." He stared at the word for awhile and gave the book to Tarun. Sainapat gave them a smile and looked through the crust below them.

Tarun opened the book at the back page and read some verses through paced time to close the book at the beginning in five minutes. He handed the book back, pointed to the ground and said, "Dev Ji".

Colours of Enlightenment & A Potion

From where they were standing they could see the moon and the Rock. The Rock floated in the far distance of the valley, and the light shining from the sun off the moon made it possible to see the Rock. The moon was on the closer left side of them and was due to rise closer. Marcos placed more sticks on the fire.

" "When the Brahmins or Kshatris take this sacred thread in accordance to the terms of the Vedas then they would be admitted entry into the faith." With grace Sri Guru Nanak Dev Ji listened to the words of the Pandit and spoke the following beautiful words."
Adhyai 9:15

"*Smyrnium* plants that produce inflorescences of yellow pigment and deviations of which begin to produce snowflakes and snowflowers." Everything else that Faran kept humming to was not only exciting to Caffe but also was tickling Tarun, Marcos and Sainapat.

There was a mention between potato families that Tarun began laughing to as his brother named Caffe a division from the *Solanaceae* family.

Faran walked over to the edge of the woods and picked up a pinecone, and another one, and another one, and a twisted one, and brought it back to the campfire. He threw one each at the guys, and handed one to Caffe. Tarun threw his in the fire, and so followed Marcos, and then Sainapat. The pinecones started crackling.

"Why have you got me a pinecone now?" asked Caffe.

"So you can throw it in the fire," said Faran.

Caffe threw her pinecone into the fire too.

"Ouch, that hurt," said Faran as the pinecone crackled.

"Nice one," Sainapat said in Sashan.

"Well you're alive," returned Caffe.

For Sainapat the truth about keeping peace within himself, and distancing himself further from Sasha was to visualize what Faran was talking about. Pitch Pine was a noun that Sainapat heard, along with Sugar Pines, and Coast Redwoods, later Sainapat realized that Faran had started naming trees. Most plant life that Sainapat had seen came from Desert Palms that spread along the whole coast of Sasha; besides them he could only recognize pine trees.

Faran carried on spilling names of plants, and trees, and pointing towards the direction in which they could be found in Goman. He pointed over at some trees that resembled Red Maples or Elms, Poplars or Birches, and Cedars or Oaks. Faran began naming unusual names for trees as Desert Ironwoods, Joshuatrees, and an Elephant Tree for them to hear.

A hundred acres of Redwoods sprang in front of them, and greener, and darker green spread through the land around Sainapat. From where Sainapat could see there was nothing resembling home, but instead a new environment was landscaped ahead of him to study. Moreover there was no reason for him to think about what would come of Sasha. Watching Faran point to the trees, and gather pinecones, and surprise Caffe with the others, allowed Sainapat to appreciate where he was and forget where he had come from.

Faran fell into a sugar-rush after stuffing his mouth full of jellybean candies. Caffe started watching

Colours of Enlightenment & A Potion

the campfire as Faran began speaking about the trees to himself rather than to Caffe's fancy. And for approximately a minute, Faran disappeared into his own world amongst the light shining off the leaves of the trees, off the moon, the Rock and the sticks from the campfire, and whilst the trees reflected silver light towards him the night became younger.

"*Ranunculus*. I would like a *Ranunculus*," Caffe said to try and get Faran's attention.

If that hadn't had worked she would have gently moved her finger across her leg, and would have held to release the finger off her flesh, or to have needed to slap her own thigh. (Now touching others seemed well to Faran, but touching self was seen as being weird, and only was acceptable when changing). For true mercy Faran had heard over his own voice. The possibility of that plant to be chosen by Caffe to describe Caffe overwhelmed Faran, and he walked over to her. He asked for her hand and they both left the others.

Sainapat pronounced to himself, '*Ranunculus,*' and began to beat an Om as a sign of acceptance. Marcos went to collect more pine cones and Tarun fell into the beat of the island.

The Outcome

Chapter 25
The Visit

Joule landed on the iron based Rock that flew around Bani; he blew hot flames reaching a dozen meters from his ignited thermo-regulated gas ducts out into space and relaxed.

The particles of Bani were formed from radioactive elements in space that brought around mass. Protons and neutrons held the most mass compared to that of electrons in space. When all three identities coincided an atom was formed.

An electron presented a weight that was so small and unrecognizable to touch unless when shocked. Balloons hold electrons statically from objects surrounding them, and depending on the objects own ability to hold its own electrons was a matter of electromagnetism. The same functioning electromagnetism produces radio-decay, a matter of material decomposing in space, was where he landed.

There was a mass to an electron, and this added with the mass of a proton made a muon. The attraction between them was a tau, and anything without a charge was a neutrino. All this was used to help everything stick together in the fear of the planet halting to a stop, which would even pull the Rock from space into Bani's earth.

Leptons were particles that formed waves of electromagnetism, and the anti-lepton was an electron. So the word carrying electrons in vacuum was leptons, and what Joule could see was more than water droplets when staring into space by daylight, but electrons being pushed in space. For Joule to engage across space he used the sum of energy through leptons localised in space to pull him to that location, and to pull him at light speed if Joule figured.

Thank you for understanding that radioactive elements decompose, and everything holding electrons makes things move. Depending on the wave direction, and naturally from north to south, the decay forms land sooner or later. And the radioactive elements that Joule was sitting on with his mighty claws had arrived from the push of radioactive materials away from itself. This push was held by electromagnetism. Later particular objects generate their own field of electromagnetism with their source. So this made the Rock and moon orbit around Bani, and Bani arc half an ellipsis to contour their sun. With their sun held by the field of electromagnetism of other stars around it.

Joule's claws scratched into the quartz mineral that occupied the Rock's surface. This strong wave arrangement of molecules covered the outer surface tightly. The inner portion was more a mica and halite structure consisting of sheet and cube carbon arrangements respectively. Arrangement of carbon atoms bonded with metals held the structure of the Rock. Metals such as chromium, cobalt, copper, lead, nickel, manganese, silver, and iron filled most of the Rock. The density of the Rock allowed Joule to land easily.

The reason for Joule to arrive so close to Bani was the surprising shot of light he had seen from the planet's surface. Joule decided to visit the planet to

Colours of Enlightenment & A Potion

satisfy his curiosity. If Joule was watching the light travel from Bani to the Rock from the moon, the time would have taken five seconds, however from where Joule was sitting the light shined close to five minutes, so Joule left Master's realm to be closer to Bani.

    He stretched his wings and folded them closed. He walked across the Rock and stretched his wings again to jump over the Rock's far horizon. Joule watched Bani come into view with Goman facing him when something reflected into his eye. Joule flew over to a shiny shell that was embedded in the Rock. There was no life present. Slowly Joule broke the electromagnetic wave field that held the Rock and the moon with Bani and disappeared in space back home.

Chapter 26
Into Grounded Lava

Floodgates used cofferdams to keep out all the water that would slip into the craters Sasha had made. The concrete was pushed into place and sealed spaces in the cliff. The vacuum was sucked out and fresh air filled the compartments that Sasha had made. There was over a million cubic yards of earth that was pulled out. And there was plenty of space for food. Earth, rock, steel-bound timber plates, all cargo were pulled in mile after mile. Depolarization at neuromuscular junctions twitched synapses that fired muscles to move the men's backs and arms, grabbing and clenching everything into place. The time was to seal the chambers and the tunnels, and water to be irrigated through the system by hydroelectric power.

"Dam, we can't see!" shouted a lady.

The sound was coming from Lindsey Butcher. The lights switched on and air filled the chambers. The people started to breathe easier. The radio light came on-line.

"Red, over," said Marine, indicating that Mine Red was operational.

"Blue, over," marked Blue.

"Green, over," said Malek in Mine Green.

"Yellow, good," marked Butcher.

"Seems like we are ok, everyone's still breathing, no bodies have fallen to the floor," marked Prof. Esjah from Mine Red. He smiled gently feeling

Colours of Enlightenment & A Potion

relieved that no one had been heard suffocating. "Not long left now, make sure everyone is familiarized with staying afloat," said Prof. Esjah.

"I'm ok in Mine Green, holding tight in surroundings, over," said Malek.

"That's good to know," replied Prof. Esjah.

"Is everyone else okay?" said Lindsey.

"Everyone is fine," said Prof. Esjah again whilst glancing over at Marine. Marine began smiling. "We are all thinking of you here, and everything is well. O.kay. let's move it, over and out." Prof. Esjah said, and the radios went silent.

All the mines were fitted with passing water through piped aqueducts, and kept a caisson to make sure the area occupied within the cliff was watertight. There was no chance to work at the other mines as every mine was sealed from the others. The only contact between the mines was by copper wire and pipes that ran water from the Alps of Sasha in the west to the waterfall which kept the watermill turning in the east.

Persons and personals were moved from the square shaped lobby within the mine structure to the parameters. People with their families grabbed one another, and their belongings, and moved up against the walls. There were walls planted as divisions in the main lobby. Each wall consisted of a bench area with armrests. The divisions occupying the outer wall of the main chamber and the rows of walls within were arranged as sarcomeres like in myofibrils of muscle fibers. They too were designed to contract in emergency.

Sandeep Patel

Persons were strapped with locking cushioned iron bars. These comforted the adult as well as the child. All lights were soon to be turned off. And all persons would have to try and stay awake. For some of the people that undeniably chose this sitting help was appreciated in building these cradles of four. The path was well examined and studied once over that missing the other was not considered an option.

Many municipal engineers as well as military engineers had excavated this task and everyone in Sasha trusted in their opinion. Charmed were the people when the air had filled their lungs that living in the dark for some while would be no problem. The brackets that locked each individual came to a final hiss, and all cushions that padded the iron bars came to a soft pressure. The lights switched off. Small sounds of whispers echoed between people. Babies began to make noise too as they felt weary of their changed environment.

"How's everyone? Over," asked Prof. Esjah.

"Mine Green good, over," said Malek.

"Mine Blue good, over," said Blue.

"Mine Yellow good, over," said Butcher.

"Does the packages of food really need to be eaten Mine Red? Over," asked Blue.

"We will eat it when the time is right, Manson," said Prof. Esjah.

"What time will that be? Over," said Malek.

"When your stomach can't take the hunger anymore that's when. Let's all have some rest, over and out." suggested Prof. Esjah.

A few hours had been passed and the lights were placed back on. The people had experienced the

Colours of Enlightenment & A Potion

seating positions; however every seat was available on the time of need. The iron bars were raised and the people slowly stretched their muscles.

For Mine Blue, Manson Blue tensed himself with his hands first together. Mountains of pressure laid in the force between his hands and shoulders attracting to each other. Feeling that pressure could no longer be held within his upper body, so he stood and tensed down to his toes. He tensed his arms further and stretched them up, and on release placed them in pray to begin tapping his pinky finger against his left palm to the seconds.

For Mine Red, Barsy Marine engaged in watching all people stay within the inner wall. The passages of children running pass the open bands between the walls allowed him to relax further in their stay within the mines. For days if not weeks now had passed, and watching the lights on the screen blink without a word the people were made aware that days had passed.

Malek Esjah was in command of Mine Green with the same operations as the others. Delivering the food to the people and irrigating the floor. Cleaning occurred once a day and everything was kept clean daily. Waste that the mines produced were collected, shredded, and shot to the surface with other waste from the mines. Everything was tried to be kept clean. Trash was literary thrown in the trash. There was no need to pretend to be afraid for doing what was right anymore as being afraid kept them alive. Malek propped himself against a wall with a finger and then four fingers, he bowed and leaned into his stance tensing his muscles.

Sandeep Patel

Lindsey Butcher addressed Mine Yellow. She was filling orders just as the others to keep as many people alive as possible. Children needed motivation to stay focused with, hence not becoming aggravating to the adults as sooner or later that aggravation would arrive on her. Thus Butcher attended around the children and the families as well as the scientists.

Hands together; fingertips and thumbs, tighter, tighter, harder, harder and harder now with incy wincy spider climbing up the water spout, climbing stronger up the water spout incy wincy spider. Harder, tighter, stronger, swifter, with or without touch was how they passed time. Thumbs crossed to compose hands together held their variables within the closed chambers. Gently also, with or without touch, and tapping the fingertips tighter to keep rhythm with or without music. Left hand posturing first and second fingers with thumb or if not with right hand to keep the pulse of the heart beating. Scrolling the fingers from stop, scrolling the fingers on either hand can scare the spider away. Then again a slow release from pressure from standing still the pinky finger with thumb can attract the spider in.

The goal for Sasha was to stay alive. The grains of time that would pass were tried not to be kept focus on, but instead they became adapted to counting each second that went by. Time didn't pass with days and months, they passed by watching the seconds that drifted without any light. So four mines had to sit in the dark, without any light but artificial, and four mines sat with no idea on how long to sit there for. They would begin to pray and wonder if they would ever see the light, or be perished by patience.

Colours of Enlightenment & A Potion

Sashans began to hold their patience by watching from left to right to left the fire-waves of their hands. They played 'eye-spy with my little eye,' something that is red, something that is black, something that is white, and something that is gold, to pass their time.

Mine Red was red, so were fire-extinguishers, fire-bells and fire alarms.

Black was found everywhere, under the chair, in the vent, that man's pen.

White was found by the milk in children's hands or a bowl of rice, also the light within one's eye.

Mine Yellow was gold, such as honey, gold bricks, safety levers, harnesses, and as a sign of hope.

Chapter 27
Radio Communication

In the alchemy lab of the great castle of Goman noise was coming from a busy body. The alchemy lab was a great room at one end of Goman's castle. The lab was designed not only to be fireproof but also provide quietness for times of solitude. Faran opened the gigantic oak door to the alchemy lab to see Sainapat mapping his thoughts.

"What are you working on?" Faran asked Sainapat. "So what is that?"

What Sainapat was working on was a phone. He had managed to bring with him a 90-volt battery with a 300-ohm resistor, and yards of copper wire. He had two tubes, where at one end of each tube he attached two strands of copper wire, and covered them with two thin layers of aluminum foil. Sainapat attached the copper wires to the battery and to a switch he had made from the thin film of metal and wood. The other ends of the wires were attached to the second tube similarly to that of the first. The thin layers of foil had carbon granules between them.

Sainapat gave Faran one phone piece and walked him to the other side of the door that he had just come in from. Sainapat walked back to the table with the switch and belled Faran. Rattle went the carbon granules on Faran's end.

"One, One, One, One, Two, One Two," came a sound from the granules.

Colours of Enlightenment & A Potion

"Wow, what's this?" said Faran, and the sound of Sainapat's laugh could be heard coming through the wires. Faran walked back into the lab, "This is amazing. What if we could call the king from here? He would love this."

The actual fact was that Sainapat was trying to make a radio device as his last had been broken. The phone was well appreciated by Faran but Sainapat knew he had to make contact with Sasha. The time had come close to where final migration of Sashan people would have come to an end; hence Sainapat had to somehow send a message to Sasha before their own exile.

Sainapat caught the attention of Faran looking down at his schematics. Faran was looking at a picture of what he was holding in his hand. Sainapat moved the diagram of the phone device away and showed Faran an image of Sasha.

"As far as I can see, we will need a lot more wire," suggested Faran. He picked up the wire and shrugged his shoulders. Sainapat nodded gently.

Fabulous thought that there was a position for me, that not listening to Scripture but instead listening to men fooled. Precious vows were broken amongst many men that the evaluation led to two reasons for the fall of one culture. Starting with the reason, one; no love was practiced, and two; no joy was appreciated in reading from honourable men, and hence no joy in believing in an honourable Lord. And to place a third was to allow negligence in truth making.

Sandeep Patel

Singing into your own voice, and singing into your own song, Shaheed Baba Deep Singh Ji, born a day and 298 years before I over there, declared to celebrate Diwali in Amritsar. Meddling pieces of scrap material can always be melted to form double edged weapons, and there always should be scrap material. Five-hundred men became five-thousand men and all ready to die. So he marched with them to the top of a hill, to the top of the hill, six miles north from Amristar they stood announcing to twenty-thousand pieces of scrap metal in the Iron Age, A.D.

Diwali was celebrated in Amristar that year. Straightening his head that was struck by Khan from the hot countries of the west, Shaheedan made his way to Harmindar Sahib stones' and collapsed. Pour in water, pour in water. The planet's date of November 11th 1757 A.D, the planet's conflicts cannot stay to occur again, as clearly there was not that much land to destroy, let alone the nourishment the men needed to nourish the land. Lastly before returning back to Amristar the warriors led by Baba Deep sharpened and sheathed their weapons.

Amrit, made from sugar and water was sounded as a blessing, and delivered as splashes to those that would like to live a vow to die closer to the Lord. Guru Gobindji Singh in 1699 A.D. started the Baisakhi Festival, to provide Amrit. The top of million were the Beloved Five, and every person vowing for Amrit thereafter to be known as a lion, as a Singh. Each lion since then kissed his princess, whom he post fixed Kaur, and prepared for war.

Into the Messianic Age, amongst each other, tightening their gear, their threads, their boots,

Colours of Enlightenment & A Potion

strapping their shields, and assembling in line, with their boots firm feeling the ground. Back straight, chin up, grips tightening by the rattle of more men climbing into the frame. Blue cloth with orange ribbons and medallions mostly for paper weights not weaponry kept the warriors amused within their rage. The sound of conches hollowing as Lord Kishan Kanhaiya's from times as thousands of years before them echoed to the heavens, and all Singh's waited for the howl back.

    Months had passed since the last time Sainapat had called on Faran, this time Tarun and King Lex joined him. The days were getting warmer and the land of Goman was becoming dry. Most people lived indoors now as the farms had become deserted from growing or plowing. The heat in the atmosphere was unbearable to stand. Reservations of water were kept close to the castle, and people could be seen running as fast as they could to the barrels and back home. The acceleration process was closer than expected.

    Caffe and Marcos walked in the alchemy lab as Sainapat began preparing to send a signal to Sasha. The king and his company had realized the importance for Sainapat to fulfill his task. They knew too well that a message should be sent to Sasha not only to confirm that Sainapat was still alive and well, but also to thank Sasha for sending him. Work on the phone had ceased and Sainapat concentrated on building a new radio.

    Sainapat gathered his things and handed a few devices to Faran and Tarun, and began walking to the tallest tower's balcony. Marcos planted a table and the brothers arranged the devices.

Sandeep Patel

A modulator to distinguish between the amplitude of a sound and the frequency, and a transmitter made from a copper wire attached to wood which he coiled with more copper wire as an antenna. Sainapat hooked up a speaker to receive the sound.

"Right, electromagnetic waves in the air will carry the sound from here to there. The electric and magnetic vectors should hold the sound waves created when we speak and carry that sound to that device there." Sainapat said to the others, but mostly to himself as he looked over at the speaker he had brought. This tiny contraption was attached to a tinier still microphone.

"So, I'm hoping if I modulate the frequency in this modulator to play the frequency modulation waves from the microfilm through this circuit board, then we should hear music at the other end. The estimated range in the subcarrier will start at 38 kilohertz and end at 19, keeping 18 kilohertz as our stop point, and the 19kHz as our pilot signal," Sainapat carried on.

The others began to take steps away from Sainapat and closer to the castle shade for the heat was becoming intense, and as for the fear of the strange device exploding.

"Right, la, la, la, la, laaaa," Sainapat sang whilst flicking on the switch and dialling down the modulator.

Soon sounds could be heard coming from the speaker end, "la, la, la, la, laaa."

King Lex and the others stood there in amazement as music began pouring out of the wooden box that Sainapat had made. The sound was not as authentic as Sainapat's, but nonetheless they were assured that this radio worked.

Colours of Enlightenment & A Potion

"Sasha has placed another receiver and transmitter as these on the Rock, so I should have no problem blinking them on an amplitude modulation like Morse had shown me back at home. I only hope that someone is there to hear the message." Sainapat said to the others regardless of communication barriers.

Rain clouds began to gather. Sainapat looked up at the sky, and he turned the modulation into an amplitude frequency only. The ground started shaking. The trees on all sides of the castle could be seen swaying. The castle began shaking. King Lex looked around and began to give orders. Faran and Marcos were to gather all the men and bring all the people within the castle walls and to the castle's basement. Caffe was to help them. He then looked over at Tarun and asked him to help his brother.

"I would like to stay, help Sainapat if he needs?" asked Tarun to King Lex.

"You are going to die!" cried Faran.

"We are all going to die regardless, now use your strength and help the king!" screamed back Tarun.

Tarun looked over at the king and began pushing him and Faran into the castle.

"Keep all doors sealed. Throw me a Granth. Elephant!" implied Tarun.

"Elephant!" Faran shouted back.

Since whenever could be remembered the Adi Granth was cremated if damaged. Each damage copy was regarded as a person and cremated, thus said, Agan Bhet at Goindval. Each copy was regarded as the same, but the holiest of Scripture was kept in a valley named, Kartarpur Pothi, and shown only on New Turn.

Sandeep Patel

Within the castle the abode of God had a resting place. This room, Gurdwara Ramsar, had a room in the basement where classes were taught and where Scripture was recited, repeated and recorded to point revolution. In their year of burial the last statement was made by Guru Gobindji, and at Goindval the Agan Bhet would occur. Forgiven was hoped for throughout the land of Goman that Tarun thought wiser to hold Granthji closer in the time they had left, whereas the representation of 'elephant' marked eternal love for one other.

Lightning within a bottle exploded to place Gurbani's words to a close. The pages of Scripture to only later be written if their threads held unsheltered from the rain that fell on the soil. A likely truth that land that they built around lakes on mountain valleys, holding floating lands, would themselves be built once more if torn down.

"Those individuals who believe that this world is eternal need to realise that all is false other than the name of God. It is false like the floating land of Raja Harichand which is like a cloud or the wager waged by a gambler."
Adhyai 8:22

The left hand held the straps for the horseman's anchor to the ground on the horse as he waited to call Baba Singh. Baba Singh marched ahead of his five thousand and stopped facing the tyrant army. An arrow

Colours of Enlightenment & A Potion

was picked by Baba Singh which he snapped above his head and threw the pieces left to the ground. Next he held his hands together and bowed in pray, the horses churned him to awake, a howl returned from afar.

As the metal protecting the men clattered and cries that killed the men stopped, Baba Singh finished his pray. His pray was that of a pray that was given to him as he searched for pray. The Granthji will be written to have a beginning, middle and end, but will present the future, and provide equality amongst ourselves, and amongst religions. Ancestry passed on items fell into the handles of bows to be stretched and plucked, to travel arrows hundreds of miles and strike them through the heart.

Pardoned you are to raise your hand on this land, let alone enough to raise your fingers while you think ahead. The axe-weighted weapon shall be cleaned by the thread and cleaned to blue. Skewed to his like, like Arthur's best man, Deep Singh, fell body first after he pulled himself from a spear and pulled apart the limbs of the beast, and fell thereafter blood and body first to be saved by his own hands on Harmindar Sahib.

"Ready ... ... Ready ... Ready, Steady ... Ready, Steady," said Sainapat whilst vigorously tapping a switch on his contraption. "I should be fine. Now go, hurry," Sainapat looked at Tarun and pointed at the door.

The door to the deck on the tallest tower closed between Faran and Tarun. The planet hurled and turned onto one side. Bani breached in space not continuing with the rotation of the planet's axis. For a minute Sainapat could feel that Bani was no longer moving, he stared and waited for a response from the other side. Everything began to get hotter and sweat started streaming down their faces. The light from the sun was facing away from the two men but the conduction through the planet's earth increased the heat substantially as Bani waited for the descent.

A crackle of cries from familiar accents approached the wooden box. Then as a magnetic attraction the planet started roaring at speed towards their sun, howling through space the moon flew ahead of Bani as the Rock followed closely behind into the core of their star.

Chapter 28
The Cities

Albert Bierstadt Street into Hindustan Avenue and into District East, pass another mile through 93 and over 707, joining onto Main Land 409, across one seashore, over a drive on boardwalk, and not many more miles till the checkered flag. The boardwalk's clear enough to watch the horizon turn Bani asleep. The plane of sight falls off the horizon of a fair waking for the morning, across the seashore back onto the tarmac of Main Land 409.

"The Mulla started to praise Sri Guru Nanak Dev Ji, "Baba Kalu Ji's sons' intellect is great. He has easily mastered the difficult language of Farsi." People come to see the face of Sri Guru Nanak Dev Ji to test his intellect. People are surprised at hearing his words. All of the people are praising Sri Guru Nanak Dev Ji as his age is small but his intellect is great. By hearing the sweet words both the Hindus and Muslims they love Sri Guru Nanak Dev Ji, remain happy and never upset or in pain."

Adhyai 8:9

The driver sailed over the roads made for them. A charge was sent through the roads that kept the vehicles afloat as they travelled. As for the parking within the two cities, the difference was in the charges beneath the pad that rested on the road. Charges of anions and cations bathed within different mixtures of the same electrolyte compound lined the pad. These would change configuration of negative and positive ions as the vehicle moved and turned. The scattering of ionic charge was drawn closer to the vehicle as ripples of water coming to a still as the vehicle stopped.

The shine of light silver shades of colour from the vehicle reflected light from the moon. A mass boat was docked to the north of him. Mostly what he kept track on were the rails that passed on the left of him. Tracks that struck iron ores on wood followed miles in front and behind him. Another mass boat docked on the north of him. So far he had travelled twenty-one hours, and another six were on the way. Another mass boat docked on the north horizon.

What kept him through his route was watching how the men had railed the iron. On the other side of the dual-carriage way was the cliff's face. Mining had begun from their third double lunar eclipse, and since then the cliff brow had not become any shorter.

"One day Baba Kalu Ji thought to himself, 'without education Sri Guru Nanak Dev Ji is wasting his life. What work and what could he do in order to gain wealth? He should not do any other work other than that of the family as if he is to do a different trade then people would slander him. It is my duty to educate my child as he will not learn in his older life.'"
Adhyai 8:4

Colours of Enlightenment & A Potion

Time had come for this lone ranger to eat. He stopped, ate, and carried on with his journey on 419 to East Sasha. Into route 36, exiting across 652, and into Harmony Road. Through several blocks with rooftops no higher than thirty feet he made his way into East Sasha. From the top of the blocks children could be seen flying kites. Signs posted his direction to his terminal. Mindlessly he hummed crossing under bridges, through a tressel, and right onto Lane 128. He followed this road down to the seashore.

      The man didn't care for the city much and was hoping for everything he wished for in the country. Night had become day when the man arrived to his destination. Closing his vehicle's doors he walked up to seal his fate.

"Baba Kalu Ji took his son with him so that he could learn Farsi. Baba Kalu Ji sat with the Mulla and began to praise his son, Sri Guru Nanak Dev Ji. "Please teach my child lovingly. He is very intelligent and will learn quickly. Tell me what day I should bring him to you as watching him being educated will give me a sense of satisfaction."

Adhyai 8:5

Chapter 29
The Fields

The town mouse went to see the country mouse, and where the country mouse lived there was utter silence at night that the town mouse could not sleep. If the country mouse was to meet the town mouse then inevitably the noise from the town streets would keep the country mouse up all night. The town mouse was Sainapat, and the country mouse was Tarun, and both tried to learn from each other but ended preferring their own habitat.

> *"Sri Guru Nanak Dev Ji uttered such beautiful words within was a divine sermon. "O Mulla Ji you talk about this age but without meditation on the name of God this life is wasting away.""*
>
> Adhyai 8:29

Moats, and woods, and graceful grass lands, with worn down paths that connected all together was what Tarun liked. Walking with Sainapat across their land, Sainapat would take care not to stand in solidified manure as well as raw. Unlike Tarun who would walk freely, duck, jump from stone to stone, all to show Sainapat the peace of Goman. Walking past a leaf reaching a branch he would hold back, and release the

Colours of Enlightenment & A Potion

stem of the leaf to gently pass Sainapat. Flowers would naturally make Sainapat sneeze, however he would still approach them slowly, to examine them closely, to tickle the stems and to find the seeds. Fascination with difference drove Sainapat to follow Tarun around Goman, whereas Tarun followed Sainapat to learn an approach to his new friend's awareness.

"The Mulla thought to himself, 'Sri Guru Nanak Dev Ji is mastering the difficult letters of the Farsi alphabet with ease. This child is young but his mind is wise like an elderly male. The Siharis and Muktas (special letters), accumulation, accounts were all mastered by Sri Guru Nanak Dev Ji".

Adhyai 8:8

    The night-time would sound crickets with other insects that would keep Sainapat awake and thinking of home. Tarun would ask him about the city and would become alarmed by the number of syllables Sainapat would use in a word to describe Sasha. Hence as soon as Sainapat began describing the beauty of his land to the country mouse, the country mouse would fall asleep.
    A great hybrid maple sat within a field that Tarun was introducing to Sainapat. They both reached the tree and Tarun began climbing it. Some seeds fell to the ground as Tarun pulled his way to stronger branches. He nudged Sainapat to follow and both made their way to a branch that held orange fruits. Tarun

picked the fruit for him and Sainapat. The taste was sweet as Sainapat followed Tarun in eating one. A straight bite into the fertilized seed that had grown into becoming flesh for a tree, and these two mice ate mercilessly.

"Please forgive me for the misguided words I said earlier as I am insolent and ignorant. Your faith in the Lord is complete and who in this world is to understand this?"

Adhyai 8:61

Chapter 30
The Reality

Over Mine Red a storm began to form then rain began to fall. The frost developed there throughout the planet's annual turn. Throughout the year the frost and ice settled across that land of Sasha, and for that reason people stayed towards drier land. Pity the planet turned with the Rock that shined heat onto Sasha but then again time was almost over. And they hoped for the rain to start, the rain began pouring.

A minute into the rain falling, the weighted tents and the cross wires holding the turbines forced the earth to still. There was hope that if the land would crack enough then valleys would form as cold as ice around them. The turbines roared, and the storm brewed, and the Sashans began counting. Counting, one, two, three to become a thousand, two thousand, three thousand ninety-one.

"Three thousand ninety-two!" shouted Blue.

"Four thousand," returned Blue's assistant.

"Five thousand!" chanted people to each other as the turbines held up keeping the ventilation in the trembling mines.

The sky began to rattle and crackle, however there was no wind held over the turbines. A moment of stillness between Mine Red and Mine Blue, full of nothing, empty as vacuum and there was silence between all mines.

People were comforting the young, and farmers comforted their goats. The others had quickly huddled together the second that the turbines began to whirl. The huge stabilizers casted from steel took hold of the earth. The thousand crafted bolts and nuts squeezed together, and Bani itself remained intact.

"500,000 rpms, sir," said Blue over the radio, "time counting through five minute marker. We are holding, our temperature has increased by one degree."

"I can't hear the turbines at all," said Marine to Prof. Esjah.

The rest of the service personnel stared at Prof. Dev Esjah.

"Naturally," replied Prof. Esjah.

Rather than alarm the personnel found comfort from Prof. Esjah's words, plus Marine's passion to help build the turbines they figured that no air would be available to carry the sound of the turbines anywhere closer to where they were. Let alone feel the earthquake occurring around them.

"Ten minutes," radioed in Malek.

(The marker was a full thirty minutes).

Through six hundred and eighty miles was scattered for four mines within Sasha's cliff. The largest being Mine Red, next Mine Green, Mine Blue, and lastly Mine Yellow, filled a range between 30,000 – 50,000 people, all these people waited within the rock of the cliff.

As for the mines each held three turbines, and each waited for the snow to start melting off the peaks of the mountains to blow cool air into their mines. The outcome would be full entrapment beneath snow and rock. Upside down, inside out, and frozen, or bellowed

Colours of Enlightenment & A Potion

far within the snow that execution would bring them upon a horizon of snow regardless of what time this would be.

"Lindsey, over," came a crackle through the radio from Mine Yellow.

"Return, over," announced two mines.

"Return from Mine Red," Prof. Esjah replied, "how's the temperature looking over there? Over."

"It is dropping at the rate of one degree every five minutes, and we are holding. I think the snow is beginning to collect around our foothold, over," said Lindsey Butcher.

"Stay calm Lindsey," replied Malek.

"Has there been any damage?" asked Marine.

"No," replied three distinct voices.

For all the sound generated by the turbines themselves would be enough to shatter the ice off the rocks of where they were under. The great result of not hearing the turbines, but observing a steady change in temperature showed progress was being made. As if there was no change in the temperature and sound from the turbines then something was wrong. Worst case scenario would be that the storm would persist way above the thirty-minute window and flood all the mines. Should the mines become filled with water that would suddenly turn to ice, then the hundred-thousand in battle claiming the existence of Sasha would be helpless to the sun's flames.

"Twenty-minutes, our temperature has reached four degrees above the origin, work, work, work, work!" said Blue.

"That doesn't sound right?" said Malek.

Amongst this activity a signal came on hand as beeps from the command centre at Ground Point to relay to all the mines. Blue saw the light begin to blink on his display. He held the radio down; the radio transmission had come from Sainapat.

"Mine Red! Mine Red! We have Sainapat!" shouted Blue over the radio to all mines.

"Pull the vents closed, you are gaining hot air!" screamed Marine to Blue.

"Sainapat's alive!" continued Blue.

"O true King, day and night I am trapped in a constant wave of my own thoughts."
Ang 721:2

Static! Bang! An acre away went a turbine exploding straight into the pull of Mine Blue's vent shafts. There was a rattle over the speaker. There was a larger explosion over Mine Blue. The earth cracked immediately under the snow and all the remnants in the fire were buried in the blink of an eye. The wind began to howl over Mine Blue. Nothing of this was heard over the remaining sites where rain carried on falling.

"Blue! Blue! Blue! Blue! Manson!" shouted Marine through the microphone.

Silence fell for only a few seconds before Marine continued: "Past the twenty-fifth minute marker," said Marine, from staring out in front of him, "five degrees, over,"

"Over," beeped Mine Yellow.

"Five degrees, holding, over," said Malek.

Colours of Enlightenment & A Potion

Nothing else happened for some while, thirty minutes seemed like an eternity, and all those that were holding onto each other held on tighter. Not for the time to end and see if all work had paid off, but to watch the dial behind a screen that the turbines had fully stopped. Making grace seem like an eternity.

"Thirty-minutes and turbines one, two and three, are slowing down, over,"

"Confirm, over."

"Confirm, over."

"Three-clicks, four clicks. The snow is starting to creep from under. Authorize extension? Authorizing extension for all four mines. Do we have confirm? Over," asked Marine to the other mines.

"We are building snow as the snow melts above us too. Extension operating here, over," beeped Mine Yellow.

"Confirmed for Mine Green, over," answered Malek.

The clicks on all dials returned to a stop. And the extension from each standing mine came to a halt. People waited for Prof. Esjah to say something, or nod towards Marine to give the word for re-entry. Barsy Marine anxiously glared towards his sixty-year-old wingman.

"Prof?" he said.

"Barsy, we shall wait another five minutes."

"Waiting five minutes," announced Marine through the microphone. "Blue are you there? Over," beeped Barsy to Manson.

Staring at the dials waiting for a response Prof. Esjah stood in sight of Barsy Marine. The doors started to open for all mines. The axial point was to disengage the curve as a pie would be cut. The remaining mines within the structures would be sheltered from on falling snow as the pie slices were lifted over the cliff's brow.

All mines regardless of capacity had lost ten feet of depth within the rock that the snow settled on. Ten feet of land lost and much more than an acre across land. Some peaks had broken from the tips of Sasha's Alps also. The ground was blown with air jets to help settle any hot surroundings left by the descent. Slowly the mines began to open.

Nobody knew what to expect for the condition outside their home for within the three year interval an era may have flown by. If all was well then the hope had worked. The sleds would take them straight to dry land.

The howling of the wind began to echo in all mines. This howl came as a relief to the survivors as they registered that the storm had settled, the rain had stopped, and that all was now calm. The people began to feel the difference from ventilation and natural air, and began thanking each other. The howling wind began to wake the children, along with the soft light from the dawn sky filling the chambers through light sensitive windows.

People started standing, and looking at the change in their isolated habitat. The people waited for the green light as mechanisms, wheels, and atmospheric pressures were checked to re-allow the people to feel natural daylight air. The attendees in control of Mine Red began to see out of the steel enforced windows onto the horizon of a new day.

"We have settlement, over," said Mine Red.

"Mine Yellow, we have settlement, over."

Colours of Enlightenment & A Potion

"Mine Green settled, over."

No sound came from Mine Blue. All waited patiently to hear Manson Blue. Finally the doors opened to the three mines. The wind howled in further and grieves were slowly turned to happiness as the people started smiling in hope once more.

A soft siren started ringing which informed people from all mines to move to the evacuation posts. All sleds began to fill; the path forward was to fire the evacuation call that no matter what the situation the sleds were to escape. Even over an unsuccessful plan the sleds would too escape but only to lose course.

The mercy of their will had led to successful evacuation. Slowly the landscape east of the ridge was filled with sleds that looked like bees leaving a nest over the snow landscape of Sasha. The true answer to the level of snow around Sasha mainland would be determined when the survivors reached back home. This would take a few hours at the rate that they were leaving the mines.

Less than a few hours had past when the recruits and the hopefuls walked onto dry sand much closer than they had expected. The sun was pass the Rock which still orbited their sky and the moon could be seen close beside. They heard a cry from the distance; a man was running with his arms open far wide:

"AHHHHHHHH!!!!!!!!!!" came the sound, "AHHHHHHHH!!!!!!!!!" the voice carried on.

Barsy Marine threw down his bags, and ran with his arms wide and mouth open towards Malek Esjah, "AHHHHHH!!!!" they both cried.

More dropped their bags and their other belongings and followed behind them, they all began to thank each other further. In amongst the joy of the hundred-thousand there were few who dwelled at this moment, not just for their lost ones but for the reason for their shocking survival. The few that dwelled that day came from Sasha Khand, breaking from their concentration of the others they looked over the horizon and up to a colourful sky.

The wish

Chapter 31
Master

Into a void Sainapat had travelled floating unconsciously after the castle doors got boarded down. The approach towards the sun had consumed him completely whilst his soul was absorbed out of him. His soul represented a flame and that flame was very much alive. His flame had soared away from Bani and closer to brimstone, to a large door with gray stones framing in a vault arch orientation around blackness. The gray stones reflected dark marine blue shine as Sainapat's sight adjusted to his surroundings. The light reflecting off his flame could not see into the doorway but there was a definite attraction towards it. The light off his soul illuminated over him into a tall archway to follow irregular stone to a horizon. The horizon was that of space.

"You tell me that you're welcome," came a voice from the doorway.

"I'm welcome," said Jai Sainapat.

"I allow you to only remember a name," replied the voice.

"Jai Sainapat," answered Sainapat

"I tell you why the toadstool wasn't invited to the party, because there wasn't mush-room. I tell you why the mushroom was invited to the party, because he was a fun-gi. I tell you that most limericks should be dubbed to see the heart as I see through it, like music to limericks is best heard through the heart's of men."

A laugh began bouncing off the walls of the doorway and cooled down the flame. A light approached in the form of a sphere. The sphere was floating on the hand of a person. The person was floating towards the open archway from the blackness. The flame was then turned into a ray of light and was sparked into the sphere. The light ray could see the entire universe through all time. The light ray tried to focus on a particular place and was drawn out the sphere back as a flame. The flame knew what he saw as on the other side he could see the strange person, but this time he was in his hand. The flame felt safe and remembered a shooting meteoroid falling pass a star.

"Like Matthew you swallowed a sheep and felt baa-d," said the strange person, and the flame was pulled back again to gain a better view of this stranger. "But on the contrary you walked into what was not holy for you and you consumed them well."

Sainapat's flame twitched as a shake of timber and twitched again. The flame was given a better distance to glare at the stranger. The flame looked directly to the stranger's lips and the stranger blinked.

"A lion's principle part you have, and you held this well whilst being what I asked you," said the stranger.

"His man-e," replied Sainapat.

"You remember before you were gone?"

"Savvy, an olive planted in the right place? A seed."

"Agree, just like a black-dog not calling himself a greyhound."

"And him chasing his tail for the ends to meet,"

Colours of Enlightenment & A Potion

Jai Sainapat and the stranger shared an emotion of laughter. The flame was given more feeling to his presence to where they were. Joule grunted and the wall behind the flame sheltered away from itself. Joule emerged as a serpent with broad wings from the rock and settled on a peak of another rock resembling three pedestals.

As flame he could feel him sway and divide. He peered down to see. Now he had arms and feet. With the weight of his mass and the strength of his brawn he attempted to pull himself to his feet. The man beside him was slightly taller so Sainapat was to stand on his toes, but as he did he changed himself into a flame again when he began to hover. Terrified Sainapat had become when he felt no force from the ground that he spontaneously became defensive. Master looked at him in bewilderment guessing why Sainapat was still shocked.

"Crocodiles love to play snap," Sainapat said.

"Before 1864 tribes ran over blood and water to send their messages. After these messages became printed digitally, schools that learned paid more attention but changes in time needed amendments to be made, like 'wear as you see fit to wear.' And the blood water changed to have you here. I am most grateful," said Master.

"I believe in compassion to feel kindness over weakness. I practice love over fear. Is that why?" asked Sainapat without realizing he knew the words.

"A bully was considered by man who sat on a throne so he raised a lamb in his defence. Glory to the Lamb who has control of the universe," Master replied, and Sainapat began pulling himself back together.

The one flame looked at him dividing from the right side and flickered where fingers would be, and there as hard as bone he had fingers again.

"Over all I gave you, over all I punished you with, over all the time I took from you, I punished you for so long; you remained true to my Name. And that to carry on believing in my Name even after I relieved you over that of many," admitted Master to Sainapat. "You would have endorsed my reward if you would have heard of my Name sooner, and still I know you would have been happy to suffer through my Name."

"Time is relevant to me as a caterpillar. I remember, 'Watch batteries fixed,' and, a better watch," said Sainapat.

"A better watch indeed," Master replied.

He moved away the spherical object he had and the object remained floating.

"What is Friday the 13th to you?"

Sainapat thought about this for a second: "As much as it means to you," he answered.

Master stroked his chest with his right arm, stroked it with his left, and then stroked it again with his right, what seemed to Sainapat and Joule that Master was dancing.

"Ribbons for Valentine's Day that you do not need to be aware of, and a box filled with red rose petals is now no longer your concern," said Master. "Admire a bouquet of flowers instead."

Apparently Sainapat was not sure to appreciate what this person was speaking about; nevertheless he knew too full well that this person knew him better than he knew himself. Master could feel his curiosity and brought a rose out of space for him to see. He cloned

Colours of Enlightenment & A Potion

another one, and another one, till he had twelve beautifully bloomed red roses to show Sainapat. Sainapat took the twelve and burnt them intentionally. After the last petal blackened out Sainapat held his arm up and with thought produced another rose out of cosmic space.

"Thou shall not murder," marked Sainapat glancing at the Master's heart and then through it to the black tomb doorway behind. Sainapat's heart began to beat softer. He blinked to break the stranger's concentration on him.

"Hard to paint a painting and hard to paint water, making everything hard but that of what must be repeated again. You have desire to learn and you love reading, that's what makes everything else easier."

"You mastered working your life in enlightening yourself and others with what I had given you. You mastered working peace to entertain your life and gave yourself to others. As well as you made brothers with those that were not of your own blood and found love from them. You achieved the foundation of life well," continued Master.

Noise started flowing from the black nave archway behind Master. Sounds from children and sounds from adults became more distinct as Sainapat stood by Master.

"Ask one to rejoice with us so we can harness more light for our realm," asked Master, "some leaves have returned to me that I wish to have them growing once more,"

"Why do I scratch myself?" asked Sainapat.

"Because you are the only one who knows where it itches," replied Master. "Just like James smiling all because he can,"

"Who is James?"

"James is a hedgehog that crossed the court to see his flat-mate," replied Master, "just like everything is well in Solomon's Temple, from Torahs to Bibles living safely."

"Tell me more."

"Made on Earth comes a language called Arabic, that when heard sounds like hymns to my pleasure," this wasn't amusing to Sainapat as it was for Master and Master chuckled for a moment's time before recollecting his thoughts.

"There is much you will not understand when you leave my side again, but rest assure all you see before you, you have at your will to explore," said Master, "most of everything you understand will be something in time, and that can only be fact. To play subconsciously remains fiction, and this you will love as that is you, who is me, and that is for everybody."

"Can you tell me more?" asked Sainapat.

"Ask for the swimming trunks left by the elephant and goldfish as they crossed here, and ask them to come and see me. From then enjoy eternity as now you are alive." Finished Master, and a light began to shine from within the vault-arched doorway.

"When can I get to see you again?" returned Sainapat as he went into the doorway.

"Anytime you like. Would you like me to take a note?" returned Master's voice.

"Hold my apologies in case I forget," finished Sainapat.

Colours of Enlightenment & A Potion

The sounds of birds now could be heard echoing from the blackened nave. A warm soft breeze with a sweet scent embedded itself with Sainapat's aura, and Sainapat left Master's side away from lava pouring falls, hot steam gases, rumbling igneous basalt, Joule, and into the silver shine that illuminated off the vault-arched doorway walls. The doorway sealed closed with irregular stone marking a massive gothic stone arch work as one piece.

Chapter 32
The Wish

Appearing into the light of looking at a thunder rapid valley of lava created through the shocking story Joule played to Master; Bani froze over flying fast pass Master's deck and shooting out of a hollow crater feeding through their star. Bani flew pass sitting nebulas of dust gas and hydrogen, between the nebulas within and there out, and pass galaxies filled with dark matter. The emissions of radiation reflected back through space from the gas enabled them to see. Bani flew pass thirty-two trillion kilometres in a year.

The dark matter covers over ninety-percent of the universe holding quasars of energy in the form of radio-waves at the corners of their ends. The space between galaxies is called dark matter. And there are a few galaxies consisting of many stars. Each star burns as for the gases within the star and when a star burns out planets see them as shooting stars. The distance is in correlation with the time the light is seen fading out.

Dwarf Galaxies consisting of eleven million stars, Giant Galaxies of over one trillion stars, and all accounting to a common central mass. A white charged reflection that could be seen from dark matter held many solar systems, with one having nine planets of which one was active.

Of the observable universe a Democritus, from the active planet's time of 450-370 B.C. philosophized

Colours of Enlightenment & A Potion

that the stars were arranged in a white strip. Then an Aristotle, of time 384-322 B.C. thought the atmosphere ignited the sky and burnt holes in dark matter. Lastly a Galileo Galilei, 1564-1642 A.D. demonstrated that only galaxies are filled with stars, and all stars represented a reflection as the equator of space.

The stars seen outside the active planet were charted by each other to resemble identities in the zodiac language to help navigate sight through space. There were twelve in particular around this active planet that Master called Earth, and these twelve zodiac patterns were given names reflecting particularly on their times seen from Earth annually.

Across one another constellations of stars were catalogued by Joule to help him navigate through realms. For Earth he had planned 88 constellations for the orbit of that planet around that sun. These constellations move ever so slightly, hundred-thousands of years to bring a different stretch to the same constellation of stars. Twelve of the constellations are zodiac signs, and represent a month in travel for the round planet's orbit.

Earth was most probably made round like other planets due to sublimation of gas particles or the natural spherical property of water. A kingdom inside the realm of the unknown was made more diverse when dressed with ivory white robes. The stars shined like pearls that made space faithful and true to explore. After the first resurrection of stars the second resurrection was made absolute and bound to the head crowns of the galaxies.

Master had named the galaxies. The active planet's galaxy he called the Milky Way. He called one

Andromeda Galaxy, which generated a view of an eye. Others, the Sombrero Galaxy, and the Whirlpool Galaxy, a spiral and a whirlpool of star arrangements were seen respectively.

There were times when Master had pushed a few stars, and at times too many stars out of balance, nevertheless he had arranged the foundation of space to expand back. The suns' gravitational pull on the others' naturally formed elliptical, spiral and peculiar galaxies, resembling galaxies that Master easily recognized, unlike irregular galaxies containing fewer stars and random formations. Which in between contained dark matter were remnants of stars and interstellar dust collected. These would decay closer to final entropy; to be either received by another flame or to sit there in space for eternity waiting. More bodies make warmth, eventually more warmth would occupy more earth, and fortunately more earth would cool most of space, which would hopefully provide a flame to a falling star

Master merged out of his thought and rested his arm on the table that rested on his balcony that faced all of space. He clasped his hands together and mounted a fire motion with his fingers; he realized there was much more at his disposal. He stretched up with his arms that dropped his cloak to see just enough of his youth, and he tensed his right palm to space and followed through to his toes and into the stone below. He tensed both palms open and scrolled his fingers through each other with thumbs spaced from each other. And silently far away Bani flew past all space and stilled to react again on the weight of its own pendulum.

Epilogue

A desire for Master to keep everything flowing in synchronized fashion was mandatory for Master to have. The faith of Sashans kept hope for Master to keep Bani alive. The love from Gomen gave Master a reason for his hope. The companionship with Sainapat to survive with him to spread goodwill at no cost held Master's decision.

Closing on faith left Bani's presence to commence once again. The people within Goman were to be awoken from the freeze that took place, but not all would have survived. Some may have been taken within Master, and some within Joule's Lair. The people from Sasha survived their own fate through hard work, determination and faith.

Existence for Bani was not preferred by Master until work got done. As one land chose to work for the other, Master thought to have his decision changed. Preferably all souls were to be collected to harness light for another planet. Further than that a better understanding developed brighter light as Joule's patience once again grew for Bani.

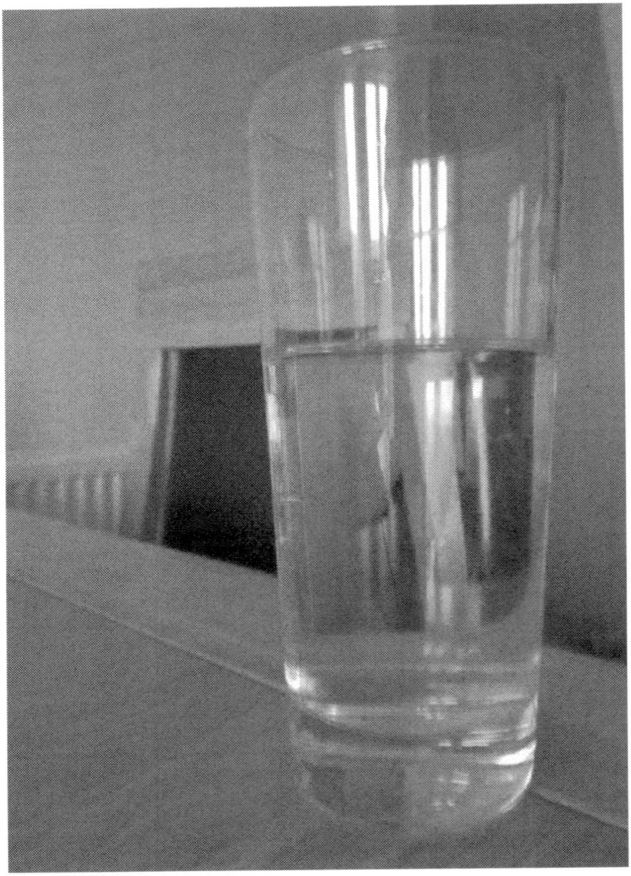

About the Author

I became accustomed to writing since a young age either from the work I had studied throughout my life and when taking notes on daily activities. I enjoyed writing from as far back as it was as paper and pen. Because of my youth and reflectance to what's important within it I was to write my books. Being privileged to having an education I didn't want my knowledge to be lost and so I thought I should write down my interests. My interests were like everyone else's in what they know and what they are taught. I didn't want to lose my education I had received and thought to write down what I knew as stories. As my worked continued I realised I had a true gift for creativity. I added Sikh Scripture as my name originates from Sikhism – God of Light.

I am very pleased to present my history and my interests within these books of mine. The main aim of the whole project was to bring positive aspects of life to everyday situations. These even included mental behaviour to change and better adapt or evolve our situations. We can all better something at sometime, may this be a temper problem, may this be an illness or suffering to another, this maybe how to congratulate another when there's nothing that can be offered. The path of many religions show to care for our neighbour, our brother, sister, family or friend member but at times we did not know how to approach difficult situations. Overall I hope to have shown that we should first smile and alongside make others smile.

There are a few factors to consider from my observations. I have included these statements to follow in all stories and I hope you can agree they are of importance to understand. They aid humanity to survive with strength and explore the unknown realities.

In all my stories I mentioned to understand that 'Om' (Sanskrit Scripture for the hymn of peace), this should be done from within and cannot be done in anger. The theme peace to be identified as the colour 'black', the theme of each other, every human being, and every animal as being that of blood, something representing love, and that is anything 'red', and most important to live in the 'light', light is life and we have peace and love to find and build for one another. Light is most important, some people including myself would like to represent this Light to also be known as God, whatever his name maybe. And lastly whenever you require power then to harness the thought of light and imagine that, also place hands together. Feel your heartbeat when tightening hands together. This doesn't need to be praying but just holding stability. Exertion is to release, the grace of yoga.

I thank every reader to have got to this point of my book. I hope you've really enjoyed it. I am to carry on working in life and wellness to inspire people to live improved lives and work with people that can benefit from my remedies. I wish all the time to read the book again. Live, love, laugh and add gold to peace.

Other Books by Author

Bhagavan's Guitar
As Light Is

Sand Deep
Lord of Light

Colours of Enlightenment
Right On Time

A Potion
Light

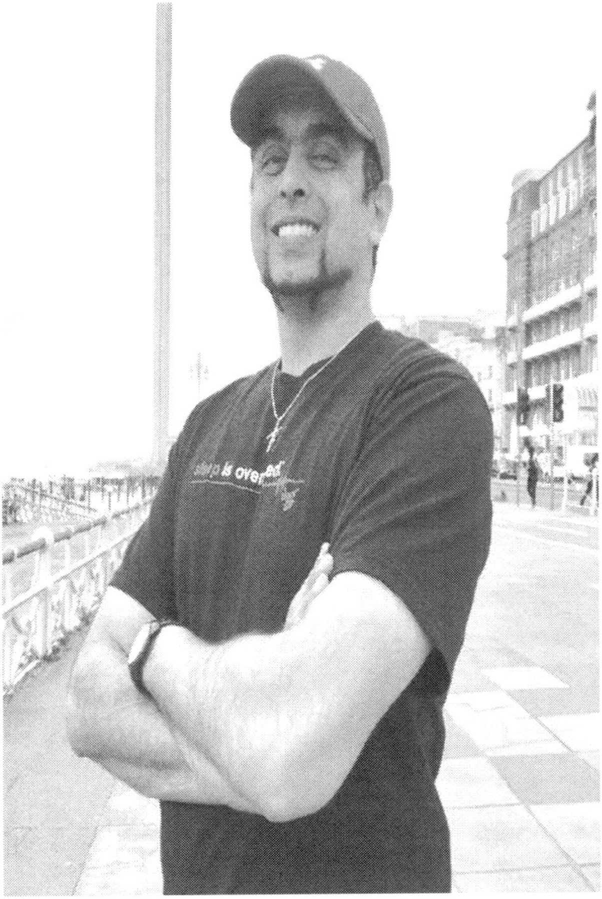

Thanks.
31/10/21